To: Katie and Emma

From: Aunt Melva and Richard

December 25, 2012

W9-BLG-335

To: Katie and Emma

From: Aunt Melva and Richard

Disney's
Treasury of
Children's Classics

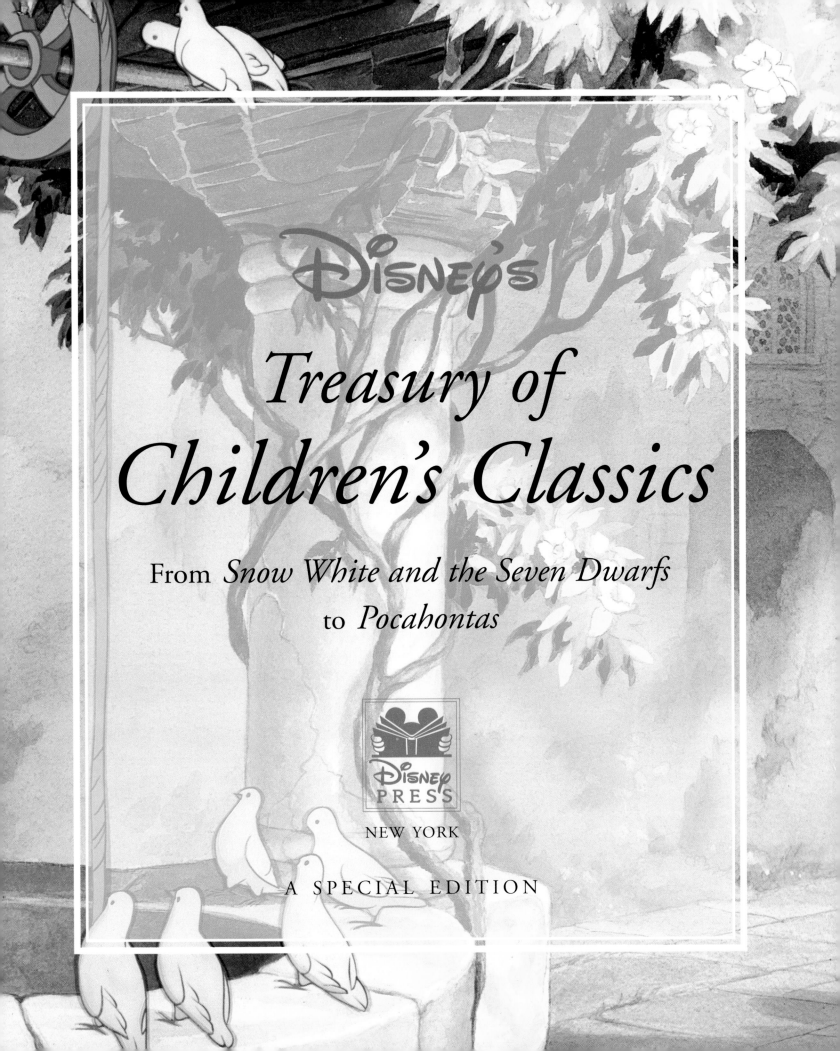

DISNEY'S

Treasury of Children's Classics

From *Snow White and the Seven Dwarfs*
to *Pocahontas*

Disney PRESS

NEW YORK

A SPECIAL EDITION

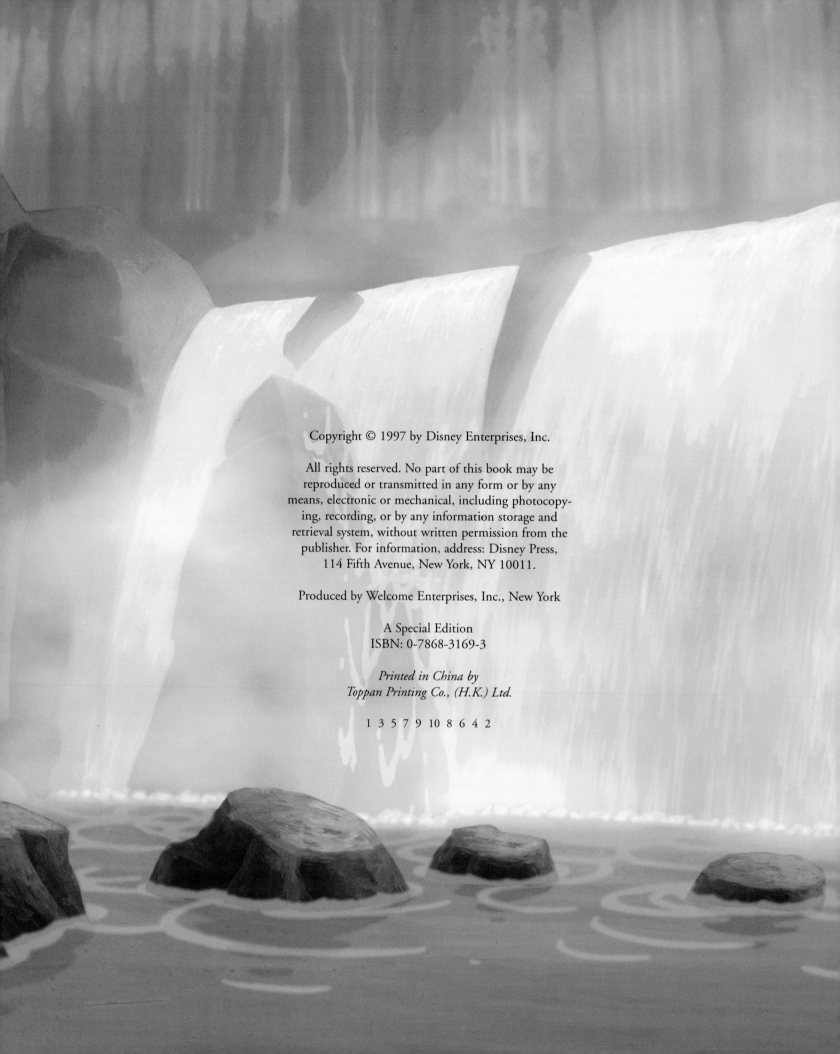

Copyright © 1997 by Disney Enterprises, Inc.

All rights reserved. No part of this book may be
reproduced or transmitted in any form or by any
means, electronic or mechanical, including photocopy-
ing, recording, or by any information storage and
retrieval system, without written permission from the
publisher. For information, address: Disney Press,
114 Fifth Avenue, New York, NY 10011.

Produced by Welcome Enterprises, Inc., New York

A Special Edition
ISBN: 0-7868-3169-3

Printed in China by
Toppan Printing Co., (H.K.) Ltd.

1 3 5 7 9 10 8 6 4 2

CONTENTS

Once Upon a Time

If You Believe

Keeping the Dream Alive

The Magic Continues

Once Upon a Time

rella

From Walt Disney's Motion Picture *Cinderella,*
based on the original classic by Charles Perrault

nce upon a time in a faraway land, a widowed gentleman lived in a fine house with his only daughter. He gave his beloved child everything her heart desired—beautiful dresses, a horse, a puppy. Still, he felt she needed a mother's care. So he married again, choosing a woman with two young daughters who, he hoped, would be playmates for his little girl.

Sad to say, the good man died a short time later, and the stepmother then began to show her true nature. She was harsh and cold, and bitterly jealous of her stepdaughter's sweetness and beauty, qualities that made her own daughters, Anastasia and Drizella, seem even meaner and uglier by contrast.

The stepsisters were richly dressed, but the poor girl was forced to wear a coarse, plain dress and apron and do all the hardest jobs in the house. She got up before daybreak, carried water, lit the fires, cooked

and washed and scrubbed. When she had done her work, she used to go to the chimney-corner and sit down there among the cinders and ashes to keep warm. Thus she came to be called Cinderella.

Her stepmother and sisters slept in beautiful chambers, but Cinderella's tiny bedroom was up in the garret under the roof of the house, where dozens of mice lived. And yet, through it all, Cinderella remained gentle and kind, dreaming that someday happiness would come to her.

She made friends with the birds who woke her each morning. She made friends with the mice who shared her garret. She gave names to all the mice, and sewed them tiny coats and hats. For their part, the mice loved Cinderella and were grateful to her because she sometimes rescued them from a trap or saved them from Lucifer, her stepmother's bad-tempered cat.

Each morning Cinderella made breakfast for the household: a bowl of milk for the cat, a bone for the dog, oats for her old horse, corn and grain for the chickens, geese, and ducks in the barnyard. Then she carried breakfast trays upstairs for her stepmother and Anastasia and Drizella.

"Take that ironing and have it back in an hour," Drizella demanded.

"Don't forget the mending and don't be all day getting it done," Anastasia scolded.

"Pick up the laundry and get on with your duties," her stepmother ordered. "Scrub the large carpet in the main hall, wash the windows, clean the tapestries."

"Yes, Drizella. Yes, Anastasia. Yes, Stepmother," Cinderella replied, as she set about her tasks cheerfully enough.

Now it happened that on the other side of town in the Royal Palace the

King and the Grand Duke were talking. "It's high time the Prince married and settled down!" said the old King.

"But, Your Majesty," replied the Duke, "first he must meet a girl and fall in love."

"You're right," the King agreed. "We'll give a ball and invite every young girl in my kingdom. He's bound to fall in love with one of them."

When the invitations to the ball were delivered, Anastasia and Drizella danced for joy. "A ball! A ball! We're going to a ball!" they exclaimed.

"I am invited, too," said Cinderella. "It says, 'By royal command, every eligible maiden is to attend.'"

The stepsisters laughed at the idea of Cinderella going to a ball wearing her apron and carrying a broom. But her stepmother, with a sly smile, said of course Cinderella could go—*if* she finished her work and *if* she had a suitable dress to wear.

"IF," laughed Anastasia.

"IF," Drizella giggled.

All day long the stepsisters were busy choosing gowns, petticoats, and ornaments to wear in their hair. All day long they talked of nothing but how they should be dressed for the ball. Meanwhile Cinderella was kept busier than ever, for it was she who had to iron the full skirts, pleat the ruffles, and tie the ribbons into bows.

When the carriage came to take the stepmother and her two

daughters to the ball, Cinderella had not had a minute to get herself ready. "Well," said her stepmother, "then you're not going. Oh, what a shame! But there will be other times and other balls." And she and her ugly daughters swept out to the coach.

Cinderella climbed the dark stairs to her room and gazed sadly out of the moonlit window at the distant castle. Suddenly, a light appeared behind her. Turning, she saw that her candle had been lit and in its glow hung a lovely party dress. Her friends the birds and the mice had made it for her as a surprise, trimming it with bits of ribbon and beads they had found about the house.

In no time at all Cinderella slipped into the dress, thanked her friends, and ran down the stairs, calling, "Please wait, I'm coming, too!" But when Anastasia and Drizella saw her they were furious. "My beads!" screamed one. "My ribbon!" howled the other. "You're a little thief!" And they snatched at Cinderella's dress until it was torn to rags.

In tears, Cinderella ran across the yard to the garden. There she flung herself on a bench and sobbed, "It's just no use. Nothing will help. I give up." But at that moment, out of a cloud of magic stardust, appeared a round-faced little woman in a hooded cloak, "Nonsense,

child," she said in a sweet voice. "Dry those tears—you can't go to the ball looking like that."

Cinderella stopped crying and asked, "Who are you?"

"I'm your fairy godmother," said the woman, "and we don't have much time. I think the first thing you'll need is a pumpkin." Cinderella couldn't guess why, but she obediently fetched a large pumpkin. The godmother waved her wand over it and sang the magic words, "Salaga-doola, menchicka boola, bibbidi-bobbidi-boo." The pumpkin slowly rose on its vine, while its tendrils curled into wheels. In no time it had become a handsome coach.

"Now," said the godmother, "we'll need some mice." Four of Cinderella's little friends scurried forward, and once again the god-mother sang the magic words as she touched the mice with her wand. Four dapple-gray horses appeared and were hitched to the coach.

Then the godmother changed Cinderella's old horse into a proud coachman, and Bruno the dog into an elegant footman. "And now for you, my dear," said the fairy godmother, tapping Cinderella with her wand. Instantly the torn dress became a lovely silken gown. Peeping out from under its skirt were dainty glass slippers, the prettiest in the whole world.

As Cinderella got into the coach, her godmother commanded her, above all things, not to stay at the ball past twelve o'clock. For if she stayed one minute longer than midnight, the coach would become a pumpkin again, her horses mice, her coachman an old horse, and her footman a dog, while she herself would be dressed in rags. Cinderella promised to leave the ball before midnight, and she set off joyfully for the Royal Palace.

The ball had already started when she arrived, and the Prince was politely bowing to the two-hundred-tenth and -eleventh young ladies—Anastasia and Drizella. Suddenly, the Prince looked up and saw in the doorway of the palace the most beautiful girl he had ever beheld. Entranced, he walked past the sisters toward Cinderella, took her hand, and led her into the great hall among all the company.

The King's son wouldn't dance with anyone else the rest of the evening, and not for a minute would he let go of Cinderella's hand. Her

sisters and her stepmother, never recognizing Cinderella, wondered who the beautiful stranger might be. All the ladies studied her clothes and headdress and vowed to copy them the very next day. But the old King chuckled contentedly because his plan had worked—the Prince had indeed found the bride of his dreams.

When the palace clock began to strike midnight, Cinderella remembered her promise. "I must go," she cried in a panic, and, freeing her hand from the Prince's, she ran through the palace and down a flight of stairs, with the Prince and the Duke in pursuit. One of her tiny glass slippers fell off, but she ran on and leapt into her waiting coach.

The clock was still striking as the coach sped away from the palace. As it passed through the gates, the clock struck twelve. Coach, horses, and all vanished, and in their place was a pumpkin, some mice, a dog, an old horse, and Cinderella in her ragged dress. All that remained of the magical evening was one glass slipper sparkling on her foot.

The next morning the King's son had it proclaimed throughout the land that he would marry the girl who had lost her slipper at the ball the night before. He sent the Grand Duke to travel about the kingdom in search of the girl whose foot would exactly fit the glass slipper. The Duke tried the little slipper on every princess, every duchess, and all the Court, but in vain. Finally he came to Cinderella's house.

The stepmother, in great excitement, went to rouse her lazy daughters. "We haven't a moment to lose," she cried. "There is a chance that one of you can become the Prince's bride if the glass slipper fits you!" And she sent them scurrying down to the Duke with the warning, "Don't fail me."

Then she followed Cinderella, who had gone to her room to make herself presentable for the Duke, and locked her in. No one else was to have a chance at so great a prize.

When Cinderella heard the click of the lock she realized, too late, what had happened. "Please, oh please, you must let me out!" she called, rattling the doorknob. But her stepmother dropped the key in her pocket and walked away, laughing her meanest laugh. She did not

24

know that two little mice followed her down the stairs, never taking their eyes off the pocket where the key rested.

Meanwhile Drizella and Anastasia were arguing over the glass slipper, each claiming it as her own. The stepmother watched as first Anastasia and then Drizella tried to squeeze a large foot into the tiny slipper, without success. She did not notice that two quiet mice were busily stealing the key to Cinderella's door from her pocket and carrying it away.

The Grand Duke took the slipper from the unhappy stepsisters and prepared to be off with it to the next house, when Cinderella called from the stairs, "Please wait, Your Grace. May I try the slipper?" The

26

stepmother tried to block her path. "It's only Cinderella, our scullery maid," she told the Duke, but he brushed her aside. "Madam, my orders were 'every maiden in the land.'"

The wicked stepmother had one more trick left. She tripped the Duke's servant, who was carrying the glass slipper, and it fell to the floor, where it shattered into hundreds of pieces. "Oh! this is terrible!" cried the Duke. "What will the King say?"

Cinderella reached into a pocket under her apron. "See," she said, "I have the other slipper." The Duke slipped it on her foot, which, of course, it fit perfectly. Thereupon the fairy godmother appeared, and touched Cinderella with her wand, and all could see that she was indeed the unknown beauty who had captured the Prince's heart at the ball.

Cinderella was driven to the Royal Palace in the King's own coach. There, amid great rejoicing and the ringing of all the bells in the kingdom, Cinderella married her Prince.

AND THEY LIVED HAPPILY EVER AFTER.

CINDERELLA

The Story of the Production

One of the great Disney animation classics, *Cinderella* is based on the rags-to-riches fairy tale written by Charles Perrault nearly three hundred years ago. The Disney Studio spent $2.5 million and six years —from 1944 to 1950—on the production, experimenting with new techniques, modeling on the characters to give them roundness, and embellishing the artwork with extravagant detail.

Cinderella's musical score has six songs, each woven into the picture and making an important point in the story: "Cinderella," "So This Is Love," "A Dream Is a Wish Your Heart Makes," "Cinderella's Work Song," "Bibbidi-Bobbidi-Boo (The Magic Song)," and "Sing, Sweet Nightingale."

Besides a cast of nine actors and actresses who were responsible for the voice characterizations, a staff of more than sixty animators, artists, writers, directors, musical directors, and editors were involved in the production—all under the exacting supervision of Walt Disney himself. Since its premiere in 1950, the picture has been released every seven or eight years and has played in a dozen languages to audiences on all seven continents.

The multiplane camera can shoot several layers of animation painted on glass against an opaque background, thus producing a marvelous illusion of depth. Here a crew of ten technicians operates the complex machine; the man at the upper left is Card Walker who, many years later, became Chairman and Chief Executive Officer of Walt Disney Productions

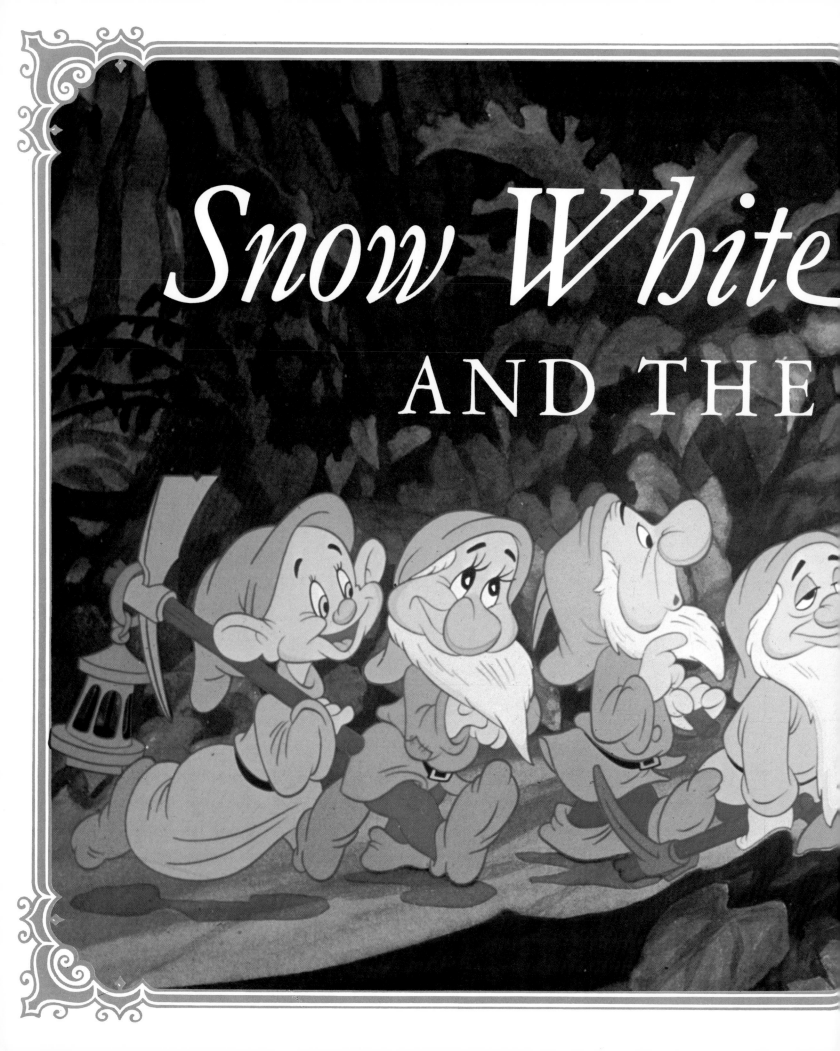

SEVEN DWARFS

From Walt Disney's Motion Picture *Snow White
and the Seven Dwarfs*, adapted from Grimms' Fairy Tales

nce in midwinter when the snowflakes were falling from the sky like feathers, a Queen sat sewing at a window with an ebony frame. As she was sewing and looking out at the snowflakes, she pricked her finger with her needle and three drops of blood fell on the snow. The red looked so beautiful on the white snow that she thought to herself: "If only I had a child as white as snow and as red as blood and as black as the wood of my window frame." Some time later she gave birth to a daughter who was as white as snow and as red as blood, and her hair was as black as ebony. They called her Snow White, and when she was born the Queen died.

A year later the lonely King took a second wife. She was beautiful, but she was cruel and jealous and couldn't bear the thought that anyone might be more beautiful than she. She had a magic mirror and every day when she looked into it she asked:

Mirror, mirror on the wall,
Who is the fairest of us all?

and the mirror answered:

You, O Queen, are the fairest in the land.

That set her mind at rest, for she knew the mirror told the truth.

But as Snow White grew, she became more and more beautiful, and the Queen feared that someday the girl would be the fairest in the land. So she dressed Snow White in rags and forced her to live with the servants and to slave from sunrise to sundown.

All the while that Snow White cheerfully scrubbed floors and dusted and carried water from the well, she dreamed that her Prince Charming would come and carry her off to his castle in the clouds. One day, as she was drawing water from the well, her friends the pigeons told her a secret. It was really a wishing well! "Make a wish into the well," they said, "and if you hear it echo, your wish will come true."

Snow White spoke into the well, "I'm wishing for the one I love to find me today."

Before the echo could repeat the whole wish, a handsome Prince on horseback rode up and saw Snow White. He looked at her with such admiration that Snow White grew embarrassed and ran off to her room. But the jealous Queen had been watching from her window, and she turned yellow and green with envy.

Looking into her mirror she demanded:

Mirror, mirror on the wall,
Who is the fairest of us all?

and this time the mirror replied:

Her lips blood red, her hair like night,
Her skin like snow, her name—
Snow White!

The Queen was in a terrible temper and she sent for her huntsman.

"Get that child out of my sight," she stormed. "Take her far into the forest, kill her, and bring me back her heart in this box, to prove you have done it."

The huntsman was saddened at these words but he did not dare to disobey his Queen. He took Snow White deep into the forest, and as he watched her happily picking wild flowers he knew he could not hurt this lovely girl.

Kneeling before Snow White he said, "I cannot kill you as the Queen commanded. Run away and hide, but do not come back to the palace because the wicked Queen will surely harm you."

The huntsman left Snow White then, and on his way home he killed a young boar and put its heart in the box for the Queen, as proof that he had carried out her orders.

Alone in the great forest, Snow White was frightened by everything she saw, every strange sound she heard. She ran and ran until just before nightfall she saw a tiny cottage, not much larger than a doll's house. No one was at home, so she opened the little door and went in. There were seven dusty little chairs, and seven dirty little dishes, seven little shirts that needed washing, and dirt and cobwebs everywhere.

"From the look of this place, it belongs to seven untidy little children," Snow White said, and she went about sweeping and cleaning and scrubbing and laundering—all with the help of some friendly woodland creatures who had followed her. They sang and danced and whistled while they worked, and in no time at all the little house was spotless.

Then Snow White went upstairs and there she found seven little

beds, each with a name carved on it: "DOC, HAPPY, SNEEZY, DOPEY, GRUMPY, BASHFUL, SLEEPY." "What funny names for children!" said Snow White and she yawned, "I'm a little sleepy myself." And flopping down across the beds, she fell sound asleep.

When it was quite dark the owners of the little house came home. They were seven dwarfs who went off to the mountains every day with their picks and shovels to mine diamonds. They no sooner had lighted their seven candles than they saw that someone had been in their house. "The whole place is clean!" Doc exclaimed. "There's dirty work afoot," growled Grumpy.

Cautiously they tiptoed up the stairs, and there they found Snow White, asleep on their beds. "What is it?" Bashful and Happy asked. "Why," said Doc, "I think it's a girl!" "She's mighty purty," Sneezy said. Bashful sighed, "She's beautiful. Like an angel." At that Snow White woke up.

When she saw the seven dwarfs she was startled. "Why you're not children at all. You're little men," she exclaimed. But they were friendly, and asked her name and how she came to their house.

Snow White told them how her stepmother had tried to have her killed and that the huntsman had spared her life. "The Queen will never find me here and if you let me stay, I'll keep house for you and do the cooking, make the beds, wash, and sew," she promised. The dwarfs whispered together and then they said, "If you keep everything neat and clean you can stay with us and you'll want for nothing."

So Snow White stayed and kept the house in order. In the mornings the dwarfs went off to look for diamonds, and in the evenings when they came home, dinner was ready. Snow White was alone all day and the kindly dwarfs warned her, "Watch out for your Stepmother. She's full of black magic and she knows everything. Don't let anyone in while we're away."

In the meantime, the Queen had been given the box with the heart, which she believed was Snow White's. She felt sure she was again the most beautiful of all. One day she went to her mirror and asked:

Magic mirror on the wall,
Who now is the fairest one of all?

But the truthful mirror answered:

Over the seven jewelled hills,
Beyond the seventh fall,
In the cottage of the seven dwarfs
Dwells Snow White, fairest one of all.

Then the Queen stamped her foot in a fury. The huntsman had 'tricked her, and Snow White still lived. As long as the girl lived, the Queen could not be the fairest one of all, and she *had* to be or jealousy would leave her no peace. At last she thought up a plan. She stained her face and hands and dressed in black rags like a toothless old peddler woman. No one would ever recognize her. She went to a secret room that no one else knew about and there she made a poisoned apple. It was beautiful, juicy-looking, shiny red, and anyone who saw it would want a bite. But one taste and the person's eyes would close forever in the Sleeping Death.

Pleased with herself, the Queen made her way to the little cottage in the forest. Hiding behind a tree she watched the seven dwarfs say good-bye to Snow White. "Don't let anybody in the house," they warned her. Then they marched off to their mountain, singing "Heigh-ho, heigh-ho, it's off to work we go. . . ."

No sooner were the dwarfs out of sight than the ragged old woman went to the window and asked Snow White for a drink of water. "Thank you, my pet," she said, when the girl handed it to her through the

window. "Now here's an apple for you," and she cackled wickedly. "Wait till you taste it, dearie, it's delicious!" Snow White reached for the poisoned apple, though her friends, the woodland creatures, tried to keep it from her. No sooner had she taken a bite than she fell to the floor, as if dead.

The birds and animals hurried through the forest to fetch the dwarfs, while the Queen laughed. "Now I'll be the fairest in the land," she said as she slipped away into the forest.

The dwarfs dashed up to the cottage too late to save Snow White.

But they saw the wicked Queen running into the woods, and they ran after her as fast as their little legs would carry them. They chased her to the top of a high cliff, and there the Queen tripped and plunged over the edge. With a terrible scream, she vanished forever.

Sadly the dwarfs returned home. Heartbroken, they looked at their beautiful Snow White, her cheeks and lips still red, as if she were asleep. The dwarfs made a crystal coffin for Snow White and set it in a glade in the forest. Night and day they kept watch over it.

A long time passed, and one day Prince Charming heard about the beautiful Princess asleep in the forest. He wondered if it was the girl he had lost his heart to long ago near the wishing well, and whom he had been seeking ever since. He rode deep into the woods and there he found her, the Princess he loved truly. Leaning over, he kissed her lips. Snow White opened her eyes as if awakening from a deep sleep; the spell of the poisoned apple had been broken by Love's First Kiss.

And Snow White's dearest wish came true. Her Prince rode off with her to his Castle in the Clouds, amid the cheers and good wishes of the dwarfs and forest creatures.

SNOW WHITE AND THE SEVEN DWARFS

The Story of the Production

Walt Disney's first attempt at making a feature-length cartoon was *Snow White and the Seven Dwarfs,* a milestone in motion picture history. Based on a fairy tale by the Brothers Grimm, Disney's eighty-three-minute entertainment is one of the most popular and beloved movies ever made. Once known as Disney's Folly, it is now called Disney's Masterpiece.

"You should have heard the howls of warning when we started making a full-length cartoon," Walt Disney recalled years later. "But there was only one way we could do it successfully and that was to plunge ahead and go for broke—shoot the works. There could be no compromising on money, talent, or time. Well, as everyone knows, the picture did make money, and if it hadn't, there wouldn't be any Disney Studio today."

Production began in 1934 and was completed in 1937. More than 750 artists worked on the picture, creating at least one million drawings, of which over 250,000 were used. Studio chemists in the Disney paint laboratories ground their own pigments from special formulas and mixed 1,500 colors and shades for the characters and backgrounds. The multiplane camera, invented and developed by Walt Disney Studio

Walt Disney accepts a special Academy Award from Shirley Temple in 1939—one large and seven dwarf-sized Oscars for *Snow White*

Adriana Caselotti,
the voice of Snow White

technicians, first reached a high degree of perfection in *Snow White and the Seven Dwarfs*. With it, animated scenes achieved a three-dimensional quality because characters and backgrounds could be photographed on several levels or planes.

The Academy of Motion Picture Arts and Sciences gave *Snow White* a special award in 1939, with nine-year-old Shirley Temple making the presentation to Walt Disney of a large golden Oscar and seven miniature replicas. There are eight songs in the picture, several of which are now considered "standards" in the trade: "I'm Wishing," "One Song," "With a Smile and a Song," "Whistle While You Work," "Heigh-Ho," "Bluddle-Uddle-Um-Dum," "The Dwarfs' Yodel Song," and "Some Day My Prince Will Come." The songs have been translated into thirteen languages and are well known throughout the world, wherever this record-breaking picture has played.

Sleeping Beauty

From Walt Disney's Motion Picture *Sleeping Beauty*,
from the story by Charles Perrault

 n a faraway land, long ago, lived King Stefan and his fair Queen. For many years they had longed for a child and finally their wish was granted. A daughter was born and they called her Aurora, after the goddess of the dawn, for she filled their lives with sunshine.

To celebrate her birth, a great holiday was proclaimed throughout the kingdom. Knights and ladies, townspeople and peasants, all dressed in their finest clothes and bringing gifts, came to the palace at the King's invitation to see the new baby and wish her well.

King Hubert, who ruled the neighboring country, arrived with his young son, Prince Phillip. The two kings had long dreamed of uniting their lands by the marriage of their children, and on this occasion they announced the betrothal of the infant Princess Aurora to Prince Phillip.

Suddenly, gliding down a shaft of sunlight that slanted into the Great Hall, the tiny figures of three good fairies appeared. Waving their magic wands they floated over to examine the display of the baby's presents. Then they approached the cradle to bestow their gifts on Princess Aurora. "Little Princess, my gift shall be the gift of beauty," said Flora as her wand showered sparkles of fairy dust. "Tiny Princess, my gift shall be the gift of song," said Fauna.

53

But just as the third fairy, Merryweather, was about to bless the infant with her gift of happiness, a wind blew the castle doors open. There was a blinding flash of lightning, and Maleficent, the evil witch, stood in the center of the hall, furious at not being invited to the festivities. Raising her arms she announced, "I too shall bestow a gift on the child. The Princess shall indeed grow in grace and beauty, beloved by all who know her. But before the sun sets on her sixteenth birthday, she will prick her finger on the spindle of a spinning wheel and—die!"

The poor Queen lifted her baby from the cradle and held her close as if to protect her from the witch's terrible words. The guards encircled Maleficent and lunged at her with their spears, but with her powerful magic she surrounded herself with flames and vanished in a puff of smoke.

Merryweather, who still had her gift to give, quickly waved her wand above the baby saying, "Do not despair, O King and Queen. Though I have not the power to undo this fearful curse, I can help." Then, as her wand created magic pictures in the air, she chanted,

Sweet Princess, if through
This wicked witch's trick
A spindle should your finger prick,
A ray of hope there still may be

In this gift I give to thee.
Not in death but just in sleep
This fateful prophecy you'll keep
And from this slumber you shall wake
When true love's kiss the spell shall break.

King Stefan, still fearful for his daughter's life, decreed that every spinning wheel and spindle in the kingdom should on that very day be burned. A huge bonfire was built in the courtyard and every spinning wheel was destroyed.

The three fairies were not sure that that was enough to keep the Princess safe from harm. They persuaded the King and Queen to let them hide the baby Princess. They would take her to live deep in the forest, all of them disguised as peasants.

And so for sixteen long years the Princess, called Briar Rose by the three good fairies, grew up with them, hidden away in a woodcutter's cottage, with birds and forest creatures for her friends.

Maleficent tried in vain to find the girl, but the good fairies kept her whereabouts well concealed. All these years they lived as mortals, never using their magic for fear that if they did, Maleficent would be able to trace them by its telltale glow.

But on the Princess's sixteenth birthday, Flora, Fauna and Merryweather wanted to surprise her with a cake and a new dress. They sent her out to pick berries in the woods and then they set to work baking a cake and sewing a dress. The cake was a disaster, the dress was awful. "I'm going to get our magic wands," Merryweather declared. "You know, I think she's right," Fauna agreed. It was the only way they had ever made anything.

The wands sent their rays of colored magic shooting around the room, and soon turned the cake into a pastry cook's masterpiece, the dress into a beautiful gown. Unfortunately, the colored sparkles from

their magic drifted up the chimney and out into the sky above the cottage. There Maleficent's raven, who had been hunting for the Princess, saw the magic traces and flew back to his mistress to report that he had found the fairies' hiding place at last.

Meanwhile, Prince Phillip, who happened to be riding through the forest, heard a sweet song. Searching for the singer he found Briar Rose dancing with the woodland creatures and he joined them. As they sang together he and the girl fell in love on the instant. But it was growing late and Briar Rose had to leave.

"When will I see you again?" the eager Prince asked her. "Come to the cottage in the glen this evening," the girl said. "I will be there with my three guardians." And she hurried home to tell Flora, Fauna and Merryweather the wonderful news.

The fairies had news of their own for the girl. "You are really the Princess Aurora, my dear," began Flora. "And tonight we're taking you back to your father, King Stefan." Sadly Briar Rose allowed herself to be led away from the cottage before Prince Phillip came for their meeting. The fairies brought her to her room in the castle where she threw herself

on the bed, sobbing. "Let her have a few moments alone," said Flora, as they closed the door behind them. "Poor dear."

King Stefan and King Hubert had been celebrating the return of the Princess and toasting the future union of their children and their kingdoms. At that moment the arrival of Prince Phillip interrupted their revelries.

"Father," he announced excitedly, "I have just met the girl I am going to marry. Not Princess Aurora, but a peasant girl."

On hearing this, King Hubert raged at his son. When that did no good he pleaded and cajoled, all to no avail. Prince Phillip insisted he would marry the girl he loved. And he galloped off to meet Briar Rose at her cottage in the woods, leaving his father in despair.

All this time Princess Aurora had been weeping alone in her room. There Maleficent, disguised as a wisp of smoke, cast a spell on the girl and led her to a secret room in which there was a magic spinning wheel—the only one left in the entire land. "What can this be?" Aurora wondered. And then she heard a voice commanding, "Touch the spindle!" Her hand reached out to the spindle, it pricked her finger, and at once the Princess fell to the floor in a swoon.

When the three fairies found her stretched out on the stone floor they berated themselves for having left the Princess unguarded even for a minute. They carried her to the finest apartment in the palace and laid

her on a bed all embroidered with gold and silver. The Princess was as beautiful as a little angel, her cheeks still rosy, her lips coral. And indeed, although her eyes were shut, she breathed very softly; so they knew she was not dead.

"Come," said Flora, "we'll put everyone in the castle to sleep until the Princess awakens!" The fairies sprinkled sleep-dust on King Stefan,

his Queen, King Hubert, the soldiers and guards, the flag-carriers, the servants—even on the fountains in the courtyard and the candles in the banquet hall. Then they flew off to find Prince Phillip, for only he could awaken the Princess.

When Phillip arrived at the cottage in the forest, Maleficent's henchmen were awaiting him. They chained him and locked him in the witch's dungeon, where he was taunted by Maleficent. She showed him a picture of his peasant girl, Briar Rose, asleep in the tower of King Stefan's castle, and told him she was the Princess Aurora, doomed to sleep until his kiss awakened her. Then, laughing cruelly, Maleficent left the Prince tugging at his chains, locked in the dungeon. It was there the three fairies found him and released him. Arming the Prince with the mighty Sword of Truth and the enchanted Shield of Virtue, they helped him escape from Maleficent's castle.

   When Phillip reached the castle of King Stefan, he found the walls overgrown with a forest of thorns while a fire-spouting dragon—

Maleficent in disguise—guarded the drawbridge. The fairies sprinkled magic dust on the Prince's sword, chanting,

Now, Sword of Truth, fly swift and sure
That evil die and good endure.

At which the sword flew straight to the dragon's heart, slaying the beast, who turned back into Maleficent as it died.

The Prince ran up the steps of the tower, two at a time, past all the sleeping courtiers, until he reached the chamber where Princess Aurora—his beloved Briar Rose—lay. Gently he kissed her. The Princess awakened, smiled at Phillip, and the whole room lit up. The fountains in the courtyard started to play again, candles flamed once more, the court awoke, and trumpets sounded from the balcony as the Prince and Princess walked down the Grand Stairway hand in hand.

Then before the delighted eyes of King Stefan, the Queen and King Hubert, Phillip and Aurora began to dance to the strains of a romantic waltz. Watching from the musicians' balcony, Fauna started to cry.

"Why Fauna," Flora exclaimed, "Whatever is the matter now?"
Fauna, sobbing, said, "Oh, I just love happy endings!"
And indeed Phillip and Aurora lived happily forever after.

SLEEPING BEAUTY

The Story of the Production

The third, and most ambitious, of Walt Disney's fairy-tale presentations, *Sleeping Beauty* was six years in the making at a cost of $6 million. It was released in 1959.

This animated feature was far more challenging than its predecessors because of the new large Technirama 70mm projection process it employed. Walt Disney explained that the wide screen "imposed added labors on the artists [300 in all]. They had to move their characters in larger fields of action. Every phase of artistry and mechanics, which together comprise the art of animation, had to be revamped."

The richly colored backgrounds were modeled after Renaissance paintings, and as for the characters in Charles Perrault's seventeenth-century classic, Disney instructed his animators to "make them as real as possible, near flesh-and-blood, and sympathetic." One million drawings later, Disney himself called the perfected process "the art of painting in lifelike motion."

The fidelity of the sound, too, was improved to do full justice to Tchaikovsky's lilting *Sleeping Beauty* ballet music that serves as the picture's score. Five songs—"Once Upon a Dream," "I Wonder," "Hail the Princess Aurora," "The Skump Song," and "Sleeping Beauty Song"—contribute to the charm of one of Disney's best-loved films.

The color laboratory in the Studio's ink and paint department prepares the special colors for each production, selecting the pigments and making certain that the paint batches remain consistent

If You Believe

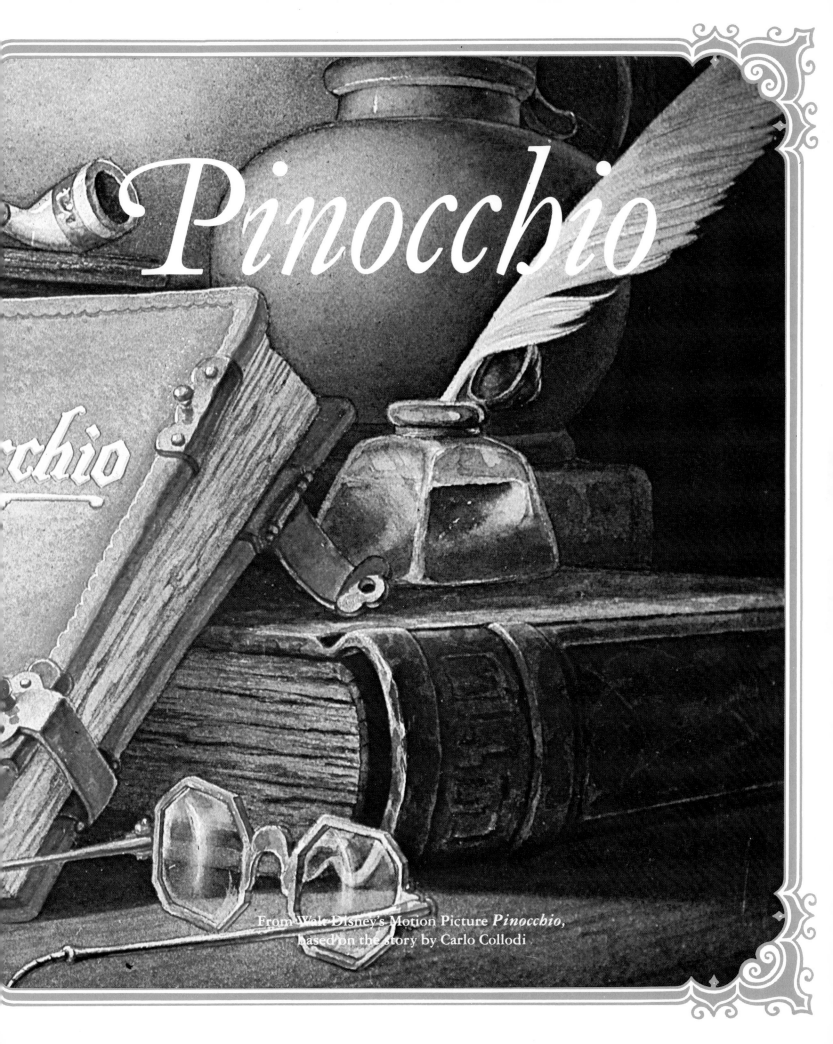

Pinocchio

From Walt Disney's Motion Picture *Pinocchio*,
based on the story by Carlo Collodi

There was once a poor woodcarver named Geppetto who made fantastic clocks and music boxes and every kind of toy you can imagine, each one a work of art. Geppetto, who almost never had enough to eat, thought that if he made a clever wooden puppet that could dance and turn somersaults in the air he could travel around the world with it and earn his bit of bread and glass of wine. So he found a good smooth piece of wood and, taking up his tools, he carved a little boy, painted him in bright colors, and gave him the name of Pinocchio.

The puppet could walk and dance very well if Geppetto pulled its strings. But the woodcarver, who lived a lonely life with only his goldfish, Cleo, and his cat, Figaro, for company, thought, "Wouldn't it be wonderful if Pinocchio was a real boy?" That night when everyone was sound asleep the Blue Fairy came down from her star in the sky and touched Pinocchio with her wand. The puppet's strings disappeared at her touch, while the Blue Fairy recited these words:

Little puppet made of pine,
Wake! The gift of life is thine!

Pinocchio was startled to find that he could move by himself and could even talk. "Am I a real boy?" he asked in amazement. But the fairy explained that to become a real boy he would have to prove himself brave, truthful, and unselfish, and would have to learn to choose between right and wrong. "Then, some day you *will* be a real boy, Pinocchio," she promised.

The Blue Fairy appointed Jiminy Cricket—a talking cricket, who had lived a hundred years and more in the house—to be Pinocchio's conscience and to teach him the difference between right and wrong. As she faded away in the glow of her bright star, her voice drifted back, "Remember, Pinocchio, be a good boy and let your conscience be your guide."

The next morning when he awoke, Geppetto was overjoyed to find that Pinocchio was truly alive. "You must go to school now," he told the puppet, "to learn things and get smart, so you can become a real boy." And the old woodcarver sold his only coat in order to buy Pinocchio schoolbooks and a shiny red apple like the other children's. Pinocchio was so grateful that he threw his arms around Geppetto's neck and thanked him again and again. "I shall learn to read at school today, Father," he promised, and off he skipped, with Jiminy Cricket at his heels.

But on the way to school Pinocchio was stopped by a couple of scheming rascals, J. Worthington Foulfellow, the fox, and his companion Gideon, the alley cat. The minute they laid eyes on the puppet without strings they knew he would be worth a fortune to Stromboli, a showman who owned a traveling puppet theater. "A little wooden boy! What an act!" They convinced Pinocchio that the theater was an easier road to success than school. Jiminy Cricket tried his best to persuade the puppet that he must turn his back on temptation and go to school instead, but Pinocchio, happily trusting his new friends, refused to listen. "Hi-diddle-dee-dee," he sang, "an actor's life for me."

Pinocchio was a great success on the stage, where the audience rained gold and silver coins on him. When Stromboli realized how much money he could make, he placed the valuable puppet in a cage. Pinocchio wept then for his father, Geppetto, and his good conscience, Jiminy, neither of whom he expected ever to see again. But Jiminy Cricket did not give up so easily, and that night he found his way to poor Pinocchio's cage.

While Jiminy was trying to comfort the puppet, the Blue Fairy appeared again. When she asked Pinocchio why he hadn't gone to school, the puppet invented a long story about being kidnapped by two monsters. As he told it, his wooden nose grew longer and longer with each lie, until finally it was like a small tree with branches and leaves sprouting from it.

Pinocchio was frightened. "What's happened?" he asked. "You are telling a lie that keeps growing and growing, as plain as the nose on your face," the fairy replied. Pinocchio promised to be truthful and good from then on, so the Blue Fairy touched his cage with her wand. "This is the last time I can help you," she said, as she freed him. Pinocchio, his nose back to normal, set off to race Jiminy Cricket back to Geppetto's house.

Meanwhile, at the Red Lobster Inn, those two scamps, J. Worthington Foulfellow and Gideon, were plotting new mischief. They had found a wicked coachman who collected stupid little boys who played hooky from school. "I takes 'em to Pleasure Island," he explained, "and they never comes back—as boys." The coachman winked an eye. "I'll pay you a gold piece for every boy you bring me. We leaves at midnight."

Once again Foulfellow and Gideon tricked Pinocchio into going with them. The puppet had been racing Jiminy Cricket home when he met the fox and the cat. They convinced Pinocchio that he needed a vacation at Pleasure Island for the sake of his health, and they personally handed him over to the coachman with the ticket for his fare. With a full load of boys, the coach, pulled by six little donkeys, clattered off to the ferry-boat dock. Luckily Jiminy Cricket had run after Pinocchio and, just in time, he hopped up on the lantern under the coach.

At Pleasure Island Pinocchio became friendly with a tough boy named Lampwick. "This is a great place—no school, you can fight and wreck the place and no one stops you. Take all the cake, pie, dill pickles, and ice cream you want. Stuff yourself. It's all free," Lampwick told him gleefully.

The boys destroyed books and pictures, broke windows, set fire to houses, chopped up furniture, smoked cigars, played cards, and chewed tobacco. "Bein' bad is lots of fun, ain't it?" Pinocchio said to Lampwick, trying to copy the older boy's way of talking. They were playing cards and smoking when Jiminy Cricket finally found Pinocchio. "Look at yourself!" he scolded. "How do you ever expect to be a real boy?"

But Pinocchio was having such a good time he refused to leave when Jiminy asked him. He didn't hear the coachman say to one of his helpers, "Give a bad boy enough rope and he'll soon make a jackass of himself." He didn't see the coachman loading a boat with little donkeys. But Jiminy, who had gone down to the dock alone, saw what was happening. The little donkeys brayed and the coachman cracked his whip at them. "Quiet!" he ordered. "You boys had your fun. Now pay for it!"

Jiminy sped back to Pinocchio. "Hope I'm not too late!" he panted. Lampwick had already been turned into a braying donkey, and Pinocchio had grown donkey's ears and a tail. Jiminy managed to get him to the shore before he got any worse, and the two of them swam for the mainland.

Geppetto, in the meantime, had gone out to search for his missing son. When Pinocchio and Jiminy Cricket finally came to his house it was dark and empty. They were sitting sadly on the curb, wondering what

could have happened to the kindly old man, when a dove dropped a note at their feet. Jiminy read the message aloud—Geppetto, while trying to get to Pleasure Island to find Pinocchio, had been swallowed by Monstro the Whale. He was still alive, in the whale's stomach, at the bottom of the sea.

"I'm going to find him," Pinocchio declared. He set off for the ocean with Jiminy hopping along behind him. "He's a whale of a whale," the cricket warned, "and besides it's dangerous." But Pinocchio was determined to find his father. When they got to the ocean they plunged into the water and swam until they saw the huge dark shape of Monstro.

When the whale opened his jaws, Pinocchio and Jiminy swam into his mouth. There, inside the enormous creature, were Geppetto and his little raft. "Father," cried Pinocchio. "Pinocchio! My son!" Geppetto exclaimed, hugging and kissing the puppet.

Together they figured out how to escape. They built a fire inside the whale and, when the smoke made Monstro sneeze, they were ready on the raft and quickly paddled out of his open mouth. Everything worked according to plan until the enraged whale caught sight of the little raft as it headed for shore. He pursued it and smashed it into splinters with his great tail, knocking Geppetto unconscious. Pinocchio bravely rescued his father and then tried to divert the angry whale while

Geppetto was carried safely to shore by a big wave. After being trapped under some rocks, the puppet was finally washed ashore, half drowned.

Sadly Geppetto carried Pinocchio home and put him to bed. He wiped away a tear as he looked at the donkey ears growing out of Pinocchio's head and thought of how brave the puppet had been. Suddenly the room glowed with bright blue starlight and the Blue Fairy appeared at the bedside. "Awake, Pinocchio, awake!" she said. "You have been brave, truthful, and unselfish."

Pinocchio sat up and opened his eyes. "Father!" he called. "I'm alive!" Then, looking at his hands, he continued, "And I'm real! *I'm a real boy!*" Geppetto, Cleo, and Figaro were overjoyed, and hugged and kissed the good-looking little boy with dark brown hair and blue eyes, who appeared so happy and full of joy.

Jiminy Cricket smiled. "He deserved to be a real boy," he said. At that there appeared on his lapel a badge of solid gold with "Official Conscience" spelled out on its ribbon. "Oh, thank you, Ma'am," the cricket chirped, but the Blue Fairy had already vanished. Only a brilliant star winked at Jiminy, its beams sparkling on his golden badge.

Contentedly the cricket sang his favorite song:

When you wish upon a star
Your dream comes true.

PINOCCHIO

The Story of the Production

How do you follow the outstanding accomplishment of *Snow White and the Seven Dwarfs*, Walt Disney's first feature-length cartoon, which won worldwide audience acceptance and a Special Academy Award in 1939? Why, you start right in on a new feature, embellish the animation, and, in the words of Milt Kahl, one of the animation directors, "Spend money and creative energy like they have never been spent since."

That's what Walt Disney did with his second full-length animated feature, *Pinocchio*. He built up his modest cartoon factory from a staff of three hundred to one of nearly two thousand, and experimented with new techniques with bold self-assurance. The excitement—and money—generated by the success of *Snow White* were lavished on Carlo Collodi's nineteenth-century children's classic about the wooden puppet who became a real boy.

Pinocchio revolutionized animated special effects, paving the way for *Fantasia*. Disney and his artists conceived the impossible, and the technicians created a fairyland of imagination and dramatic visual effects. The picture won two Academy Awards for 1940, the year of its release: Best Original Musical Score and Best Song, "When You Wish Upon a Star," sung by Jiminy Cricket. "Give a Little Whistle," "Little Woodenhead," "Hi-Diddle-Dee-Dee," "I've Got No Strings," and "Turn on the Old Music Box" were the other songs, all of them designed to carry the major story points and advance the action.

Pinocchio has been released on an average of every eight years since its premiere and has attracted a larger audience each time.

Walt Disney and the marionette star
of his 1940 feature, *Pinocchio,* seem
to be congratulating each other on a
superlative production

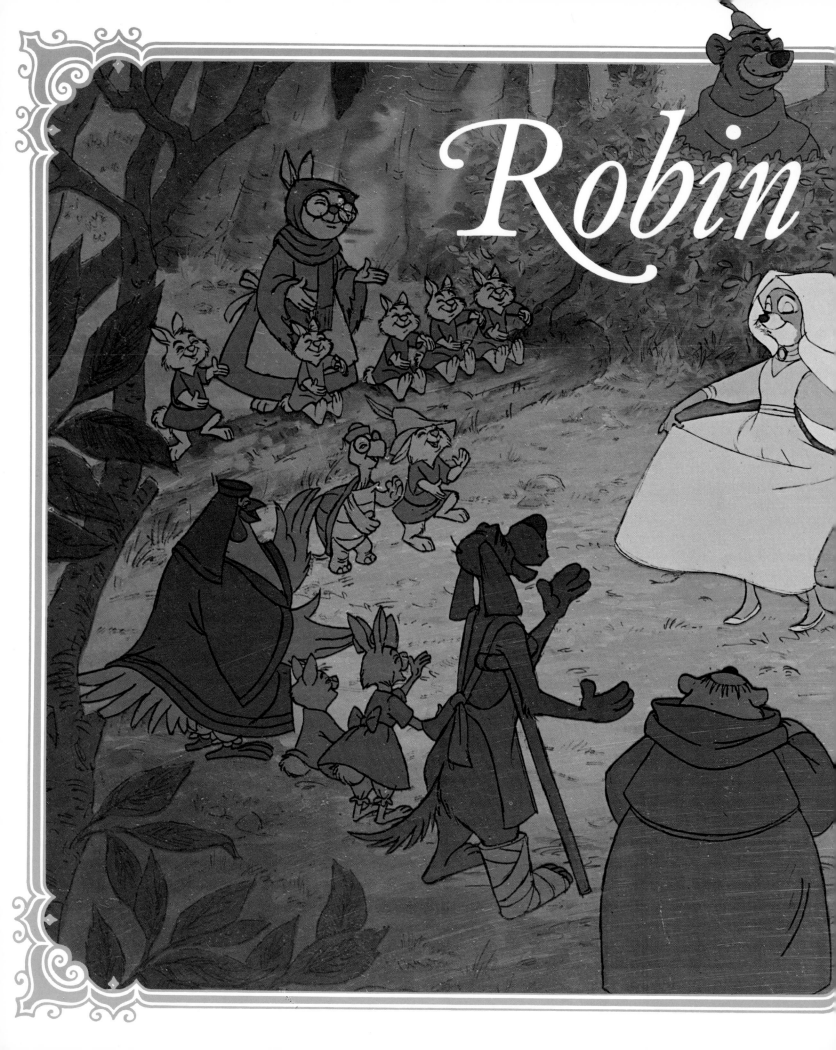

Robin

Hood

From Walt Disney Productions' Motion Picture *Robin Hood*

 he animal kingdom has its own version of the Robin Hood legends, the tales of the English hero of the common people, whose adventures were first sung by medieval minstrels. Allan a Dale, a sweet-voiced rooster, who was Robin Hood's favorite singer, presents their version.

One fine spring day, Robin Hood, a clever fox, and Little John, a large bear, were walking through Sherwood Forest, dressed from top to toe in Lincoln green. All the members of Robin's merry band wore Lincoln green and lived deep in Sherwood Forest as outlaws. Yet they were beloved by the country people because none ever came to Robin in time of need and went away empty-handed.

Now the times were troubled because good King Richard had gone off on the Third Crusade, leaving his brother Prince John, a scrawny and tyrannical lion, to rule England. Prince John's chief adviser was Sir Hiss, a wily snake, and between the two of them they had put a heavy burden of taxes on the poor people. This fine spring day, Prince John's

entourage was making its way through Sherwood Forest on the way to
Nottingham to tax the people there. As Prince John said to Sir Hiss,
"Rob the poor to feed the rich. Am I right, counsellor?" and he and Sir
Hiss chuckled gleefully as they fondled the bags of gold they had already
collected.

Robin Hood and Little John saw the royal entourage in the
distance, and Little John asked, "Are we good guys or bad guys? You
know, out robbing the rich to feed the poor?" But Robin Hood

corrected him. "*Rob* is a naughty word. We never rob, we just *borrow* a bit from those who can afford it." Then he pointed to the Royal Coach. "And here comes another collection day for the poor."

The two outlaws quickly slipped into disguises as gypsy fortune tellers, and ran ahead to the side of the road. When the Royal Coach passed, they offered to tell Prince John his fortune. Cleverly, Robin Hood and Little John flattered the Prince and in a very short time they had tricked him out of his jewels, his money bags, and even the royal robes. Then off they scampered into the depths of Sherwood Forest, loaded down with their loot.

Prince John was furious upon discovering that he had been tricked, and when he arrived at Nottingham he wanted revenge. His helpless subjects paid dearly for his humiliation. He taxed the heart and soul out of the poor people of Nottingham, and if they couldn't pay, they were carted off to jail. But most of all, Prince John wanted to catch that scalawag Robin Hood and punish him.

He told the Sheriff of Nottingham, a villainous wolf, to announce an archery tournament with the first prize a golden arrow and a kiss from his niece Maid Marian, a beautiful vixen. Prince John knew that Robin Hood had loved Marian a long time ago, before he became an outlaw, and he was sure that such a prize would lure Robin out of his hiding place.

Nottingham was a fair sight on the day of the archery match. All along the green meadow outside the town wall stretched rows of benches for people of rank and quality. At the end of the range, near the target, was a raised platform bedecked with ribbons, pennants, and garlands of flowers for the Prince, Maid Marian, and the royal party. The poorer folk sat or lay upon the green grass near the railing that kept them off the archery range. The very best archers of Merry England had come to this shooting match, and they gathered in the great tent, inspecting their bows and arrows and talking of the good shots they had made in their day. The Sheriff looked about for Robin Hood, but did not see him among the archers. "He is too big a coward to appear," he thought.

But the Sheriff was mistaken. Robin, who was one of the best archers in England, would not have missed this tournament for all the world. He and his Merry Men were there in various disguises, mingling with the crowd. Some were friars, some beggars, some peasants; Robin himself was a stork, while Little John got himself up as the Duke of Chutney and sat on the royal platform at Prince John's left hand.

The tournament had narrowed down to two contestants, the Sheriff of Nottingham and a talkative stork who spoke every time the Sheriff was about to make his shot. "Listen, Scissorbill, if you shoot half as good as you blabbermouth, you're better'n Robin Hood," said the irritated Sheriff. "He's scared of me. That's why he didn't show up today." Then the Sheriff shot his last arrow and it went straight to the bull's-eye. He was certain he had won the contest. But the stork had one more arrow and, drawing his trusty bow, he loosed the string. The arrow flew so true that it knocked the Sheriff's arrow off the target and lodged dead center in the bull's-eye.

The stork strode confidently up to the royal platform to receive his prize. But Prince John knew there was only one archer in all the land who could shoot like that. He tapped the stork on each shoulder with his sword, causing the disguise to fall away. "I sentence you to instant and immediate death, Robin Hood!" proclaimed Prince John. The Sheriff and the executioner seized the outlaw and bound him with stout ropes. Maid Marian pleaded for his life in vain, and all of his friends were in despair—when suddenly the Prince said, "Let him go!" Little John, as the Duke of Chutney, had quietly put his knife to the Prince's back and forced him to withdraw his orders.

Then the Merry Men of Sherwood came forward out of the crowd and battled with the royal guards. In the confusion Robin escaped with Maid Marian. They made their way to the hiding place deep in Sherwood Forest, and when all the band was together again the forest rang with their songs and laughter as they waited for the day when good King Richard would return to England and reclaim the throne from his unjust brother.

Once again an enraged Prince John, advised by Sir Hiss, punished the people with taxes four times greater than before. Soon the prisons were filled with poor people unable to pay, among them Robin's friend, kindly Friar Tuck, a badger. Once again, hoping to lure Robin Hood out into the open, the Prince set a trap. He announced that he would hang the good Friar for treason the very next morning. Secretly he hoped it would prove to be a double hanging, for surely Robin would come to Nottingham to save his friend, and this time they would be ready for him.

Robin and Little John stole into the town late at night. "A jailbreak is the only chance he's got," Robin Hood decided. Silently Little John crept up behind the sentry, who had just called out the time and his "All is well." Little John pulled him over the castle wall, where Robin Hood took his keys and donned his uniform. They tiptoed past the Sheriff of Nottingham, who was snoozing at the prison gate, and in short order they unlocked all the barred doors and freed the villagers who were imprisoned.

"I'll just drop in on the royal treasury, for good measure," Robin said. He tossed a hook and rope to the balcony of Prince John's bedchamber and shinnied his way up. From the balcony he shot an arrow, attached to a rope, through a prison window where Little John waited. Little John threaded the rope through an iron ring and shot it back to Robin Hood, making a perfect double clothesline and pulley. Then Little John sat back to wait for the fun.

Cautiously Robin Hood entered Prince John's chambers, where the Prince and Sir Hiss were snoring in their beds. Bags of gold were everywhere, even under the Prince's pillow. Robin stealthily removed them, one by one, to the balcony. There he fastened them to the

clothesline, and Little John then reeled them toward himself at the window of the jail. Friar Tuck helped pull the bags in, chuckling, "Praise the Lord and pass the tax rebate." Soon all the freed villagers were loaded down with gold. Led by Little John and Friar Tuck, they marched out of the jail in the dawn's first light, past the empty gallows that Robin Hood had helped them to cheat.

Robin took the last two bags of gold, leapt from the balcony to the clothesline, and rode off on it. Sir Hiss and Prince John awakened just as Robin fled, and Sir Hiss tried to recapture the last bag of gold. When he pulled at it, it split open, showering coins down on the villagers below, who happily ran off with them.

The Prince and Sir Hiss were strung out on the clothesline, screaming for help. Their cries alerted the guards, who charged after Robin, but he was too fast and clever for them. Meanwhile, Little John, the Friar, and the villagers clambered onto a two-wheeled cart and crossed the drawbridge just in time. Robin Hood held off the guards and then dived from the palace wall into the moat, where no one dared follow him. It was a time of narrow escapes and wild excitement, not soon forgotten in the town of Nottingham.

But, all's well that ends well. King Richard, a lion-hearted lion, returned from the Crusade and set his kingdom straight. Maid Marian and Robin Hood were married (the King joked that he had an outlaw for an in-law) and went to live quietly and lawfully in Sherwood Forest. And as for Prince John, Sir Hiss, and the Sheriff of Nottingham, they too found a new home—in the Nottingham prison.

ROBIN HOOD

The Story of the Production

In this, the first cartoon feature conceived and created without Walt Disney, the talented team he had forged at the Studio carried his work forward. While *The Aristocats* was still being drawn, Ken Anderson, art director and developer of new projects, scouted stories for the next feature, which was to be taken from the classics.

Robin Hood was the choice, but it was given a unique "unclassic" twist worthy of Walt Disney himself. Wolfgang (Woolie) Reitherman, the producer-director, pointed out that this version of the age-old tale is presented "as seen through the eyes of the animals of Sherwood Forest who knew Robin best." This unusual gambit had the double virtue of originality and practicality—playing to the greatest strength of the Studio artists, who drew animals with human foibles superlatively well.

So we find the Disney Robin Hood a bold and crafty fox, Little John a large, fun-loving bear, Prince John a neurotic lion, Sir Hiss (a pure Disney invention who didn't exist in the original Robin Hood tales) a sycophantic snake, the Sheriff of Nottingham a villainous wolf, Friar Tuck a badger, and Maid Marian a lovely vixen. The voices for the characters were supplied by actors whose gestures and mannerisms added immeasurably to the personalities as they took shape on the drawing boards. The characteristics of Peter Ustinov himself lurk behind the expressions and movements of Prince John; Phil Harris, who was the happy-go-lucky Baloo in *The Jungle Book* and O'Malley in *The Aristocats,* lends his voice and personality to Little John; Terry-Thomas, the gap-toothed British comedian, used his distinctive sibilance for Sir Hiss; Andy Devine of the gravel voice spoke for Friar Tuck; and Brian Bedford, a British Hamlet, was the polished, sophisticated voice of Robin Hood.

Describing the conditions under which the Disney team worked, Reitherman explained, "The atmosphere in the Studio was alive with creativity, a marriage of many minds and talents. From our imagination we created frame-by-frame spontaneity. We've sustained that feeling through many cartoon features from *Snow White* to *Robin Hood* because no picture has ever been the same. We were always trying new methods, new techniques, pioneering one thing or another."

Robin Hood, released in 1972, was a worthy successor to the animated features previously created under Walt Disney's personal supervision.

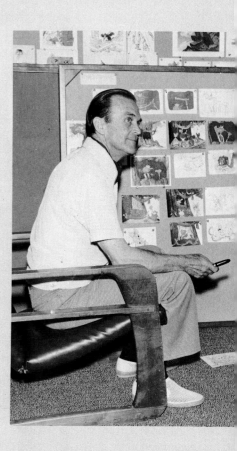

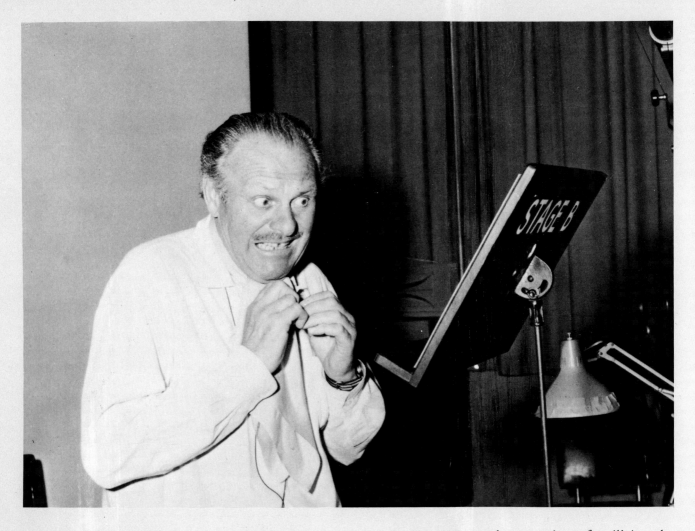

Terry-Thomas becomes the crafty villain as he records the voice of Sir Hiss, the sly snake

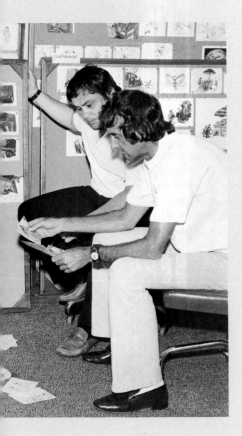

Art director Ken Anderson and two assistants decide on set and character designs

Ichabod Crane

From Walt Disney's Motion Picture *The Legend of Sleepy Hollow,*
based on the original story by Washington Irving

If we could journey back to that time in American history when Manhattan was but a Dutch market town, we would discover in the bosom of one of those spacious coves which indent the eastern shore of the Hudson River a small rural port generally known by the name of Tarry Town. This name was given in former days by the good housewives of the countryside because of the natural inclination of their husbands to tarry about the village tavern on market days.

About two miles from this village there is a little valley among high hills which is one of the quietest places in the whole world. This sequestered glen has long been known as Sleepy Hollow, and its rustic lads are called the Sleepy Hollow Boys throughout the neighboring country. A drowsy, dreamy influence seems to hang over the land. Some say the place was bewitched in the early days. The whole neighborhood abounds with haunted spots, strange sights, and twilight superstitions. The dominant spirit that haunts this enchanted region is the apparition of a figure on horseback without a head, who has sometimes been seen by the country folk galloping along in the gloom of night as if on the wings of the wind. This specter is known as the Headless Horseman of Sleepy Hollow.

Into this quiet valley there came, late one drowsy autumn afternoon, an itinerant schoolmaster from Connecticut, by name of Ichabod Crane. To see him strolling along with his coat flapping and fluttering around him, one might well mistake him for some scarecrow escaped from a cornfield. He was tall and exceedingly lank; his head was small and flat on top with a long, pointed nose that looked like a weather vane perched on his spindle neck.

As Ichabod walked down the main street of the village reading a book, the townspeople were astonished at the sight of their new schoolmaster, but they soon found that he did his work well. He ruled over the children in his one-room schoolhouse by bearing in mind the golden maxim, "Spare the rod and spoil the child." Ichabod Crane's scholars certainly were not spoiled.

But after school he was the companion and playmate of the children, and would even walk some of the smaller ones home, especially if they happened to have pretty sisters or mothers noted for their good cooking.

According to country custom in those parts, Ichabod boarded and lodged at the houses of the farmers whose children he instructed. He lived with each family a week, and went the rounds of the neighborhood with all his worldly goods tied up in a large cotton handkerchief.

Ichabod found other ways to increase his slender income—he was the singing master of the neighborhood and taught the young people to sing psalms. On Sundays, when he led the choir, his nasal voice resounded far above all the rest of the congregation. There are peculiar quavers still heard in that church and even half a mile off on a still Sunday morning, which are said to be descended from the nose of Ichabod Crane.

The females of the neighborhood found the schoolmaster to be vastly superior in taste and accomplishments to the rough Sleepy Hollow Boys and their leader, Brom Bones. Ichabod was invited to tea at the farmhouses, or would take a Sunday stroll with a whole bevy of country damsels along the banks of the millpond while the more bashful country bumpkins hung sheepishly back, envying him.

It was inevitable that Ichabod would become an object of ridicule to Brom Bones and his friends, but he didn't mind. He was content in the women's admiration of his great learning, for he had read several books quite through and was a perfect master of Cotton Mather's *History of New England Witchcraft,* in which, by the way, he most firmly believed.

There came a time, however, when the teacher's path was crossed by a being that causes more perplexity to mortal man than ghosts and goblins. That being was a woman, Katrina Van Tassel, the eighteen-year-old daughter and only child of old Baltus Van Tassel, the wealthiest farmer in the county. She was a blooming lass, plump as a partridge, ripe, melting, and rosy-cheeked. And a coquette.

Now there was no doubt that the fair Katrina was the richest prize in the countryside. And the schoolmaster, being an ambitious man, at once began to fill his mind with hopeful suppositions.

"Ah, Katrina, my love, my treasure," he sang to himself, "who can resist your grace, your charm? And who can resist your father's farm?"

From the moment Ichabod decided to gain Katrina's affections his peace of mind was at an end. He had more real difficulties than a knight-errant of yore who had only giants, dragons, enchanters and suchlike to contend with. Ichabod had to win his way to the heart of a country flirt who was surrounded by a number of rustic admirers, including the most formidable obstacle of all—Brom Bones himself. Brom was famed for his great skill in horsemanship, being as dexterous on horseback as a Tartar. He was foremost at all races and cockfights and, with the leadership that bodily strength confers in rustic life, he was the umpire in all disputes. He was always ready either for a fight or a frolic, but had more mischief than ill will in his makeup. And with all his overbearing roughness, there was a strong dash of waggish good humor at bottom.

Such was the rival with whom Ichabod Crane had to contend. Brom had cleared the field of all other suitors and the fair Katrina often wished some champion would appear and, for once, take the field openly against the boisterous Brom, if only because competition would lend some spice to the courtship. And so she did not altogether discourage the schoolteacher's attentions.

In this way, matters went on for some time. It was upon the occasion of her father's annual Halloween frolic that Katrina chose to stir up the embers of the smouldering rivalry. Thus, one invitation in particular carried a most personal and provocative summons.

The gallant Ichabod was in a transport of joy. To him this invitation could mean but one thing. He spent at least an extra half hour at his toilet, brushing and furbishing up his best—and indeed only—suit of rusty black, and admiring himself in a bit of broken looking glass that hung in the schoolhouse. "Just be your own charming self and the fair Katrina is yours for the asking," he told his reflection. So, gaily bedecked and nobly mounted on a broken-down plowhorse he had borrowed for the occasion, Ichabod rode forth like a knight of old to keep a tryst with his lady fair.

In all the countryside there was nothing to equal a merrymaking at
Mynheer Van Tassel's farm. Neighbors from miles around, dressed in
their best, came to partake of the ample charms of a genuine Dutch
country tea-table in the sumptuous time of autumn. Such heaped-up
platters of cakes of various kinds known only to experienced Dutch
housewives! There was the doughnut, the crisp and crumbling cruller,
sweet cakes and shortcakes, ginger cakes and honey cakes—a whole
family of cakes. And then there were apple pies, peach pies, and
pumpkin pies, besides slices of ham and smoked beef; and, moreover,
delectable dishes of preserved plums and peaches and pears and quinces;
not to mention broiled shad and roasted chicken; and with the motherly
teapot sending up its clouds of vapor from the midst. Ichabod Crane did
ample justice to every dainty.

The sound of music from the common room summoned all to the
dance. Ichabod prided himself on his dancing as much as upon his
singing voice. Not a limb was idle, and to have seen his loose frame
clattering about the room you would have thought Saint Vitus himself,
that blessed patron of the dance, was cutting the figures before you in

person. The lady of his heart was his partner while Brom Bones, sorely smitten with love and jealousy, sat brooding by himself in a corner.

There was no doubt that Ichabod was the man of the hour, but Brom Bones was a stubborn suitor and was determined that, by fair means or foul, his time would come.

When the night grew late, Van Tassel always called upon his guests to tell ghostly tales of Halloween. Brom knew there was no more firm believer in spooks and goblins than Ichabod Crane, and he moved close to the teacher and began to tell a fearsome story of his midnight

adventure with the Headless Horseman. Ichabod listened with eyes popping as Brom told of being pursued by the Horseman, who was looking for a head to replace his own. Dramatically, Brom finished his tale:

> Now if you doubt this tale is so, I met this spook just a year ago, and I didn't stop for a second look, but made for the bridge that spans the brook; for once you cross that bridge, my friends, the ghost is through—his power ends.

Laughing at the terrified teacher, Brom continued, "So when you're riding home tonight, look out! Beware! Make for the bridge with all your might because the Headless Horseman will be down near the hollow, looking for a head to take."

The party now gradually broke up. The farmers gathered their families in their wagons, and some of the girls left on horseback with their favorite young men. Only Ichabod lingered behind, according to the custom of country lovers, to have a moment alone with the heiress, fully convinced he was now on the high road to success. What was said between them no one knows, but something must have gone wrong, for Ichabod came out after a very short time looking quite unhappy and discouraged. Had the girl only been playing one of her coquettish tricks, encouraging the poor teacher in order to speed the conquest of his rival?

Looking neither to the right or left to gloat over Van Tassel's rich barns and fields, which he had so often dreamed of owning, Ichabod went straight to the stable. With several hearty cuffs and kicks he roused his old horse, who had been soundly sleeping, dreaming of mountains of corn and oats and whole valleys of timothy and clover.

It was at the very witching hour of night that Ichabod pursued his travel homeward. The sky grew blacker as, one by one, the stars winked out and driving clouds obscured the moon. Never had the schoolmaster felt so melancholy, so utterly alone. And the nearer he approached the hollow the more dismal he became.

Once inside the murky glen, Ichabod felt more afraid, for now the forest seemed to close in behind him and every detail of Brom's story returned to haunt him. He tried to whistle a song, but the blowing leaves, an owl's whoo-whoo, the croaking of a frog warning "Headless Horseman, Headless Horseman," filled him with terror. And then he heard the sound of hooves in the distance, coming closer. Suddenly there was wild laughter, and a black horse carrying a headless rider reared up beside him. Ichabod's terror increased when he saw that the head, which should have rested on the rider's shoulders, was carried before him

instead. A sword whizzed past his ear. Ichabod's old horse ran as fast as he could with the other pursuing him. Once again the terrible rider slashed at Ichabod's head with his sword. "If I can but reach that bridge," thought Ichabod, "I am safe."

A convulsive kick in the ribs and the old nag sprang upon the bridge, thundered over the resounding planks, and gained the opposite side. And now Ichabod cast a look behind to see if his ghostly pursuer had vanished. Just then, to his horror, he saw the headless rider rise in his stirrups and hurl the grinning head at him. Ichabod tried to dodge the horrible missile, but too late. It hit his head, tumbling him from his horse.

The next morning they found the old horse cropping grass near his master's gate, but not a trace of the schoolteacher. On the far side of the bridge, however, there was discovered the hat of the unfortunate Ichabod, and close beside it—a shattered pumpkin.

It was shortly thereafter that Brom Bones led the blooming Katrina to the altar. Now rumors persisted that Ichabod still lived, married to a wealthy woman in a distant county. But of course the old country wives, who are the best judges of such matters, refused to believe such nonsense. They knew the schoolmaster had been spirited away by the Headless Horseman, and it is a favorite story often told in the neighborhood round the winter evening fire. Even today, a plowboy, loitering homeward on a still autumn evening, has sometimes thought he heard a voice in the distance chanting a melancholy psalm in the tranquil solitude of Sleepy Hollow.

THE ADVENTURES OF ICHABOD AND MR. TOAD

The Story of the Production

Walt Disney, the master of entertainment, combined a colonial American folk tale, Washington Irving's *Legend of Sleepy Hollow*, with a droll British fantasy, Kenneth Grahame's *Wind in the Willows*, to make a rousingly successful animated feature. Bing Crosby narrated and sang the tale of the ludicrous Yankee schoolmaster, Ichabod Crane, and his devastating courtship. Basil Rathbone, crisply British, told of the reckless capers of Mr. Toad of Toad Hall.

To capture the authentic feeling of the Hudson Valley country and the traditions of a colonial farming community like the one at Sleepy Hollow, Disney personally visited the region around Tarrytown. The results of his careful research can be seen in the accurate details of costumes, buildings, and landscape rendered by the animation artists.

But the Disney version of *Ichabod* is more than the tale of a playful yokel who uses a fearful legend to get the best of his rival for the hand of the local belle. Brom Bones, a hulking but harmless jokester, becomes a menacing demon on his wild midnight chase after the terrified schoolteacher. In those scenes he is a match for any of the most fiendish Disney villains. The dark scarlets, fierce purples, and livid magentas of the Headless Horseman chase scenes raise the emotional pitch—color in action being used in a masterly fashion to heighten the drama.

The Adventures of Ichabod and Mr. Toad was released in 1949. Bing Crosby and his Rhythmaires sang three songs, "Katrina," a sweet ballad; "Ichabod," a light, rhythmic chant; and "Headless Horseman," a fantastic jitter-song very popular on Halloween.

In 1978 Ichabod's story was re-released as *The Legend of Sleepy Hollow*.

The hands of animator Frank Thomas creating the character of Ichabod in action-packed line drawings

118

Painting a cel is delicate work. No smudges, specks, or fingerprints can mar the celluloid sheet, and the execution must be meticulous because the slightest flaw will be magnified enormously on the motion picture screen

Adapted from the Walt Disney Motion Picture *Peter Pan*,
based upon *Peter Pan* by Sir James Matthew Barrie, by arrangement
with The Hospital for Sick Children, London, England

WALT DISNEY'S

Peter Pan

r. and Mrs. Darling lived near a little park in Bloomsbury, a quiet part of London, with their three children, Wendy, John, and Michael. The children's nursemaid was a shaggy St. Bernard dog called Nana, who always knew exactly what medicine to give for a cough or a cold and could carry a spoon of the stuff in her mouth without spilling a drop. She was a treasure, Mrs. Darling often said.

At bedtime Wendy used to tell her younger brothers exciting stories about Never Land, a magical place where children remained young forever and had adventures with mermaids, Indians, pirates, fairies, and a remarkable boy named Peter Pan. "He has sometimes come to the foot of my bed and played on his pipes for me," Wendy confided to them. "The last time, Nana caught him at it and nipped off his shadow as he escaped."

One evening Mr. and Mrs. Darling were going out to a party. As they kissed the children good-night, Mr. Darling said to Wendy, "You're growing up, dear, and it's time you had a room of your own. This is your last night in the nursery." It so happened that on this same night the extraordinary adventures of the Darling children began.

A moment after Mr. and Mrs. Darling left the house, the nursery windows blew open and in flew Peter Pan and a fairy no larger than your hand. Her name was Tinker Bell and she moved in a sparkling shower of fairy dust. She flew about the room, searching for something, and finally landed in a dresser drawer full of sewing things. There, sure enough, was Peter Pan's lost shadow. Peter woke Wendy by playing on his pipes and asked her if she would be good enough to sew his shadow back to his feet again.

"I'm so glad you came tonight," Wendy told him as she sewed. "You see, I have to grow up tomorrow, and I might have missed you."

"I'll take you to Never Land with me. You'll *never* grow up there and you can tell stories to my Lost Boys every night," Peter said.

So they roused Michael and John out of their beds and, with a sprinkling of Tinker Bell's fairy dust, away they all flew, heading for Never Land, while Nana barked frantically down in the backyard.

Of all delightful islands, Never Land is the snuggest, with adventures all close together. The Lost Boys were looking for their leader, Peter Pan; the Indians were looking for the pirates; the pirates, led by the fierce Captain Hook, were after Peter, too. Peter had once, in a fair fight, cut off the Captain's hand, in place of which he now wore a hook. Worse yet, Peter had thrown the hand to a crocodile, who liked the taste so much that he had followed the Captain ever since in hope of getting the rest of him. Fortunately, the crocodile had also swallowed an alarm clock with a loud ticktock, which gave Hook fair warning when the creature was nearby. It was a sound that frightened the Captain out of his wits.

The Darling children looked down at their first glimpse of Never Land. "Oh, Peter," Wendy exclaimed, "it's just as I've dreamed it would be—Mermaid Lagoon, the Indian encampment—oh, and there's Captain Hook's pirate ship!" At that moment they heard the boom of a cannon from the ship, for Hook had seen Peter Pan in the sky. "Look out!" Peter yelled. "Tinker, take Wendy and the boys to the island. I'll stay up here and draw Hook's fire." But Tinker Bell was jealous of Wendy's friendship with Peter, and she purposely flew so fast that the children could not keep up with her.

Tinker zoomed down through the trees, to a hollow stump that was the entrance to the secret underground room where the Lost Boys lived. With the loveliest tinkle, as of golden bells (for that is the fairy language), she told the boys that Peter wanted them to attack the Wendy Bird and its brothers. When the children appeared, the boys pelted them with sticks and stones. Luckily, Peter Pan arrived just as the Lost Boys yelled "Hurray! We got the Wendy Bird!" He was very angry. "I bring you a mother to tell you stories and you knock her down," he scolded. And when Peter heard that it was Tinker's fault he sent her away for a week as punishment.

Then, Peter and Wendy flew off to Mermaid Lagoon while John and Michael joined the Lost Boys to fight the Indians. Wendy was enchanted by the mermaids' lovely lazy singing as they played in their lagoon. But Peter suddenly heard something in the distance. Leaping upon a rock that hung out over the sea he looked down and saw in a cove beneath him a boat from the pirate ship. "It's Hook!" he cried. At that dread name the mermaids plunged into the lagoon and disappeared. Captain Hook and his First Mate Smee had tied the Indian Princess Tiger Lily to a rock in the water. Peter and Wendy flew closer, but remained hidden.

"Now, me dear princess," said Hook, "you tell me the hiding place of Peter Pan and I'll set you free. Otherwise the tide will come in soon and you'll drown." Tiger Lily, however, bravely refused to betray her friend.

Peter tried to trick the two pirates into setting Tiger Lily free by imitating spirit voices. But Hook was suspicious and climbed up the rocky cliff with his sword drawn. When he saw Peter he shouted, "Hah! Pan, I'll get you for this!" Then he and Peter fought a fierce duel, to the very edge of the cliff. "I say, Captain, do you hear something?" Peter asked. There was a loud TICKTOCK, which so frightened the pirate he slipped and fell over the edge. There he hung by his hook, just above the hungry jaws of the crocodile.

Peter rescued Princess Tiger Lily in the nick of time, and he and Wendy flew with her to the Indian village where they all enjoyed a happy celebration with her father, the Chief. Meanwhile Smee saved his captain from the crocodile, who had already eaten Hook's trousers and was snapping his jaws for more.

Back at the pirate ship Captain Hook had the banished Tinker Bell brought to him. He slyly offered to sail away with Wendy who, he understood, had come between the little fairy and Peter. If Tinker would tell him how to find Peter's secret hiding place, where Wendy was living, Hook and the pirates would take the girl far away. Jealous little Tinker was delighted. She gave him the directions but added,

"You mustn't harm Peter!" The pirate assured her, "I won't lay a
finger—or a hook—on Peter Pan." Then, laughing nastily he said,
"Thank you, my dear," pushed Tinker Bell into a glass lantern, and shut
it tight.

Gleefully the pirates listened to Captain Hook's instructions for
finding Peter Pan's hideout and kidnapping him and all the others.
They set out through the forest, found the entrance in the hollow tree,
and hid themselves near it until the children came out. Below, in the
hideaway, Wendy was tucking the Lost Boys into bed as she sang them a
lullaby about home and mother. Instead of falling asleep, they all
became so homesick that they decided to leave at once and return to their
families. All except Peter Pan. "Go on!" he told them, "but I'm
warning you. Once you're grown up you can never come back!" Wendy
looked at him sadly and said, "I must go home to my mother and father.
They'll miss us dreadfully." She followed the eager boys to the door.
"Good-bye, Peter," she whispered.

As the children scrambled out of the hollow tree they were captured by the pirates and carried off, struggling, to the ship. Captain
Hook and Smee remained behind with a gift for Peter—a package with a
bomb inside. "I gave my word not to lay a finger, or a hook, on Peter
Pan, and Captain Hook never breaks a promise. But when Pan opens
this, it will blast him right out of Never Land!"

Aboard the ship the pirates told the children they must join the crew. "Unless you do," Hook threatened, "you'll walk the plank." "Oh, no, we won't," Wendy insisted. "Peter Pan will save us." Then Captain Hook told her of his little joke. "We left him a surprise package, you might say, that will explode as soon as he opens it. He won't be saving anyone, including himself."

When Tinker Bell, imprisoned in the lantern, heard those words she was sorry she had caused such terrible trouble for Peter and the children. Desperately she broke the lantern open and flew away to warn Peter.

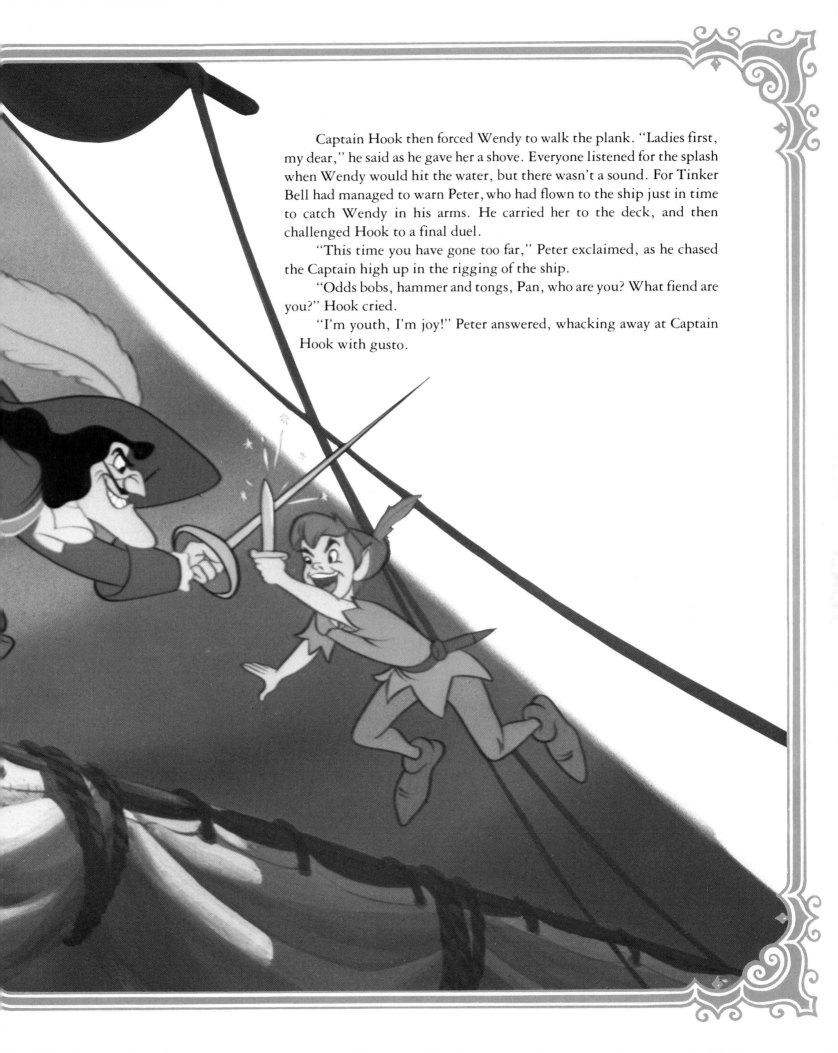

Captain Hook then forced Wendy to walk the plank. "Ladies first, my dear," he said as he gave her a shove. Everyone listened for the splash when Wendy would hit the water, but there wasn't a sound. For Tinker Bell had managed to warn Peter, who had flown to the ship just in time to catch Wendy in his arms. He carried her to the deck, and then challenged Hook to a final duel.

"This time you have gone too far," Peter exclaimed, as he chased the Captain high up in the rigging of the ship.

"Odds bobs, hammer and tongs, Pan, who are you? What fiend are you?" Hook cried.

"I'm youth, I'm joy!" Peter answered, whacking away at Captain Hook with gusto.

The boys chased the frightened pirates into their rowboat, and they rowed toward land as fast as they could, never once looking back. Hook took a tremendous swing at Peter, lost his footing, and plunged down into the sea below—where the crocodile waited. When last seen, the crocodile was chasing Hook, who was swimming after the pirates in the rowboat, who were rowing frantically for shore.

Now Peter Pan became captain of the ship. Tinker Bell, who was happy she had saved Peter and was his friend again, sprinkled the ship with fairy dust. The homesick boys hoisted the anchor and raised the sails, and the craft moved out to sea.

"Where are we sailing, Peter—I mean, Captain Pan?" Wendy asked.

"To London, madam," came the answer.

"Oh, Michael, John," Wendy called, "we're going home!"

At the nursery window Wendy, John, and Michael stood looking up at the starry sky. There, silhouetted against the pale moon, was what seemed to be a pirate ship under full sail, trailing fairy dust as it moved away into the distance. It had brought them safely back to the nursery, where the gangplank had been lowered through the open window. They had said good-bye to Tinker Bell and Peter Pan, and now they wanted to watch until the great ship sailed forever out of their sight.

Mr. and Mrs. Darling returned from their party and came up to the nursery with Nana.

"Oh, Mother," Wendy exclaimed, embracing Mrs. Darling, "we're back!"

"Back from where?" her mother asked.

"Never Land!" John and Michael shouted. "We came back on that ship way up in the sky." Mr. Darling looked out of the window where his children were pointing to something that appeared at first to be a cloud against the moon.

"You know," he said, "I have the strangest feeling that I've seen that ship before. A long time ago. When I was very young."

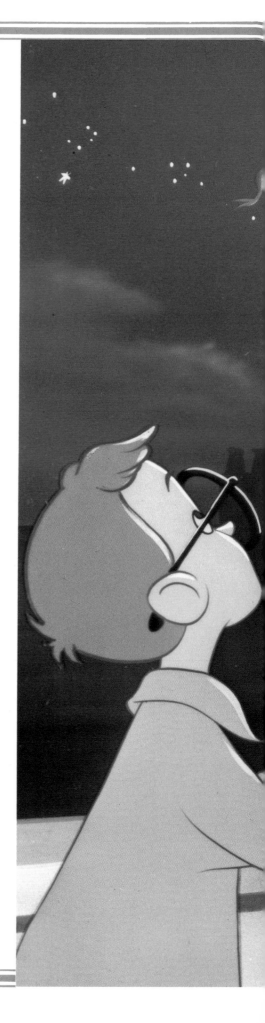

Kathryn Beaumont, whose voice and personality were used for the animated Wendy, watches layout artist Charles Phillipi make the first sketches

PETER PAN

The Story of the Production

The magical world of Peter Pan has never been so perfectly realized as in this animated feature. The landscape of Never Land, peopled by colorful and whimsical characters, was expanded to the furthest limits of fantasy by Walt Disney's imaginative genius. It was one of his most ambitious undertakings, in preparation for ten years and in active production for three more before its release in 1953.

During those thirteen years, every one of the Studio's top animators, background painters, and character developers worked on some aspect of the picture. More than nine hundred painted backgrounds were created, a record number at that time, and more than half a million drawings and sketches were made! The production cost $4 million, a much larger sum in 1953 than it is today.

Disney carefully read James M. Barrie's stage directions for the play *Peter Pan* as well as annotated scripts from later performances, which gave him many more clues for his production. When the animated feature was completed, he believed his screen version approximated what Barrie himself might have done had the technique of animation existed when his play was produced in 1904.

The role of Peter Pan has always been played by an actress, from the original Maude Adams to the more recent Mary Martin. Disney broke with that tradition and used the voice and personality of a real boy, Bobby Driscoll. The animators gave the cartoon character angular and manly gestures and action, in place of the more feminine tomboyishness that had become typical of Peter Pan, the boy who would not grow up.

Another unusual aspect of this picture for Disney is that most of the characters are people (Tinker Bell and the Mermaids have human forms), with the exception of Nana, the St. Bernard nursemaid, and the ticking crocodile that is Captain Hook's nemesis. It is the only Disney picture in which there are so few animal characters, and it illustrates the artists' greatly increased proficiency in animating the human body.

Youth, joy, and adventure come shining through this most beautiful version of a treasured classic, which, like its hero, refuses to grow old.

Alice in

From Walt Disney's Motion Picture *Alice in Wonderland*, an adaptation of Lewis Carroll's *The Adventures of Alice in Wonderland* and *Through the Looking Glass*

Wonderland

lice was beginning to get very tired of sitting by her sister on the riverbank and of having nothing to do. Once or twice she had peeped into the book her sister was reading, but it had no pictures or conversations in it. "And what is the use of a book," thought Alice, "without pictures or conversation?"

The hot day made her feel very sleepy, as she sat stroking her cat Dinah, when suddenly a White Rabbit with pink eyes ran close by her. Alice was not at all surprised to hear the Rabbit say, "Oh! my fur and whiskers, I'm late! I'm late! I'm late!" But when the Rabbit actually *took a watch out of its waistcoat pocket,* and looked at it, and then hurried on, Alice started to her feet. It flashed across her mind that she had never before seen a rabbit with either a waistcoat pocket or a watch to take out of it and, burning with curiosity, she ran after it just in time to see it pop down a large rabbit hole.

In another moment down went Alice after it, never once considering how in the world she was to get out again. The rabbit hole was very, very deep, but she fell very, very slowly and had plenty of time, as she went down, to look about her. The walls of the hole were lined with cupboards and shelves; here and there she saw maps and pictures hung on pegs. She took down a jar from one of the shelves as she passed. It was labeled "ORANGE MARMALADE," but to her great disappointment it was empty. Down, down, down—would the fall *never* come to an end? Suddenly, thump! thump! down she came upon a heap of sticks and dry leaves, and the fall was over.

Alice was not a bit hurt, and she jumped to her feet in a moment. Before her was another long passage; the White Rabbit was still in sight, hurrying down it. Away went Alice like the wind. She was close behind the Rabbit, but when she turned a corner, it was no longer to be seen.

Alice was in a long hall with doors all around it, but they were all locked. Behind a curtain, there was one small door, and when Alice peeked through its keyhole she saw a lovely garden. The Doorknob of this door startled Alice by speaking to her. "You're much too big to get through. Simply impassable." "You mean impossible," said Alice. "No," said the Doorknob. "Impassable. Nothing's impossible. Try the bottle on that table, next to the little gold key."

Alice took the bottle, which was labeled "DRINK ME," but the wise little girl was not going to do that in a hurry. She looked first to be sure it wasn't marked "poison." "For," Alice told herself, "if you drink much from a bottle marked 'poison,' it's sure to disagree with you sooner

or later." This bottle had no such warning, so Alice drank it—and found herself growing smaller and smaller and smaller until she was only ten inches high. Just the right size for going through the door to the garden. But she had left the key on the table.

"Try the box," said the Doorknob. And Alice noticed a little box marked "EAT ME" on the floor. When she nibbled the cookie inside it, she immediately grew bigger and bigger until her head struck against the roof of the hall. "Curioser and curioser!" cried Alice. "Good-bye, feet!" When she stopped growing, she had become more than nine feet high. She at once took up the little golden key, but now, of course, she was much too big for the door to the garden.

Then Alice began to cry, and she cried and cried until there was a great pool of her tears. She saw the little bottle bobbing on the water and quickly drank the few drops remaining in it. Immediately she shrank to a tiny size and fell into the empty bottle. Riding safely within the bottle, Alice was swept on a wave of her own tears through the keyhole.

With the help of several strange creatures she encountered, Alice crawled out of the bottle and set off to explore the new land and to search for the White Rabbit. On her first adventure she met two fat, quarrelsome brothers, Tweedledee and Tweedledum, who insisted on reciting poems to her. First they did "The Walrus and the Carpenter," and Alice listened politely. When it was over she wanted to leave, but the Tweedle Twins insisted on another recitation, "Father William." While they were reciting the third verse, Alice quietly slipped away.

Soon she came upon a neat little house on the door of which was a bright brass plate with the name "W. RABBIT" engraved upon it. Just then the upstairs shutters flew open and the White Rabbit himself appeared. It called out, "Why, Mary Ann, what are you doing here? Run in this moment and fetch me my gloves."

The White Rabbit hurried out of the house, and waited impatiently while Alice searched inside for the gloves. She found a cookie jar labeled "TAKE ONE," so she did. Next thing she knew, Alice was growing again. She grew so huge that her arms and legs burst through the windows and doors, and she filled the little house until finally she split it apart. The White Rabbit, seeing the ruination of its home, cried out, "Help! Monster! There's a monster in my house!"

Its cries brought a Dodo and a lizard, both of whom tried to get Alice out of the house, but with no success. It was Alice herself who spied a carrot growing in the garden. "I wonder what will happen if I eat it," she thought and, reaching a giant hand out of the window, she picked it. As soon as she took a nibble she became small again. But by that time the White Rabbit had run off, muttering, "I'm late, I'm late. The Queen will be so angry! Oh no, can't wait, good-bye, hello, I'm late, I'm late, I'm late!"

Little Alice tried to follow the Rabbit through the garden, but it was too fast for her again. Noticing a cloud of smoke, Alice traced it to a large mushroom on which a caterpillar sat, contentedly blowing smoke rings as it puffed on its hookah. "Who are you?" the caterpillar demanded, when it saw the girl. "And exacticaly what is your problem?"

"Well," Alice answered, "it's exacticaly—I mean exactly—this: I should like to be a little larger, sir."

"Why?" the caterpillar demanded, blowing a beautiful question mark out of smoke.

"Well," said Alice, "three inches is such a wretched height."

The caterpillar, insulted at these words, said angrily, "*I* am exactly three inches high and it is a very good height indeed." And before Alice

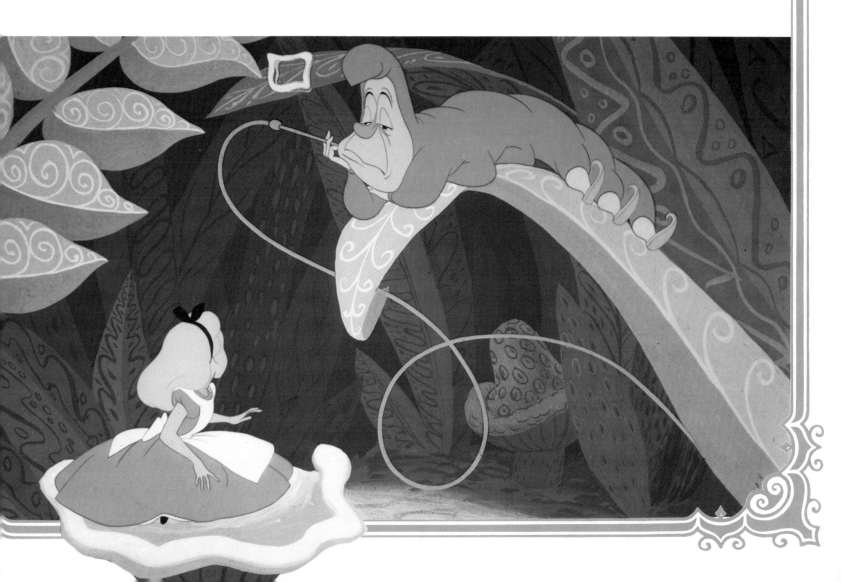

could apologize, the caterpillar had disappeared in a thick cloud of its own smoke. In its place a butterfly appeared. "By the way," the butterfly said, resuming the conversation (for, indeed, the caterpillar had changed into the butterfly), "I have another helpful hint for you: Eat one side of this mushroom and it will make you grow taller. And the other side will make you grow shorter." With that it flew away.

Alice nibbled from both sides of the mushroom until she had reached her normal size. "There," she sighed, "that's much better. I think I'll save these," and she pocketed two pieces of the magic mushroom, one from each side.

And now Alice found herself in a dark forest with no idea where to go to find the White Rabbit. The signs posted on the trees only added to her confusion. Looking about, she was startled to see a Cheshire Cat sitting on a bough of a tree grinning down at her. And since it had *very* long claws and a great many teeth, she felt it ought to be treated with respect.

"Cheshire Puss," she began timidly, "would you tell me please which way I ought to go from here?" "That depends on where you want to get to," said the Cat.

"I don't much care," Alice answered. "I'm looking for the White Rabbit."

"Well," said the Cat, "in *that* direction lives a Hatter and in *that* direction lives a March Hare. They're both mad."

Alice looked frightened. "We're all mad here," the Cat said. "I'm mad; you're mad or you wouldn't have come here." Then the Cheshire Cat began to vanish quite slowly, beginning with the end of its tail and ending with its grin, which remained some time after the rest of it had gone.

"Well, I've often seen a cat without a grin," thought Alice, "but a grin without a cat! It's the most curious thing I ever saw in all my life!"

Alice then decided to walk in the direction of the March Hare's house. A table was set out under a tree in front of the house, and the March Hare and the Hatter were having tea at it. A Dormouse was fast asleep between them and the other two were using it as a cushion, resting their elbows on it and talking over its head. They were having an unbirthday party. When they saw Alice coming they cried out, "No room! No room!"

"There's plenty of room," said Alice indignantly, sitting down in an armchair at one end of the table. It was the maddest tea party Alice had ever attended. What with changing seats and changing cups every few minutes, and the Hare and the Hatter trying to stuff the poor Dormouse into a teapot, and the conversation making no sense whatsoever, Alice was growing more and more bewildered. Abruptly the Hatter took his watch out of his pocket and asked, "What day of the month is it?" Alice thought a bit and then said, "The fourth."

"Two days slow," sighed the Hatter, shaking his watch and then holding it to his ear. "I told you butter wouldn't suit the works," he added, looking angrily at the March Hare.

"It was the *best* butter," the March Hare meekly replied. "Yes, but some crumbs must have got in as well," the Hatter grumbled. "You shouldn't have put it in with the bread-knife." Turning to Alice, he asked, "Do you think some tea might help it?"

"Really, now you ask me," said Alice, very much confused, "I don't think . . ."

"Then you shouldn't talk," said the Hatter.

This piece of rudeness was more than Alice could bear. She got up in great disgust and walked off. "I will find that White Rabbit," she thought angrily, "and ask him how to get home. I've had quite enough of this place."

Just then she noticed a little path between tall hedges. She followed it and soon found herself in a beautiful garden among bright flower beds and cool fountains. A large rose tree stood near the entrance of the

garden. The roses growing on it were white, but three playing-card
gardeners were busily painting them red. When Alice asked them why,
the Three of Clubs answered:

> We planted white roses by mistake,
> The Queen she likes them red.
> If she saw white—
> She'd raise a fuss,
> And each of us
> Would quickly lose his head.

At this moment the Two of Clubs called out, "The Queen! The
Queen!" The three gardeners immediately threw themselves flat on
their faces. There was a sound of many footsteps and Alice looked round,

eager to see the Queen. Soldiers and courtiers, among them the White Rabbit, formed a grand procession, and last of all came the King and Queen of Hearts.

When they reached Alice, the Queen said severely, "Who is this?" No one answered. "Idiots!" said the Queen, tossing her head impatiently. "What's your name, child? Look up. Speak nicely." Alice curtsied and replied politely. "But," she thought, "they're only a pack of cards after all. I needn't be afraid of *them*."

So when the Queen demanded to know who were the three cards lying on their faces, Alice, surprised at her own courage, answered, "How should *I* know? It's no business of *mine*."

The Queen turned crimson with fury. "Off with her head!" she screamed.

"Nonsense," said Alice very loudly and decidedly, and the Queen was silent.

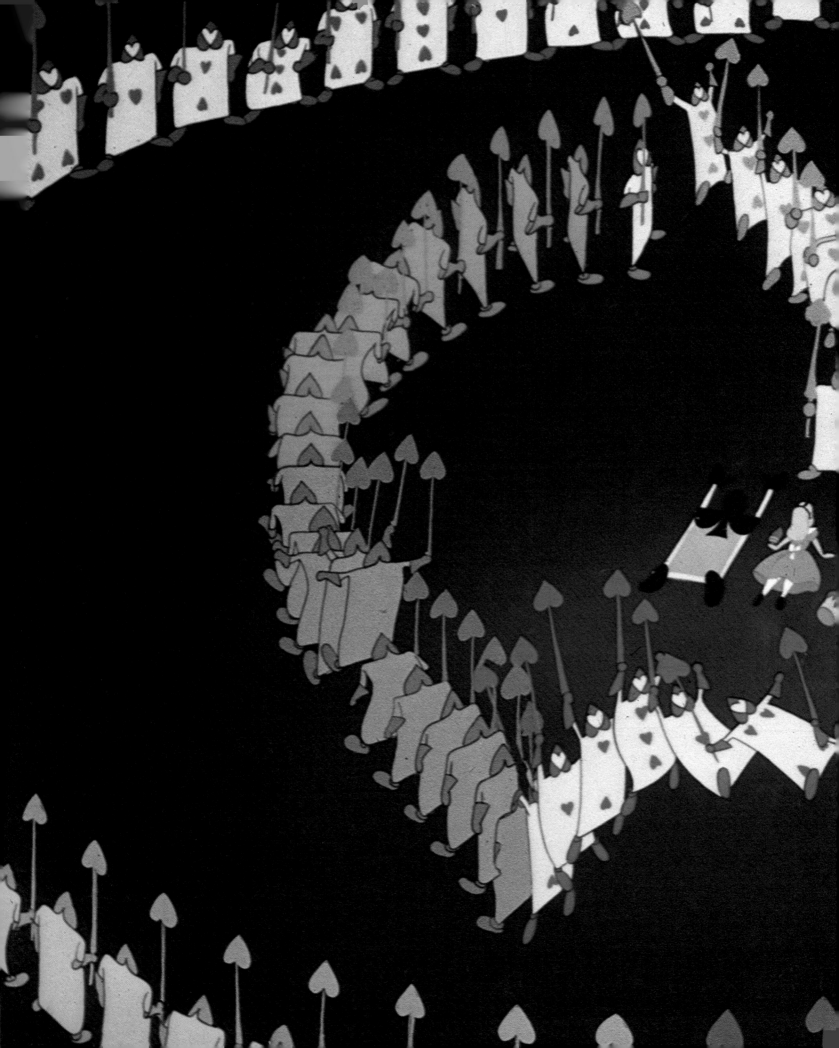

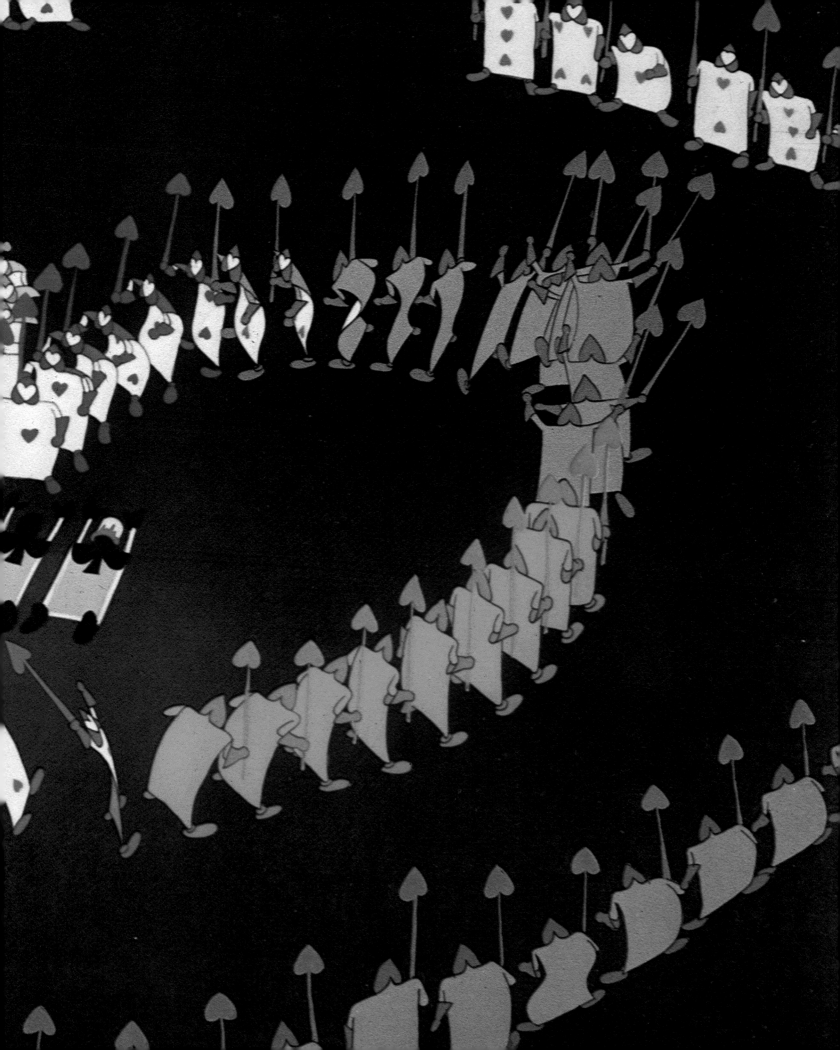

"Can you play croquet?" shouted the Queen. "Yes!" shouted Alice. "Come on, then," roared the Queen.

Alice was given a flamingo for a mallet and a hedgehog for a ball. The players all played at once without waiting for their turns, quarreling and fighting, while the Queen went about stamping and shouting "Off with his head!" or "Off with her head!" In the midst of the turmoil the Cheshire Cat appeared. Then it disappeared, and appeared again somewhere else. The Queen was provoked by its pranks and, since Alice talked to the Cat and seemed to be its friend, the Queen demanded that she be put on trial.

Alice was then put in the prisoner's dock, where she became truly alarmed about what might happen to her. The White Rabbit—late as ever—read the charges. Then the Queen banged her fist on the bench and shouted, "Sentence first, verdict afterward! Off with her head!" Alice, really frightened, put her hand in her apron pocket and felt something there. It was the mushroom. She popped both pieces in her mouth, one after the other. Suddenly she grew to her full size, and the tiny cards jabbing her ankles were nothing to fear. Alice picked up a handful and flipped them away. "Why, you're nothing but a pack of cards," she said.

At this the whole pack rose up into the air and came flying down upon her. Alice gave a little scream and tried to beat them off—she found herself lying beneath a tree on the riverbank with Dinah in her lap. Some leaves were fluttering down upon her face.

"Wake up, Alice dear," said her sister. "What a long sleep you've had!"

"Oh, I've had such a curious dream," said Alice, "a dream of Wonderland."

"Well now, run in for your tea; it's getting late."

So Alice got up and ran off, thinking what a wonderful dream it had been, all on a happy summer day.

ALICE IN WONDERLAND

The Story of the Production

On a "golden afternoon" in 1862—July 4th to be exact—Charles Lutwidge Dodgson, an Oxford mathematics don, took three little sisters boating on the Isis. The middle sister, ten-year-old Alice Liddell, asked for a story from the young man, one "with plenty of nonsense in it," to while away the time. Wishing to please the child he started with these words: "Alice was beginning to get very tired of sitting by her sister. . . ." And thus one of the great classics in the English language was born. "The interminable fairy tale," as Dodgson called it, went on for many future meetings. Eventually the author hand-lettered the whole story, drew thirty-seven illustrations for it, and presented the charming manuscript book to Alice Liddell for Christmas in 1864. He titled it *Alice's Adventures under Ground*.

Revised and expanded, the book was published on July 4, 1865, the third anniversary of the boating party. John Tenniel drew the illustrations, some of them not unlike the author's; the title became *Alice's Adventures in Wonderland;* and the author signed himself Lewis Carroll—all three names were destined for worldwide fame.

In 1949, Walt Disney chose Alice's fantastic adventures as an ideal vehicle for animation. For nearly two years he and a staff of 750 artists worked on the production, transposing Carroll's text and Tenniel's illustrations to their medium as faithfully as possible.

During a story conference on *Alice in Wonderland,* Winston Hibler, Ted Sears, Walt Disney, and Ed Penner review sketches and storyboards

Alice in the recording studio—
Jerry Colonna, Kathryn Beaumont,
and Ed Wynn create the sound
track for the March Hare's and Mad
Hatter's tea party

For the voices of the zany characters that Alice meets in Wonderland, a cast of highly idiosyncratic comedians was assembled: Ed Wynn's giddy giggle became the Mad Hatter's; Jerry Colonna's vocal eccentricities helped to delineate the March Hare; the Cheshire Cat's voice was Sterling Holloway's; Richard Haydn's supercilious tones made the Caterpillar a standout. Verna Felton spoke commandingly for the terrible-tempered Queen of Hearts. J. Pat O'Malley, a man with many vocal talents, provided voices for Tweedledee and Tweedledum, the Walrus, the Carpenter, and the Oysters. A British actress, Kathryn Beaumont, supplied Alice's girlish voice, as she was later to do for Wendy in *Peter Pan*.

Alice in Wonderland was a musical, and among its best songs were "I'm Late," "Alice in Wonderland," "All in a Golden Afternoon," "Unbirthday Song," and "Very Good Advice."

With this feature, released in 1951, Walt Disney succeeded in bringing Alice to the screen in a form which pleased both the traditionalists and the large new audience not previously acquainted with her and her curious companions.

157

From Walt Disney's Motion Picture *Bambi*, adapted from
the story by Felix Salten. The edition containing the full text
of *Bambi, a Life in the Woods* by Felix Salten is published in the
U.S. by Simon & Schuster and in the United Kingdom by Jonathan Cape Limited

Bambi

e came into the world early one morning, in the middle of a little forest glade screened in by leaves and branches on all sides. There was barely room for him and his mother. The baby fawn stood swaying on wobbly legs, as if surprised to find himself out in the strange world.

"What a beautiful child," said a magpie, perching on a nearby branch. "How remarkable that he can stand up by himself after just being born!" Her chirping and chattering aroused the other forest creatures, who hurried to the thicket to admire the new baby. "It isn't every day," said the owl, "that a Prince of the Forest is born. Congratulations."

The mother didn't answer because she was busy washing the fawn, licking him gently with her warm tongue. His little red coat with fine white spots was still somewhat mussed, and on his baby face there was still a deep, dreamy expression. The fawn sank down and snuggled sleepily against his mother, hunting eagerly until he found nourishment for his life. While he suckled, his mother continued her warm caresses. "Bambi," she whispered. "My little Bambi."

By early summer Bambi was frisking along behind his mother as she walked the narrow paths that ran through the woods. Wild flowers twinkled like white, yellow, and purple stars among the green leaves. The voices of a thousand woodland creatures murmured and buzzed and hummed. And one creature, a little bunny named Thumper, thumped.

"Good morning, Prince Bambi," someone called from overhead. Bambi turned his head upside down, and there, to his astonishment, he saw a family of opossums hanging from a branch by their long thin tails. The next thing he knew, he tripped over a rock and went sprawling.

His mother turned back and licked him comfortingly. Thumper hopped over and said, "Come on, Bambi. Get up, and try again." When Bambi stood up on his spindle-legs, Thumper and his sister frolicked around him. Thumper thumped on a log with his hind legs. "I'm thumpin'," he announced. "That's why they call me Thumper." Bambi looked at him admiringly, but said not a word.

A family of birds flew past and alighted on the branches of a tree where they warbled their little song. Bambi looked at them curiously. "Those are birds," Thumper told him. "Say 'bird,' Bambi." "Bur, Bur," said Bambi. The rabbits hopped about excitedly. The young Prince had spoken his first word! Bambi was so pleased with himself he kept saying "Bur. Bur. Bur," until suddenly he said it right, "BIRD!"

Just then a butterfly flew into the clearing and settled down right on Bambi's tail. Bambi spun round to look at it. "Bird," he said. "No, Bambi, that's a butterfly," Thumper explained. Bambi leapt toward a bush of bright flowers that resembled the butterfly. "Butterfly!" he said proudly. "No," Thumper corrected him again. "That's a flower," and he bent down to smell a blossom. Bambi, too, put his head down to smell the flower, but found himself face to face with a small skunk, who had hidden behind the bush. "Flower!" he exclaimed. "No," said Thumper, rolling on the ground with laughter. "That's no flower, that's a skunk!" The skunk, however, liked his new name. "The Prince can call me Flower if he wants to," he said. "I don't mind."

There was a sudden flash of lightning and the rumble of thunder in the distance. "I think I'd better go home now," said Thumper. "It's going to rain." And off he ran. Bambi had no idea what "rain" meant, but the loud noise frightened him and he ran to find his mother. They both made their way to the thicket, where they lay down to sleep. But Bambi was soon awakened by the splashing sound of water, the fresh, wet, earthy smell, and the plop of a raindrop that now and then landed on the tip of his nose. So this was rain! The lightning flashed again and the thunder boomed closer. Bambi snuggled nearer to his mother. She bent her head over, covering him and shutting out the noise and the wet. Very soon Bambi fell back to sleep.

One morning Bambi followed his mother out of the forest and into the big open meadow. "We must be careful here," she warned. "There are no trees and bushes to hide us, so we must be sure it's safe." She stopped at the edge of the wide open space and stood motionless as she sniffed the wind, looked in all directions, and, with head held high, listened intently. At last, she said, "Come on, Bambi, it's all right."

There were other deer out in the meadow, nibbling at the sweet clover. And there was a pond with a duck and a frog. Bambi's eyes grew larger and larger as they surveyed this broad new world. He drew back, startled, when a strange fawn bounded over to him. He had never seen one before. The fawn, trying to be friendly, edged closer to Bambi. He backed away, stumbled over a root, turned and dashed off to his mother. The strange fawn followed. Bambi's mother looked down at him, amused at his shyness. "That's little Faline," she said, "your Aunt Ena's daughter. Run along and play with her."

Bambi turned slowly toward Faline. Suddenly she gave a leap and rushed away. In a moment Bambi darted after her. They ran in a broad circle, they leapt into the air three, four, five times. Bambi had never felt so wildly happy. The sweet smell of the meadow, the open sky, the warmth of the sun made him leap for joy.

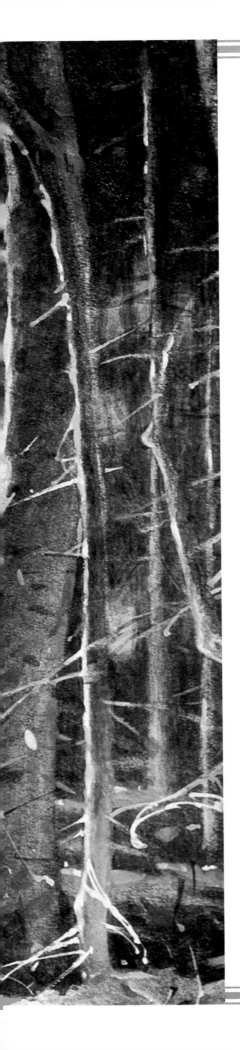

Then something happened that was more exciting than anything else that had happened to Bambi that day. Out of the forest came the sound of hoofs beating on the ground. Branches snapped and someone burst out of the thicket. He looked like Bambi's mother but was larger, and his head was crowned with gleaming antlers. He was stately and noble, his head held royally high and his splendid antlers rising above it. Bambi was overcome with admiration. In the hush that fell over the meadow the stately stag passed by in silent splendor. The fawns didn't dare to breathe until he had disappeared into the thicket.

"Who was that?" Bambi whispered to his mother. "That was your father," she said. "Of all the deer in the forest he is the bravest and wisest. That's why he's known as the Great Prince of the Forest."

"How handsome he is," Bambi sighed. His mother smiled down at him. "If you are cunning, my son, and don't run into danger, you'll be as strong and handsome as your father someday, and you'll have antlers like his, too."

Time passed; the leaves fell from the trees and the cold winds blew through the forest. One morning Bambi awoke in the little thicket next to his mother to find that the world had changed overnight. It smelled different, and when Bambi peered out, the trees and bushes were covered with whiteness. "Mother, look," he cried. "What is that white stuff?" "That's snow," she answered. "Winter has come."

At first it was fun to play with Thumper and Faline and his other friends in the soft white snow. But then Bambi noticed that life had become much harsher. Before, they had all lived a rich life with plenty to eat in meadow and forest, and Bambi, who had known only abundance, thought he would always have plenty to eat. But now it grew harder and harder to find food. Bambi had to dig the snow away with his little hoof to find one withered blade of grass. The icy crust cut his delicate legs.

Bambi's mother taught him how to feed on the bark of a tree. She could stand on her hind legs and reach up high to rip a piece of bark off for him to share. But as winter wore on, the trees were stripped of their bark by hungry deer, and there was less and less to eat. "Winter sure is long, isn't it?" Bambi complained. "It seems long, but it won't last forever," his mother assured him. "I'm *so* hungry," Bambi sighed.

So, although the meadow was dangerous except in the evening or early morning, Bambi's mother took him there one afternoon. Pawing aside the snow, she called, "Look here. Grass, new spring grass!" Lowering their heads, the two deer ate hungrily, two dark shapes alone in the middle of the great white meadow.

All at once they heard the magpies warning, "Look out! Look out!"

Bambi and his mother raised their heads and sniffed the air. And there it was, a heavy wave of scent that meant Man. At the same moment they heard the crash of a gunshot. "Run, Bambi. Don't look back—keep running no matter what, to the thicket," and Bambi's mother was off with a bound that barely skimmed the snow.

The thunder of Man's guns was all about, and then the sounds grew fainter as Bambi ran deeper into the forest. Outside their thicket he waited for his mother, calling her as he wandered through the trees. "Mother! Mother!" There was no answer.

Bambi's eyes widened in astonishment when out of the winter twilight the Great Stag appeared. "Your mother can't be with you anymore," he said in his stern but gentle voice. "Now you must be brave and learn to walk alone. Come, my son," he added as he turned and moved off through the trees. There was nothing for Bambi to do but to follow.

Time passed and it was spring, when all the forest animals fall in love, or as the owl put it, "become twitterpated." They had all grown during the winter, and his friends almost didn't recognize Bambi, who had traded in his spots for a pair of small antlers. Flower the skunk was the first of the group to fall in love. He saw a pair of mischievous blue eyes peeking out of a clump of black-eyed Susans. There was a soft giggle, and the blue eyes winked. Then a little girl skunk emerged and kissed Flower. From that moment on, Flower followed her about, completely "twitter-pated."

Thumper was next, losing his heart to a honey-colored bunny. Bambi vowed such foolishness was not for him, but when he saw his old playmate Faline, now a beautiful young doe with a soft tan coat and large brown eyes, he became as "twitterpated" as any creature in the forest.

"Will you stay with me, Faline?" he asked her. Faline moved toward Bambi and was about to answer when a rival buck named Ronno moved roughly between Faline and Bambi. Shaking his antlers and pawing the ground, he dared Bambi to take one step closer to the doe. Bambi, enraged, charged at the buck, and they fought, antler to antler, while Faline watched and wished very hard that Bambi would win. Pushing and straining, Bambi finally braced with his hind legs and hurled himself at Ronno. The buck fell to the ground, while Bambi stood over him, victorious. Then he led Faline away. "You were wonderful," she said softly. All that summer they were together.

Once again the autumn winds were blowing. Bambi awoke one morning and sensed that something was wrong. Leaving Faline in their
thicket, the young buck explored the forest, searching for the danger.

At the edge of a cliff he was joined by the Great Stag. They looked
down into the valley in the early morning mist, and saw a campfire and
movement. And smelled that fearsome smell. "Man," said the Stag in
his deep voice. "There are many this time. More than I have ever seen
before." The crows flew off to caw their warning. "Quickly," the Stag
commanded. "To the hills!"

Bambi went to join Faline, but she had left their thicket in search
of him. Each called through the forest to the other. "Bambi!" "Faline!"
Meanwhile pheasants, quail, rabbits, birds, and every animal large and
small hurried to make their escape from Man. Shots rang through the
forest.

Then a pack of savage hunting dogs raced through the woods. They
were chasing Faline. The doe bounded away, her heart pounding as the
dogs snarled at her heels. She leapt up to a rocky ledge, and turned to see
the dogs scrambling below her and barking loudly. She was cornered
and could go no further. "Bambi!" she called.

Bambi had heard the barking and when he recognized Faline's call

169

he came running. He charged the pack of dogs and then reared up on his hind legs, using his sharp front hoofs to slash at any dogs who attacked. They kept a respectful distance. "Jump, Faline," he called to her, "and run home." When he thought Faline was safe, Bambi turned and ran at top speed, once even leaping over a fallen tree. There was an unexpected crash of sound and at the same moment a sharp pain in his leg. Bambi stumbled and fell, wounded by a gunshot.

He had not lain there long when squirrels, rabbits, and other small animals ran past him. "Get up, Bambi! Get up! The forest is on fire!" they cried as they fled toward the stream to safety. And then, as smoke began to drift into that part of the forest, the Great Stag appeared. "Get up, Bambi," he ordered. Bambi struggled to rise and the Stag encouraged him. "Get up, Bambi. You can," he said. "Now, follow me."

As Bambi limped behind the Stag, the smoke stung his eyes and every now and then a flash of flame jumped from one tree to another. "Man caused this, too, with a little cinder from his campfire," said the Stag. "We must follow the stream to the island. The fire can't reach us

there." They both plodded through the water, with hundreds of other creatures around them. At the tip of the island various small animals huddled, and in the tree branches families of birds stared across the river as their forest home was destroyed. Bambi was in despair when out of the gloom he heard his name called as only one creature in the whole world could call him. "Faline!" he responded joyfully. The two were reunited at the water's edge and they stood, shoulder to shoulder, watching the terrible spectacle in silence.

Another spring came, flowers bloomed once again, tender green leaves sprouted on live trees, covering the charred remains of the fire. Flower and Owl and Thumper had families, and they all were hurrying to the thicket to see Faline and her twin fawns.

Bambi and the Great Stag looked on from a distance. "Don't follow me any further, Bambi," said the Great Stag in a calm voice. "My time is up and I must look for a resting place. Good-bye, my son. I loved you dearly." Soundlessly he disappeared into the bushes without stirring a leaf.

Bambi was now the Great Prince of the Forest.

BAMBI

The Story of the Production

When Walt Disney read Felix Salten's *Bambi, a Life in the Woods* in 1937 (the year that *Snow White* was released) he knew at once that he wanted to make an animated feature based on the book. The story of a deer's life from birth to maturity was written with great feeling and tenderness by the well-known Austrian author.

In order to capture the beauty and sensitivity of the book, Disney realized that a great deal of careful naturalistic detail would be required. During the three years of planning before animation was begun, he sent artist Maurice Day on a five-month trip to the Maine woods to photograph and sketch animals, bushes, trees, cloud formations, bark patterns, snowdrifts, and fire-ravaged forests. Other artists were sent to western woodlands. Back at the Studio, an imaginary forest setting was charted and mapped so that each animator would have a guide for the position of every tree and rock in his background scenes.

The multiplane camera, which gives depth of detail from foreground to background, was used extensively in filming *Bambi,* with as many as nine separate levels being photographed at one time. The scenic artists who painted the forest scenes worked in oils rather than the customary tempera to achieve greater richness of detail and perspective.

Although animals like Thumper the rabbit, Flower the skunk, and the wise owl are amusing cartoon characters, the deer and other forest creatures are rendered with greater fidelity to nature. Two live fawns, two skunks, some squirrels, birds, rabbits, chipmunks, and other denizens of the forest were kept in an animal compound at the Disney Studio in Burbank during the entire production time. They served as living models for the animators, who attended special art classes in drawing animals and their movements.

Bambi was released in 1942, five years after it was first planned. It is unique among Disney's animated features for its poetic naturalism and scenic grandeur.

A life class for the Disney artists brought the woodland creatures right into the Studio

Peter Behn, the voice of Thumper, feeds the rabbit model while animators Ollie Johnston, Milt Kahl, and Frank Thomas look on

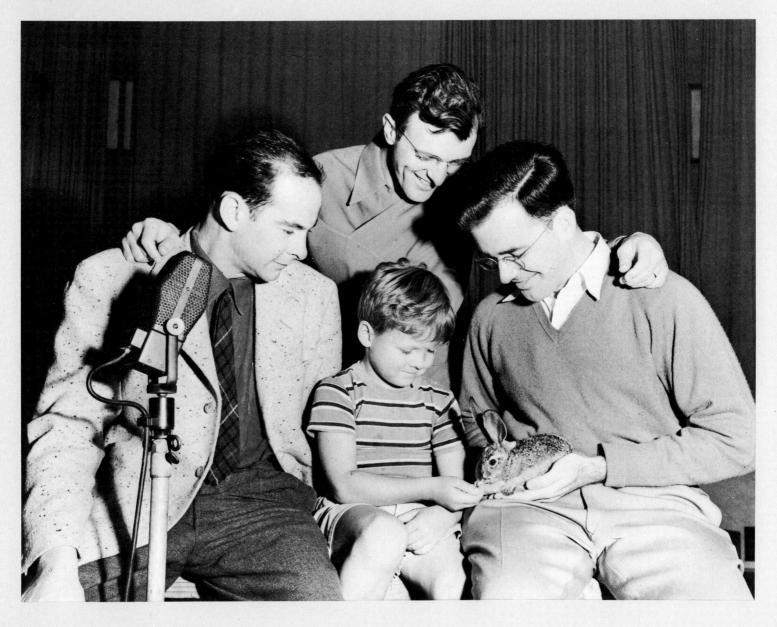

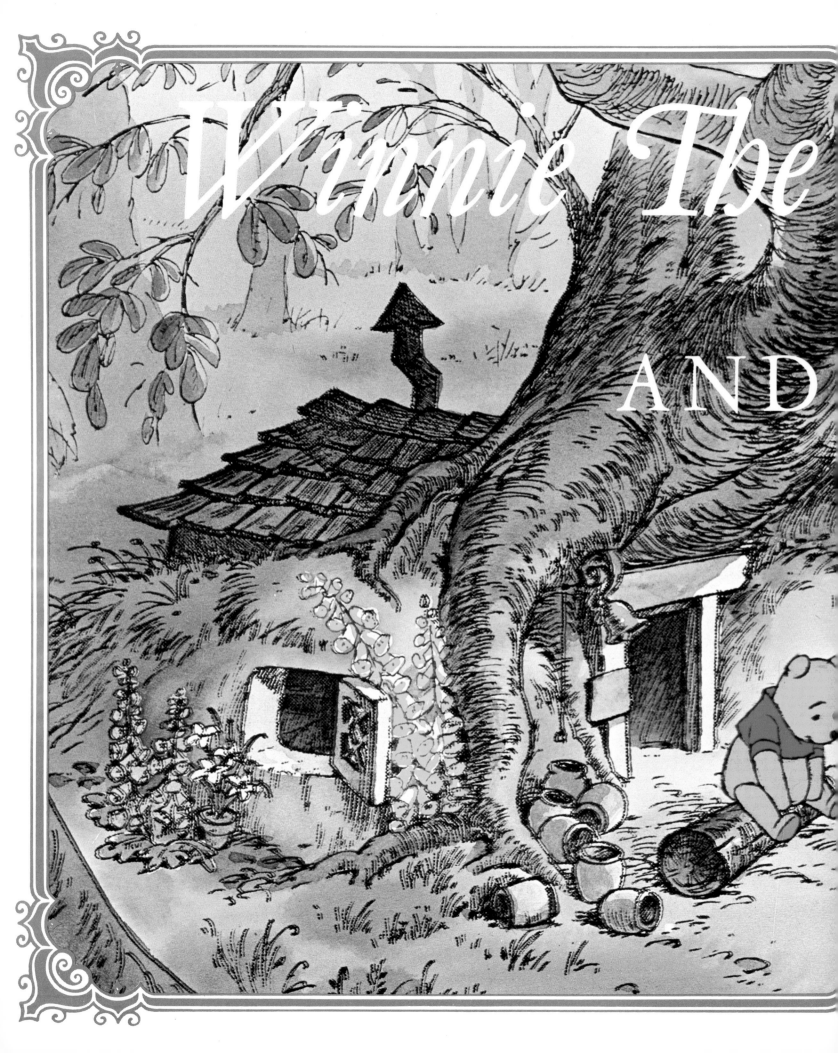

Pooh
The Honey Tree

From Walt Disney's Motion Picture *Winnie the Pooh and the Honey Tree*, based on the books by A. A. Milne, published in the United States by E. P. Dutton & Co. Inc. and in the United Kingdom by Methuen and Company, Ltd.

ike most small boys, Christopher Robin had toy animals to play with, and they all lived together in a wonderful world of make-believe.

His best friend was a bear called Winnie the Pooh, or Pooh for short. Now Pooh had some very unusual adventures, and they all happened deep in the Hundred Acre Wood, where Christopher Robin played. It was the enchanted neighborhood of Christopher Robin's childhood.

Winnie the Pooh lived in the Hundred Acre Wood all by himself under the name of Sanders, which means he had the name over the door in gold letters and he lived under it.

One day when Pooh was sitting by the fire warming his hands, he heard his clock strike. When he heard that sound, he knew it was time for something, but what could it be? Since he was a bear of very little brain, he had to think about it in the most thoughtful way he could.

"Oh yes!" he said at last, getting to his feet. "Time for my Stoutness Exercises." And he stood before his mirror and began to touch his toes and straighten up while he sang a little song:

When I up-down,
Touch-the-ground,
It puts me in the mood,
Up-down, touch-the-ground,
In the mood for food.
I am stout, round,
And I have found,
Speaking poundage-wise,
I improve my appetite
When I exercise.

After finishing his exercises Pooh wondered what to do next. It was about eleven o'clock in the morning, just the time for something sweet, so he went to his cupboard and took down a jar of honey. But the jar was empty.

"Oh bother," said Pooh. "There's only a little left." And he pushed his face deep into the honey pot so he could lick the last bit.

While he had the honey pot over his face, a bee flew in the window and buzzed past Pooh's ear. "That buzzing noise means something," said the bear. "The only reason for making a buzzing noise, that *I* know of, is because you're a bee!" He pulled the pot off his face and watched

the bee fly out the window. "And the only reason for being a bee is to make honey." Pooh followed the bee outdoors and watched it fly into a hole in a nearby tree. "And the only reason for making honey is so *I* can eat it!"

Eagerly, Pooh headed for the tree and started to climb. He climbed and he climbed and he climbed, and as he climbed he hummed a little hum to cheer himself up. The climb was getting harder and harder and Pooh was swinging dangerously on a very thin branch. *Crack!*

"Oh, help!" said Pooh, as he dropped to the branch below.

"If only I hadn't—you see, what I meant to do-oo!" he said, bumping from branch to branch.

"It all comes, I suppose, from," he sighed as he flew gracefully into a prickly bush, "from *liking* honey so much. Oof! Oh bother!"

He crawled out of the bush, brushed the prickles from his nose, and sat down to think again. And the first person he thought of was Christopher Robin.

So Winnie the Pooh went to see his friend Christopher Robin, who lived in a tree trunk in another part of the forest where he could be near his friends and help them.

Christopher had just finished nailing on Eeyore's tail. The donkey, who was forever losing his tail, looked at it gloomily. "Thanks," he said. "It's not much of a tail, but I'm sort of attached to it."

Just then Pooh arrived. "Good morning, Christopher Robin," he called.

"Good morning, Winnie the Pooh," said Christopher Robin.

"If it is a good morning," said Eeyore, "which I doubt." And he jogged off.

Pooh looked at the toys in front of Christopher's house. "I just said to myself coming along: 'I wonder if Christopher Robin has such a thing as a balloon about him?' I just said it to myself, while thinking of balloons and wondering."

"What do you want a balloon for?" asked Christopher, as he untied a blue balloon.

Winnie the Pooh looked carefully in all directions to be sure that no one was listening. Then he put his paw near his mouth, and growled in a deep whisper, *"Honey!"*

"But you don't get honey with a balloon!"

"I do," said Pooh.

"How?" asked Christopher, handing him the string of the balloon.

"I shall fly like a bee, up to the honey tree, see?" And Pooh floated up in the air with the balloon.

Christopher caught him just in time. "Oh, Pooh, you can't fool the bees that way."

"Wait and see," said Pooh.

He went to a very muddy place that he knew of, and rolled and rolled in the mud until he was black all over. "Now," he explained, "I'll be a little black rain cloud under the sky-blue balloon."

Christopher Robin smiled at Pooh affectionately. "Silly old bear," he said.

They walked over to the honey tree together, Pooh holding on to the balloon and Christopher Robin holding on to Pooh. Pooh pointed up at the hole and asked Christopher to aim him at the bees. Christopher gave the bear a little lift in the right direction, let go suddenly, and there was Pooh Bear, floating gracefully up into the sky, level with the bees' nest, but about twenty feet away from it.

"Hooray!" Christopher Robin shouted.

"How do I look?" Pooh called down.

"You look like a chubby bear holding on to the string of a balloon," said Christopher. "Careful, Pooh. Hold on tight!"

"I'm only a little black rain cloud," Pooh sang. "Pay no attention to little me."

Pooh Bear floated closer to the hole and reached a paw in for some honey. A bee flew out and buzzed around his nose.

"Christopher Robin," Pooh called, "I think the bees s-u-s-p-e-c-t something. Go home and get your umbrella and walk around saying, 'Tut-tut, it looks like rain.' I think it would help fool the bees."

Christopher returned with his umbrella and Pooh sang a little Cloud Song, such as a rain cloud might sing. But the bees were buzzing more suspiciously than ever. Some flew out of their nest and gathered round and round the cloud as it began the second verse of its song. One bee even sat down on the cloud's nose.

Then a swarm of angry bees attacked the balloon. It began to lose air and Winnie the Pooh floated slowly down toward the ground.

"Christopher Robin!!" Pooh called. "Oh bother! I think I shall come down." But Christopher caught him before he could hit the ground. Using the umbrella as a shield they splashed across a mud pond, leaving the angry bees behind.

"I've been thinking, Christopher Robin," said Pooh, as they sloshed across the pond. "And I have come to a very important decision. Christopher Robin, *you never can tell with bees.*"

WINNIE THE POOH AND THE HONEY TREE

The Story of the Production

In 1966, Walt Disney released the first animated featurette based on A. A. Milne's children's classic, *Winnie-the-Pooh*. Running a little under half an hour, the film version of this enchanting adventure of a small boy, Christopher Robin, and his favorite toy bear, Winnie the Pooh, has been seen by millions of new fans in theaters and on television. In bringing Milne's characters to life through animation, Disney and his creative staff remained faithful to Ernest H. Shepard's original book illustrations, themselves almost as famous and beloved as the stories.

A. A. Milne, an English novelist and playwright, wrote a book of verse about his four-year-old son in 1924, *When We Were Very Young*. This was followed by a second book of verse, *Now We Are Six,* and by two volumes of stories about Christopher Robin and his toy animals, *Winnie-the-Pooh* and *The House at Pooh Corner*. Christopher and his stuffed toys all lived in a delightful woodland, very much like that surrounding Milne's country house in Sussex. Shepard, a friend and neighbor, captured the characters and setting with inspired authenticity in his drawings for all four books. The books have been translated into twelve languages and have sold close to fifteen million copies.

At the Walt Disney Studio in Burbank, an actor dressed as Winnie the Pooh cavorts in front of the Animation Building

John Lounsbery, one of Disney's
veteran animators, brings Eeyore,
the dolorous donkey, to life

Wolfgang (Woolie) Reitherman, the director of the film, also directed Disney's *The Sword in the Stone, The Jungle Book, Robin Hood,* and *The Aristocats.* Working closely with Reitherman on the animation were eleven of Disney's veteran artists, including Hal King, John Lounsbery, John Sibley, Walt Stanchfield, and John Ewing. One team of artists painted the colorful scenes against which the animated characters performed, and another created the layout designs.

Sterling Holloway, the well-known Hollywood character actor, spoke for Winnie the Pooh, while Sebastian Cabot handled the background narration. The director's ten-year-old son Bruce Reitherman was the voice of Christopher Robin. Richard M. and Robert B. Sherman, who won Oscars for their music for *Mary Poppins,* composed five songs for the *Pooh* film. The entire score was arranged and conducted by Buddy Baker.

All this for a twenty-six-minute cartoon—no wonder *Winnie the Pooh and the Honey Tree* has succeeded so well as a recreation in another medium of a treasured children's classic!

The

From Walt Disney's Motion Picture *The Jungle Book*, inspired by the Rudyard Kipling "Mowgli" stories

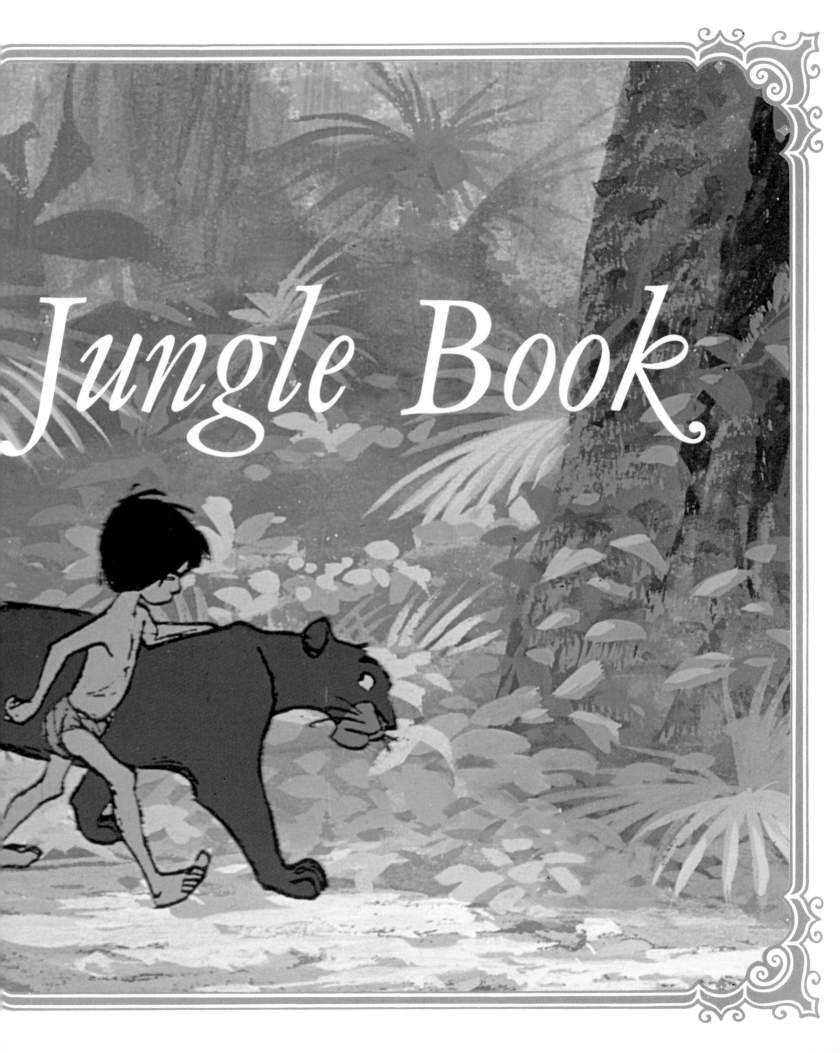

Jungle Book

any strange tales are told of the wild jungles in India, but none so strange as the story of Mowgli, the mancub, who was found by Bagheera, the black panther, in a basket by the riverbank. Bagheera carried the basket to a wolf family with young cubs and asked if they could feed and care for the mancub, too.

"I have never seen one," said Mother Wolf. "How little! How naked, and—how bold! See, he looks up and is not afraid."

The hungry little creature snuggled up to Mother Wolf with the other cubs. "Lie still, little frog," she told him. "Mowgli, Mowgli the Frog, I shall call you." And the wolves kept Mowgli and raised him like one of their own.

Ten times the rains had come, and Mowgli had grown as strong and hardy as his wolf brothers, with whom he had become a great favorite. Then, one night under a full moon, the elders of the Wolf Pack gathered at Council Rock for a very important meeting. Bagheera watched and listened from the limb of a nearby tree while they spoke. The Pack was alarmed because Shere Khan, a man-hating tiger, had returned to their jungle after a long absence. They feared he would surely kill the half-grown mancub and any wolves who tried to protect him.

Finally Akela, their leader, spoke. "It has been decided. The mancub can no longer stay with the Pack. It is too dangerous for the rest of us. He must leave at once." In vain Father Wolf pleaded that Mowgli could not possibly survive alone in the jungle. Then Bagheera, springing lightly from the tree, said he would take Mowgli to a man village several day's journey away, and leave him safely with his own kind.

Early the next morning Bagheera and Mowgli set out for a walk in the jungle. When night fell, Mowgli wanted to return to his wolf family, but the panther explained that he could not ever go back because Shere Khan had sworn to kill him. At this Mowgli grew very unhappy. "I *will* go back," he declared. "I can look after myself!" But the black panther would have no disobedience. "Enough," he growled. "We'll spend the night up in this tree. Things will look better in the morning."

No sooner had Bagheera dozed off than Kaa, a slippery python, slithered up the tree to the branch where Mowgli crouched, too unhappy to fall asleep. In the special way that pythons have, Kaa hypnotized Mowgli and coiled himself around his body. He was just about to open his jaws and swallow the mancub when Bagheera wakened. In a flash the panther knocked Kaa out of the tree and snatched Mowgli from him. "So, you can look after yourself, can you?" he sneered at the frightened mancub.

At daybreak Mowgli was awakened by a loud military voice shouting drill commands:

Hup, two, three, four,
Keep it up, two, three, four.
By the ranks or single file,
Over every jungle mile.

It was Colonel Hathi, the elephant, noisily drilling his troops. Mowgli, enjoying the new game, mischievously fell in behind the smallest baby elephant. But the Colonel saw him and trumpeted, "I say, what happened to your trunk?" Then, looking more closely, he bellowed, "A mancub! This is treason!" He knocked Mowgli to the ground and was about to stamp on him when Bagheera leapt between them. He apologized to the outraged elephant for Mowgli's bad manners and explained that he was taking him back to a man village.

But Mowgli still didn't want to go to the man village and he still missed his wolf family. He stubbornly grabbed a small tree and hung on while Bagheera tried to push and then to pull him on his way. In exasperation the black panther gave up. "All right, mancub," he snarled. "You're on your own," and he padded off into the jungle.

Mowgli sat down against a rock, alone and not quite sure which way to go next. While he was wondering, he heard a carefree song, and then the singer appeared. Baloo the bear came rollicking through the jungle, singing a jaunty song and dancing a few shuffling steps. He stopped short when he saw Mowgli. The bear and the mancub struck up a conversation, and sang and danced and played games together merrily. They went fishing, swam in the river, and had a fine lazy time. "Stay

away from the man village," Baloo growled. "They'll ruin you. They'll make a man out of you. And you're going to make one swell bear."

All this time, a band of monkeys had been watching the two friends from high in the treetops. At a signal from their leader, two monkeys swiftly swung to the ground, grabbed Mowgli, and carried him off to the ruins of an ancient temple where their king, Louie, was waiting.

Meanwhile, Baloo called to Bagheera for help and, hoping to save the mancub, he and the panther raced through the jungle to the ruins. They were in time to hear King Louie demand that Mowgli give him the secret of Man's Red Flower. (By Red Flower the king meant fire, only no creature in the jungle will call fire by its proper name, since every beast lives in deadly fear of it.) But Mowgli didn't know how to grow the Red Flower and said so. Before the angry ape king could punish the mancub, his attention was caught by a large female ape dancing across the room. It was Baloo in disguise, waving and smiling at King Louie, and soon the infatuated ape king and all the monkeys were dancing wildly after

Baloo. The ruins shuddered and shook, and the temple pillars began to totter. Just before the building collapsed, Bagheera snatched Mowgli out of danger and in the confusion they and Baloo made their escape.

They were not to be together for long. Mowgli, fearing that Baloo also wanted him safely in the man village, ran away alone into the jungle. He wandered into a rocky place where a flock of ugly vultures had gathered. Seeing that the mancub was sad, the vultures tried to comfort him with jokes and funny dances. In the midst of their merrymaking, Shere Khan, the fierce tiger, stalked into the clearing. "Run, friend, run," the vultures shrieked as they flapped their wings and took off into the sky.

"I won't run from anyone," Mowgli declared. He picked up a club and prepared to hit the tiger. With a terrible roar, Shere Khan opened his mouth and bared his claws. Just as he was about to leap at the mancub, Baloo arrived, grabbed Shere Khan by the tail, and stopped him short, in mid-leap.

Meanwhile, the vultures returned to help Mowgli. One of them lifted the mancub in his powerful talons and flew off to a nearby tree, which had been struck by lightning and was aflame. "Fire, Mowgli, that's the only thing Old Stripes is afraid of. Get the Red Flower," he said, setting Mowgli on the ground. Mowgli picked up a burning branch and ran with it to Shere Khan. "Up, dog," he cried. "Up when a man speaks or I will set your coat ablaze."

Shere Khan snarled at the fire, and Mowgli beat him over the head with the branch, singeing his fur. The tiger, whimpering and whining in fear and pain, ran frantically across the clearing and disappeared over the farthest hill. "That is the last we'll see of him," said Baloo. "He took off like a flaming comet."

Toward evening, near the riverbank, Baloo and Mowgli were joined by Bagheera. The panther suggested that, with Shere Khan gone from the jungle, there was no reason why Mowgli couldn't remain with his animal friends forever. But Mowgli had felt a strange restlessness ever since he had held the stick abloom with the Red Flower. Something was different about him now. He knew he was meant to be a man and not a wolf.

And then a creature such as he had never seen before came down to the river, and as he watched her, Mowgli was captivated. Singing softly, she filled a vessel with water and placed it on her head. Mowgli approached her, took the vessel gently, and placed it on his own head, just as she had. The pretty creature walked along a little path that led to the man village, with Mowgli following. The sky was just beginning to darken when Mowgli entered the gates of the village to meet those mysterious things that are called men.

"Mowgli, come back, come back," called Baloo.

"Go on, go on," urged Bagheera.

Mowgli turned briefly, waved to his friends, and disappeared behind the village fence.

Baloo shrugged. "He would have made one swell bear," he said sadly.

THE JUNGLE BOOK

The Story of the Production

Inspired by Rudyard Kipling's Mowgli stories about a boy raised by wolves in the forests of India, *The Jungle Book,* released in 1967, was the last animated feature to be personally produced by Walt Disney. Thirty years and some seventeen animated movies after *Snow White,* the picture incorporated all of the advanced techniques and perfected artistic skills that the Studio had developed. Its lush and colorful jungle backgrounds are among Disney's most beautiful.

But the greatest innovation is how closely the animated characters are patterned after living personalities, whose voices are employed for the soundtrack. Phil Harris, with his easygoing traits, became Baloo, the happy-go-lucky bear; Louis Prima's gravel voice and jazz rhythms influenced the creation of King Louie, the jiving ape-potentate; George Sanders lent his suavely villainous personality to Shere Khan, the tiger; Sterling Holloway was the sneaky python, Kaa; Sebastian Cabot, the character actor, created the stern but dedicated panther, Bagheera; J. Pat O'Malley's Englishness was transmitted to Colonel Hathi, the elephant drilling his dawn patrol; and Bruce Reitherman, the youngster who was the voice of Christopher Robin in a Winnie the Pooh film, imprinted his endearing boyishness on young Mowgli. All of these actors, with their distinctive personalities, took command of the characters on the animators' drawing boards as in no other Disney picture.

The Jungle Book is an animated musical comedy that runs for an hour and eighteen minutes. The twelve sequences that make up the feature comprise 1,039 separate scenes and 760 painted backgrounds. And for every minute of animation there are 1,440 different pictures! These mind-boggling statistics are the reality behind Walt Disney's desire to make animation "a means of bringing life and motion to fine illustrations." They indicate why he was preeminently successful in creating fluid motion from drawings, rather than the flickering images that used to play across the movie screen in animated features.

Baloo the bear and his voice
and model, Phil Harris, go into
their song and dance

206

Keeping the Dream Alive

Dumbo

From Walt Disney's Motion Picture *Dumbo*,
based on the book by Helen Aberson and Harold Pearl

he circus train was loaded and ready to start the trip north from winter quarters in Florida. But it was waiting for something. The clowns were ready, the acrobats were ready, nearly everyone was ready. The giraffes stuck their long necks through the roof of their car to find out the reason for the delay. Only the elephants knew why the train hadn't started, and the old gossips among them whispered the secret to one another. "It's Mrs. Jumbo. She's waiting for her baby."

Just then a stork carrying a large, heavy bundle flapped to a stop on the roof of the elephant car. "Well, little fella," he said to the bundle, "let's get going." Then he hollered, "Mrs. Jumbo! Calling Mrs.

Jumbo!" The other elephants waved their trunks through the hatch of the elephant car. "Over here, Stork," one of them trumpeted. The stork fluttered down to the floor of the car and deposited his bundle next to Mrs. Jumbo. "Here's your baby, Ma'am. Jumbo Jr."

Mrs. Jumbo carefully unwrapped the bundle. Smiling up at her was the most adorable blue-eyed baby elephant anyone had ever seen. The old gossips looked over the partition at the mother and her new baby. "Better than I expected," whispered one. "Isn't he adorable," said another. "Kootchy Kootchy," said a third, tickling the baby with her trunk.

At that, Jumbo Jr. sneezed—and when he sneezed his ears flopped forward. They were no ordinary large elephant ears; they were *enormous* ears, almost as big as the entire baby, and the gossips were horrified at first. Then they began to giggle and laugh at the funny-looking baby elephant. "Jumbo, indeed," giggled one. "He should be called DUMBO. That fits perfectly!"

But Mrs. Jumbo turned her back on them, wrapped the baby's ears around him, and cuddled Dumbo to her lovingly.

The circus train chugged along, and when it had to climb a mountain it struggled up the steep slope, panting, "I think I can, I think I can," and when it started down the other side it went faster and faster and huffed, "I thought I could, I thought I could." Finally the train stopped with a jolt at a little town. The circus people set up their tents and prepared to give their first show.

Dumbo watched the other elephants perform. They could do all kinds of wonderful tricks, balancing delicately with two feet on a ball or tub, standing on their hind legs with trunk raised in the air. Looking at them, Dumbo wondered if he could ever hope to perform such tricks.

His mother tried to protect him from the teasing of the circus folk and the people who came to see the "Biggest Little Show on Earth." But once they caught sight of the little elephant with the big ears people laughed. One day some children were especially unkind. When one boy actually started to pull Dumbo's ears it was too much for his mother. Mrs. Jumbo snatched the boy up and spanked him with her trunk. The Ringmaster ordered her chained, and when she tried to break loose to join Dumbo, the Ringmaster cried, "She's wild—tie down her trunk! Take her away! Put her in jail!"

Poor Dumbo. He was left alone in Mrs. Jumbo's empty stall. The other elephants would have nothing to do with him. "He's an F-R-E-A-K," they said, "and it's his fault Mrs. Jumbo is in jail." "Furthermore," said the leader of the gossips, "I wouldn't eat at the same bale of hay with him."

A tough little circus mouse named Timothy overheard all this unkind talk. "What's the matter with his ears?" he asked. "I think they're cute." Timothy decided Dumbo needed a friend and he would be it. But Dumbo trusted no one anymore, and he hid from Timothy in a haystack.

"Look, Dumbo, I'm your friend," said the mouse to the haystack. "Look what I've got for ya," and he held up a peanut. "C'mon out and be friends. Maybe together we could get your mother out of the clink."

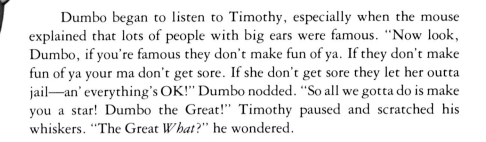

Dumbo began to listen to Timothy, especially when the mouse explained that lots of people with big ears were famous. "Now look, Dumbo, if you're famous they don't make fun of ya. If they don't make fun of ya your ma don't get sore. If she don't get sore they let her outta jail—an' everything's OK!" Dumbo nodded. "So all we gotta do is make you a star! Dumbo the Great!" Timothy paused and scratched his whiskers. "The Great *What?*" he wondered.

Now it happened that the Ringmaster wanted to build the most sensational elephant act ever seen. Timothy overheard him talking about it. "In the ring stands seventeen elephants. One climbs up on top of another until all seventeen elephants makes a tremenjus Pyramid of Pachyderms. I blow the whistle, the trumpets are trumpeting, the drums are drumming—and then comes the climax." The trouble was, the Ringmaster had not yet figured out a tremendous climax. "Maybe it comes to me in a dream," he said.

That night Timothy whispered in the ear of the sleeping Ringmaster. "The climax for your Pyramid of Pachyderms is the Little Elephant with the Big Ears, the World's Mightiest Midget Mastodon, DUMBO! He will jump from a springboard to the very top of your pyramid, waving a flag for a glorious finish."

The next day the Ringmaster got his elephants together for the premiere of their dazzling act under the Big Top. Inspiration had come to him in a dream. Dumbo would be the climax. The pyramid of elephants was a bit wobbly but ready, Dumbo was dressed in a costume with a little flag to wave. The trumpets trumpeted, the drums rolled. "You're on, Dumbo," said Timothy, jabbing the reluctant elephant with a pin. Dumbo ran toward the springboard, but just as he got to it he tripped over his big floppy ears. Instead of sailing to the top of the high elephant pyramid he sailed smack into it, knocking the elephants off balance so they flew in all directions. One elephant landed on the high wire, two more found themselves bouncing up to the trapezes, one dropped into the safety net and its weight pulled the whole tent down. It was a disaster and Dumbo's clumsiness and big ears were to blame.

In disgrace Dumbo was sent to Clown Alley. "Oh, the shame of it," said one of the elephants. "Let us take the solemn vow," said another. "From now on Dumbo is no longer an elephant."

The clowns needed Dumbo to be the baby in their burning building act. Dumbo was terrified of the flames; he was afraid of jumping from the top-floor window to the firemen's net; and worst of all, he was ashamed to be a ridiculous plaything for the clowns.

But the audience loved the act with Dumbo in it. The clowns had never enjoyed such applause. After the show Timothy tried to cheer Dumbo. "You're a big hit. You're terrific. You're colossal." But Dumbo was still sad. "Look," said Timothy, "you were such a hit the clowns are drinking a toast to you." The clowns were celebrating their new success with champagne, and a bottle of it tipped over and spilled into Dumbo's water bucket.

Timothy and Dumbo innocently drank all the water, wondering at
the strange bubbles in it. After an attack of hiccups, both fell asleep and
Dumbo had a remarkable dream of pink elephants and flying. When
Timothy and Dumbo awoke they were amazed to find themselves up on
the limb of a tree, with a flock of Crows. They knew that elephants can't
climb trees. There was only one way they could have arrived there—
Dumbo must have *flown!*

Timothy became very excited. "Your ears, Dumbo. Dere poifect
wings. You flew!"

But Dumbo didn't want to believe it. Finally, to help him, one of
the Crows used some psychology. He gave Dumbo a Magic Feather to
hold in his trunk. "Now you can fly," they all told him. Timothy sat in
the rim of Dumbo's hat, and the Crows got behind the elephant on the
branch of the tree and pushed. "Flap your ears," Timothy instructed.
"Up, down—up, down—one, two, faster, faster. Get up your flying
speed!" And Dumbo took off. "He fly just like a eagle!" exclaimed one
Crow. "Better'n an airplane," said another. "Brother, now I've seen an
elephant fly, I've seen everything!"

That day Dumbo made history. When he joined the clowns for the burning building act, instead of jumping from the top floor, Dumbo, with Timothy perched on his hat and the Magic Feather clutched in his trunk, FLEW. He flew all around the circus tent, looped up to the very top of it, zoomed down and around. The crowd, the clowns, the Ringmaster watched in amazement. Suddenly the Magic Feather blew away. Dumbo looked startled and stopped flapping his ears. "Come on

Dumbo, fly!" Timothy urged. "Open up them ears. The feather was just a gag. *You can fly,* honest, you can!"

Dumbo started to drop to the ground, but at Timothy's words he began to wave his big ears again—and he soared up, up, up, into the air. He could fly, he could really fly, all by himself!

"Wonder Elephant Soars To Fame," said the newspaper headline. "Dumbo Manager Signs Hollywood Contract." On the circus train Dumbo, Timothy, and Mrs. Jumbo, happy to be together at last, traveled in style in "Dumbo's Private Car." From that day on, Dumbo was the star of the circus.

DUMBO

The Story of the Production

Unlike Walt Disney's earlier animated features *Snow White, Pinocchio,* and *Fantasia, Dumbo* was in production only a little over a year. The picture was begun in 1940 and released in late 1941, a remarkable schedule for which there were several interesting reasons.

The original story, *Dumbo, the Flying Elephant,* by Helen Aberson and Harold Pearl, was simple, tightly constructed, and ideally suited to the animated screen, so the shooting script was developed quickly. Then the production team's enthusiasm for the picture carried them far beyond normal working hours, and their inspired overtime resulted in two or three times as much animation completed each week than for any previous feature.

The formidable technical problems that had had to be solved in each of the earlier features, using up a great deal of production time and dollars, had been mastered, and the resultant know-how was immediately available for *Dumbo.*

At this stage of the game, Walt Disney was familiar with his production artists' strengths, and he was able to cast them to their best advantage. The animators who created the unforgettable elephants in the "Dance of the Hours" sequence in *Fantasia* were turned loose on the elephants in *Dumbo.* But Disney did some less predictable casting, too. The artist responsible for Monstro the Whale in *Pinocchio* and the Devil in the "Night on Bald Mountain" sequence of *Fantasia* was chosen to animate the endearing, waiflike baby elephant, Dumbo, while the

A Disney artist, sketching at Cole Brothers' Circus, captures the authentic Big Top background

Working on the script of *Dumbo*,
Joe Grant and Dick Huemer were
inspired by a small model of the star

supervising artist of the lumbering dinosaurs in *Fantasia* was assigned to the tiniest, quickest, toughest member of *Dumbo*'s cast, Timothy Mouse.

The animators ran into an unusual problem in depicting elephants. They found that, when drawing close-ups, they had to deal with the big bulge of forehead, very small, wide-set eyes, and long proboscis, all of which made it difficult to convey emotions by means of subtle facial expressions. By taking liberties and bringing the features closer together, enlarging the eyes and fringing them with lashes, and emphasizing cheeks and jowls, which could move expressively, they solved the problem. Also, an elephant's mouth is usually hidden by its trunk, but the mouth must be seen if an animated elephant is talking. The artists got around that difficulty by having their elephants lift or gesture with their trunks while speaking. Thus the mouth could be seen, and the gestures gave added emphasis to the speech.

Dumbo never talked, but his expressions were eloquent, and his sidekick Timothy Mouse talked for both of them. Silent or not, Dumbo is one of the most successful and beloved of all the Disney characters.

Of the seven songs woven into the story line, "Casey Jr.," the train song, and "When I See an Elephant Fly" are outstanding favorites.

223

101

From Walt Disney's *101 Dalmatians,* based on *The Hundred and One Dalmatians* by Dodie Smith, published in the U.S. by The Viking Press, Inc., copyright 1956 by Dodie Smith, and in the United Kingdom by William Heinemann Limited

Dalmatians

ongo was a handsome white Dalmatian with black spots. He owned Roger Radcliff, a nice young bachelor musician who was gentle, obedient, and unusually intelligent. In fact, Pongo thought at times he was almost canine. Roger understood the barks for "Out, please!" "In, please!" "Where's my dinner?" and "Let's go for a walk." Pretty good for a human! They lived in a nice little house near Regents Park in London, but it had become very lonely for both of them.

To Pongo it was plain to see that his bachelor pet needed someone. He was too wrapped up in his work, writing songs all day and half into the night. Songs about romance, of all things, a subject he knew nothing about. So Pongo took matters into his own hands—or paws— and arranged a meeting in the park one spring day with Anita, a pretty lady who was owned by Perdita, a good-looking female Dalmatian. There's nothing like a walk in the park, in early spring, at dusk, when the lights are just blinking on all over London, to promote romance.

In a few short weeks there was a double wedding for Pongo and Perdita and Roger and Anita, and the dogs settled down to a life of pleasant domesticity with their happy pets.

The months passed peacefully, and in autumn Pongo and Perdita became the proud parents of their first litter of puppies. Fifteen beautiful little Dalmatians! When Roger saw the new puppies in the kitchen, where Nanny Cook was getting them settled, he was flabbergasted. "Fifteen puppies!" he exclaimed. "Why Pongo, boy, that's marvelous! You old rascal!" Pongo held his head high and there was a new light in his intelligent dark eyes.

Just then the doorbell rang and Nanny Cook opened it for Cruella De Vil, Anita's old schoolmate. No one liked her. She was mean and selfish, but Anita wanted to be polite to her. Cruella blew smoke in Anita's face and demanded, "Where are they?"

"Who, Cruella?" Anita asked. "The puppies, the puppies," Cruella said in a loud, rude voice. Anita picked up one of the tiny puppies. "I'll take them all, dear," said Cruella. "Just name your price." Cruella had a passion for fur coats, and she had her heart set on owning a white one with black spots. "I worship furs, I live for furs. Why, I even sleep between ermine sheets. That's why I *must* have these Dalmatians."

But Roger, who had just come into the room, said firmly, "We aren't selling the puppies and that's final!" Pongo stood by, nodding his head. "Not even one," Roger added. "No, no, and NO again."

"You'll be sorry," Cruella shouted. "I'll get even with all of you.

Fools! Idiots!" And she slammed the door behind her with a crash that broke the glass.

Anita embraced Roger. "Oh, darling, you were magnificent," she said. Roger puffed on his pipe. "That's a strange name, De Vil. If you put both parts together it spells Devil. Maybe that's why she's so mean." Pongo ran to the pantry to tell Perdita the good news. "My ole pet Roger. He told her off, Perdy. She's gone for good!"

One evening about six weeks later, Pongo and Perdita took Roger and Anita for their customary evening walk in the park. The puppies were at home, watching television before bedtime, when the back doorbell rang most unexpectedly. When Nanny Cook answered it, there stood a tall skinny man with a poker and a short fat man with a club. "Uh, we're from the gas company," said the short one; his tall partner pushed past him into the kitchen. While Nanny Cook protested, the two thugs locked her in the cellar, scooped up fifteen sleepy puppies, and stuffed

them into a large burlap bag. They carried the bag to a van waiting outside, and off they sped.

Half an hour later Pongo and Perdita brought Roger and Anita back and heard Nanny Cook banging on the cellar door. After they freed her they all searched the house to see what silver or valuables had been stolen. Everything was in its proper place except the puppies. Of the fifteen spotted Dalmatians there wasn't a trace. "Those scoundrels! They stole the puppies!" wailed Nanny Cook.

Roger was very good. He was on the phone to the police, to Scotland Yard, to the newspapers to place ads and offer "reward for return, no questions asked." The next day Cruella De Vil telephoned. "Oh, Anita," she crooned, "what a dreadful thing. I just saw the papers. Have the police been any help?" But before Anita could answer politely, Roger grabbed the phone. "Where are they, Cruella?" he demanded. "Idiot!" Cruella screamed. But Pongo, standing near the phone, nodded his head in agreement with Roger. He, too, thought Cruella was the number one suspect, although there was no proof so far.

That evening, while Perdita slept next to him, exhausted by grief, Pongo chewed on the wicker of his basket as Roger might thoughtfully smoke his pipe. In spite of his playful, charming ways, Pongo happened to possess one of the keenest brains in dogdom, and he used it now. He devised a plan.

The next day the police and Scotland Yard had nothing to report. Pongo took Perdita into his confidence. "Perdy," he said, "I'm afraid it's all up to us dogs. We must use the Twilight Bark." That is the dogs' way of keeping in touch with other canines, however distant, of passing on important news or just plain gossip.

It was a few weeks before Christmas and twilight came early. Pongo and Perdita made their wish clear to take Anita and Roger for a walk just before dusk. With the Radcliffs firmly attached to their leashes, the two Dalmatians eagerly led the way to Regents Park. At the top of a little hill Pongo and Perdita stood side by side. They barked to the south, north, east, and west, and from the distance answering barks could be heard. "Perdy, we're in luck. It's the Great Dane at Hampstead. He has a network of friends throughout the country," Pongo reported after one especially clear bark. The All Dog Alert was on its way, with news of the stolen puppies being relayed all across England. Every dog who heard it would turn detective, and their answers could be expected the following evening.

From the Great Dane to a terrier, to a Scottie, to an Afghan puppy, to a barge dog of no discernible bloodlines but much intelligence, to a goose on the river, to a horse in a barn in Suffolk, to the barnyard cat

named Tibs, to a shaggy old dog with the habit of command, called
"Colonel"—the chain of dogs relayed the message. *"Fifteen spotted puppies
dognapped from London!"*

    "Colonel, Sir," said Tibs the cat, "two nights past when I was
prowling about, I thought I heard puppies barking over at Hell Hall,
the old abandoned De Vil place." "By Jove!" exclaimed the Colonel.
"There is smoke coming from the chimney, and where there's smoke
there's fire. We'd better see what's up."

    Under cover of darkness the Colonel and Tibs stole up to the old
house. Tibs crawled through an open window and found himself in a
room full of little Dalmatians. "Are you the fifteen stolen puppies?" he
asked. "No, we're bought and paid for," one of the puppies answered.
"All eighty-four of us. There's another bunch of little ones in the other
room. They're watching T.V. with the Badun Brothers."

"Watch out for the Baduns!" warned one of the pups. "They're mean."

Tibs slipped quietly into the next room. There he saw a tall thin man and a short fat one, both with disagreeable faces. Tibs was able to count fifteen black-and-white-spotted puppies scattered about the room. The kidnapped Dalmatians! He flashed the good news to the Colonel through the open window. Back through the chain of dogs it traveled to the Great Dane in Hampstead.

The next evening in Regents Park, Pongo and Perdita heard the message, and late that night they started their journey to Suffolk to rescue their children. It took them two nights of steady running, mile after snowy mile, since they dared not show themselves in daylight. Dogs along the way, who had been alerted by the Twilight Bark, gave them food, shelter, directions, and news of the puppies. At last on a cold frosty night Pongo and Perdita found the Colonel, up to his neck in a snowdrift, keeping watch at the gates of Hell Hall.

They were just in time! The Baduns had received orders from Cruella to kill all ninety-nine Dalmatians that very night, and the brothers were trying to capture the frightened puppies. They had chased them from room to room in the dark old house, but that clever cat Tibs had led the puppies to safety every time while leading the Baduns a merry chase. Now at last, the brothers had the whole kit and caboodle cornered in the Red Room. Escape was no longer possible.

But at the very instant that one of the Baduns was saying, "Now we got 'em!" two snarling furies crashed through the window and hurled themselves at the men. Perdita fastened her jaws on the club that was raised against her darlings; Pongo went after one of the Baduns, who yelled, "I'll knock the spots off of ya, ya mongrel." The ninety-nine puppies set up a racket, but Tibs led them out through the open window in a safe and orderly retreat to the old barn.

The puppies and their parents had a happy reunion there while the Colonel stood guard outside, prepared to hold the Baduns at bay. "Are all fifteen of you here?" asked Pongo. "Twice as many," said one of his puppies. "There are ninety-nine of us now." And they told how Cruella had bought up all the Dalmatians she could find because she wanted to make coats of them. "They were going to pop us off and skin us!" said one of the pups. "Dogskin coats is what she was after."

Perdita and Pongo were shocked, and they talked together softly. Then Pongo announced, "We'll take you all home with us. Our pets would never turn you out." The Colonel called out, "Better be off. Here they come!"

So Pongo, Perdita, and all the little Dalmatians, after thanking their new friends, set off across the snow-covered fields for the long trip home.

Unfortunately one hundred and one dogs leave a lot of tracks in the snow—four hundred and four paw prints, to be exact. And Cruella (who had driven up from London expecting to collect her dogskins) and the Baduns in their van would have very little trouble following Pongo and Perdita and their charges. Halfway to London, a jet black Labrador ran out of his village with good news for Pongo. There was a truck leaving for London with room for all of them. "A ride home, everyone!" barked Pongo. "Did you hear that?"

Immediately the cold and tired puppies were cheered. The Labrador led them to a warm blacksmith's shop to wait until the truck was ready to leave. Just then they heard the roar of a motor and Cruella De Vil's red car drove slowly past, trailed by the Baduns' van. They were following the dogs' tracks and stopped near the blacksmith's shop. "Idiots!" Cruella screamed. "They've got to be near here somewhere. Find them!"

"Oh, Pongo," said Perdita, "what shall we do?" But one of their puppies accidentally found the answer. He fell into the blacksmith's ashes and in an instant became completely black. "Look," said Pongo, "he's a Labrador! Let's all do the same. Cruella is looking for Dalmatians." So all the dogs rolled in the ashes, and then one hundred and one sooty black Labradors marched out to the truck, right past Cruella's car and the Baduns' van. "I've always wanted to get good and dirty," giggled one of the pups. But just as the last of the pups was being helped into the truck by Pongo, some melting snow from the roof dropped onto it, washing off the soot and showing the white fur with black spots.

"There they go!" screamed Cruella. "My dogs! My coats! After the little mongrels," she yelled to the Baduns.

But the truck had started on its way to London, with all the dogs safely inside. Cruella's red car sped after it, with snow flying from its wheels. The Baduns were right behind her. Cruella tried to ram into the truck, but the driver yelled "Crazy woman driver!" and raced his truck across a narrow bridge well ahead of her. Cruella's car skidded wildly, the Baduns' van crashed into it, and both flipped over into a ditch. The last the cheering Dalmatians heard of Cruella was her furious voice floating up from the ditch, addressing the Baduns, "You idiots! You fools! You imbeciles!"

When the truck reached London the Dalmatians headed straight for the house near Regents Park. Nanny Cook opened the door to see what all

238

the barking was about, and she was nearly knocked over by a wave of happy black dogs. Roger said, "Why, they're Labradors." But Anita recognized Perdita, then Pongo, then some of the pups. They cleaned them up as best they could and counted them as best they could.

"One hundred and one!" Roger exclaimed. "Pongo, you old rascal!" "We'll have to buy a bigger place in the country," said Anita. "We'll have a plantation," Roger hummed. Then he sat down at the piano and sang:

We'll have a plantation,
A Dalmatian plantation,
Where our population can roam.

And they all joined in singing Roger's newest, jolliest song.

101 DALMATIANS

The Story of the Production

Animals and comedy, two of the Disney Studio's strong points, are combined in this sophisticated thriller about a dognapping case solved by dogs. Based on a successful British novel by Dodie Smith, the picture was released in 1961 after nearly three years in production, at a total cost of $4 million.

It is possible that the 150 studio artists labored so long because of the unique nature of the characters. Dalmatians wear white coats with black spots, and, according to Studio statistics, the creation of 101 of them entailed the laborious painting of a total of 6,469,952 spots! For those interested in the minutiae of animation technique, Pongo, the leading canine character, wears 72 black spots while Perdita, his mate, sports a coat with but 68; each of the 99 puppies wears 32.

This film was the first to use a reproduction process known as Xerography, in which the artists' drawings were transferred directly to

Frank Thomas, animal animator extraordinary, makes sketches for *101 Dalmatians* with the assistance of five of them

The spontaneity of the delightful sketches made from live models has been preserved by the Xerox camera, which transfers the animators' drawings directly to the cels

the cels (transparent overlays on which the characters are drawn), and from them to the film. The laborious hand-inking of thousands of cels was, therefore, no longer necessary.

One of the most impressive comic effects was the smoke emanating in curls and clouds from villainess Cruella De Vil's ever-present cigarette. Waved about in a slinky long holder, the cigarette created its own calligraphy of evil. The special effects technicians used so much smoke that, if it were compressed into a single cloud, they estimate it would blanket a city of one hundred thousand souls.

Rod Taylor, a rugged Australian actor, supplied the voice for Pongo, the picture's hero; the slightly higher tones of Ben Wright served for Roger Radcliff, the human second lead. J. Pat O'Malley was responsible for four of the "character" voices and a good deal of the authentic Cockney slang.

Not surprisingly, in a picture dealing in part with a songwriter, the songs are clever and catchy. "Playful Melody," "Cruella De Vil," and "Dalmatian Plantation" are among the brightest.

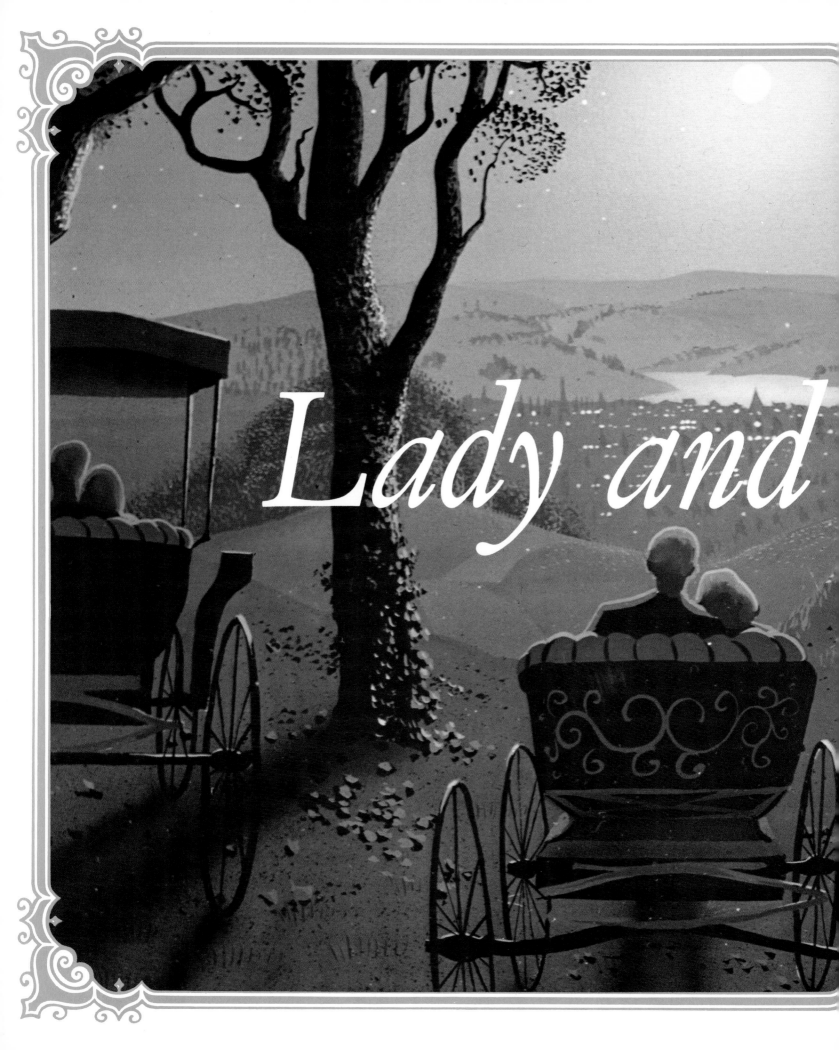

Lady and

the Tramp

From Walt Disney's Motion Picture *Lady and the Tramp,*
from the story by Ward Greene

 t was Christmas day of the year 1910 in a small American town, a very special Christmas for a young couple because it was their first one together. Jim Dear handed his wife Darling a gift box tied with a big ribbon. When Darling opened it a little cocker spaniel puppy peeked out. "Oh, I love her!" Darling exclaimed. "What a perfectly beautiful little lady!" And that is how Lady got her name.

On Christmas night Jim Dear and Darling tucked Lady into her own little basket with her own little cover. Then they turned out the lights and went upstairs to bed. Lady climbed out of the basket and followed them, howling. Three times they brought her back downstairs. Finally, being intelligent people, they understood. From that night on, Lady slept on their bed.

It was a happy life. Each morning, after waking Jim Dear, Lady would dash out through her own little door and bring in the mail and the newspaper. All day, while Jim Dear was away, she policed the yard and kept the house safe by chasing away blackbirds, butterflies, and anything or anyone she thought dangerous. In the evening when she heard Jim Dear's whistle she raced to meet him, then she raced him to the front door. Jim Dear, who was always polite, would say, "Ladies first," as he opened the front door for her. At night, when the three of them sat around the fireplace together, Lady thought there could be no happier family in all the world.

244

Her two best friends were Jock, an elderly Scottie who lived next door, and Trusty, an aging Southern bloodhound who lived across the street. One day they were joined by a stranger in town, a carefree, cocky mongrel named Tramp. Her friends noticed that something was troubling Lady and tried to help her. Jim Dear and Darling were expecting a baby and, said Lady sadly, they seemed to have lost all interest in her. "Weel now, Lassie, I wouldna worry muh wee head about that," Jock tried to comfort her.

"You see, Miss Lady," Trusty explained. "There comes a time in the life of all humans when, well, like with the birds and the bees, a stork comes, and brings a cute little bundle of joy. But they'll still love you, too. Why, Miss Lady, everybody knows a dog's best friend is his human."

Lady was cheered a little but then the stranger, Tramp, spoke up and what he said was exactly what was worrying Lady. "Remember this, Pigeon," Tramp pointed out, "when a baby moves in, the dog moves out." Poor Lady! Tears sprang to her lovely brown eyes. Tramp continued, "That nice warm bed by the fire? Forget it, you'll wind up in a leaky doghouse."

Jock was furious with the stranger for upsetting his friend. "Off with ye," he barked. "We've no need of mongrels here and their r-r-radical ideas!"

Lady thought about Tramp's warning a lot during the next
months. Then one April night there was great excitement in the little
house. The doctor came and stayed quite a while. Jim Dear ran up and
down the stairs and hardly noticed Lady. After a time a strange sound
came from Darling's room, a kind of whimpering cry. Jim Dear ran out
yelling happily, "It's a boy! It's a boy!"

For a few days Lady was kept out of the bedroom she used to share
with Jim Dear and Darling because the baby lived there with them. She
could hear Darling singing soft sweet songs, and Jim Dear would lower
his voice and walk on tiptoe when he entered the room. Lady stood
guard out in the hall, but one evening Jim Dear patted her head and
said, "It's high time you met the rest of the family, Lady," and he
brought her over to the cradle. Darling, looking happier and more
beautiful than ever, was singing the baby to sleep. As she and Jim Dear
and Lady looked down at the little pink creature, they were a happy
family once more. Lady wagged her tail joyfully. Tramp had been all
wrong.

About a month later Jim Dear and Darling were packing their suitcases for a short trip. Jim's Aunt Sarah was coming to look after the baby. "Don't worry, old girl," Jim said to Lady. "We'll be back in a few days and you'll be here to help Aunt Sarah."

But the first thing Aunt Sarah did after she arrived was to chase Lady out of the room. "Shoo! Shoo! Scat! Get out of here! You'll frighten the baby." No one had ever spoken to Lady like that before. Her feelings were hurt, and sadly she went downstairs to be by herself for a while.

In the living room an astonishing sight greeted Lady. There was Aunt Sarah's basket, and out of it slithered two of the slinkiest creatures Lady had ever seen. Slyly they looked at her and purred:

We are Siamese, if you please,
We are Siamese, if you don't please.
We are looking over our new domicile.
If we like, we stay for maybe quite a while.

Then the two cats leapt about the room and did the most outrageous things, mischief that the well-brought-up Lady would never have dreamed of. They climbed the birdcage stand, they jumped on the sofa cushions, they slid on the piano, scratching its polished surface with their sharp claws, they frightened the wits out of the goldfish when they tried to catch it. Then they started up the stairs to find the baby's milk.

Lady, horrified, could stand no more. She barked furiously and went after the cats. Guests or no guests, they could not be allowed to wreck her family's house and steal the baby's milk. Aunt Sarah heard the commotion and stormed down the stairs. There were her precious cats, chased to the top of the bookshelf by that vicious dog who had made the room an absolute shambles.

"Oh, you wicked animal!" Aunt Sarah scolded. "Attacking my poor innocent little angels!" And she hauled Lady off to a pet store and had her muzzled and leashed.

Terrified of the strange leather straps enclosing her face, Lady broke away and ran out of the pet store. She was in a strange neighborhood and had run only about a block when a pack of vicious dogs caught sight of her and gave chase. They pursued her into an alley and had her cornered when Tramp, who was lunching nearby and recognized Lady, leapt between her and the charging dogs. He was an old street brawler from

way back and, fighting furiously, he beat off the pack of dogs and chased them away.

"What are you doing in this rough part of town, Pigeon?" he asked Lady. Then he saw the muzzle. "We've gotta get that thing off. I know just the place." Taking Lady's leash in his mouth he led her to the zoo. Lady was so grateful to be protected by a big strong dog that she asked no questions.

When they reached the zoo, they went first to the alligator's cage. One look at his mouthful of teeth, and they decided to try something smaller. At the beaver's pond Tramp announced, "There's the answer to our problem." Sure enough, the beaver, though busy, was happy to oblige. With his strong front teeth, which could chew through trees, he made quick work of chewing through the leather straps—and the muzzle fell off. "Ya can keep it, friend, it's all yours," said Tramp, while Lady laughed for the first time in ages.

To celebrate, Tramp took Lady to dinner at Tony's Italian restaurant. Tony and his chef serenaded the romantic couple, and Tramp asked Lady if she would stay with him and share his happy-go-lucky life. "We'd be footloose and collar-free," he said. "It sounds wonderful," Lady sighed, "but who'd watch over the baby?" She had made a promise to Jim Dear and Darling, and she could not break it. So Tramp sadly agreed to take her home.

At home, Lady was in disgrace and Aunt Sarah forced her to stay in the doghouse, away from the baby and her precious cats. It was a rainy

night, and the doghouse leaked. Miserably, Lady kept watch over her snug warm home where a light burned in the baby's window. Suddenly she saw a dark shape scurry across the yard and up the trellis to the baby's room. A rat! Frantically she barked a warning, but Aunt Sarah only called out, "Lady, stop that racket this minute, or you'll be sorry!"

But Tramp heard the noise several blocks away and came running to see if Lady was in trouble. "A rat in the baby's room!" she told him. They both rushed to the house, squeezed in through Lady's little door, and quickly climbed the stairs to the baby's room. Tramp chased the rat all around the room, and the baby's crib was overturned, but the infant was unharmed. While Lady watched over the baby, Tramp cornered the rat at last behind the curtains and killed it.

Lady was so proud of him, and so relieved that the baby was safe. But Aunt Sarah, disturbed by the noise, came into the room, saw the overturned crib and the strange mongrel, and screamed, "Merciful Heavens! You vicious brutes!" She locked Lady in a closet and chased Tramp to the cellar. "That's it," Aunt Sarah declared. "Now I'm going to call the dogcatcher."

Tramp was taken away in the dogcatcher's wagon, and was to be destroyed the next day. Luckily, Jim Dear and Darling returned home not long after. When they released Lady from the closet she barked so urgently that Jim asked, "What is it, old girl? What are you trying to tell us?" Lady rushed over to the curtains and barked louder. Jim lifted a corner of the curtain and there lay the dead rat. Then they understood everything.

Jim immediately set out after the dog wagon but Jock and Trusty were ahead of him. Their barking made the horses bolt, and the wagon overturned. Jim Dear, arriving on the scene, said to the dogcatcher, "There's been a mistake. That dog is mine!" And he freed Tramp and brought him home to a hero's welcome.

And now it is another Christmas and the baby has grown, but so has the family. Jim Dear and Darling have quite a time getting them all in a Christmas picture, all holding still at the same time. There's Baby, and Lady, and Tramp—proudly wearing a collar, too—and four little pups. Three of them look just like their gentle mother, but the fourth one, Scamp, is a chip off the old block.

LADY AND THE TRAMP

The Story of the Production

Walt Disney wanted to do a dog story about a pretty little cocker spaniel named Lady and her human family as seen through her eyes. "We discovered during our preliminary conferences that we had only half the story we wanted," said Walt. "Our prim, well-bred and house-sheltered little Lady, when confronted with a crisis, just up and ran away, and all our cajoleries couldn't lure her back again. We had forgotten one all-important thing—a dog is entitled to some natural animal life aside from being man's best friend and his most tolerant critic. It was when we ignored this that we got into trouble storywise and dogwise."

Then Disney read a story by Ward Greene about a raffish dog, "Happy Dan, the Whistling Dog," and it struck him that a dog like Greene's mutt, who wore no man's collar, might be the perfect foil for Lady. He got in touch with the author, they conferred, "and exchanged doggish anecdotes and family experiences involving our own pets. It wasn't long before Ward had whistled up the Tramp and," said Disney, "it didn't take much urging to incite Ward to write a book about their amazing adventures, upon which we based our picture."

Peggy Lee, the singer and composer, wrote five of the picture's songs with Sonny Burke. She sang "He's a Tramp," the lullaby "La-La-Lu," and the unforgettable "Siamese Cat Song."

One of Walt Disney's innovations in the making of this feature was to construct a miniature Victorian Gothic mansion, furnished down to the last detail. Celluloid cutouts of the principal characters, in the proper scale, were used to work out positioning and relationship to the backgrounds. Everything was to be shown through the eyes of the canine characters, from a very low angle, and the model house helped solve problems of perspective. It also unified the work of the picture's many artists and directors—all backgrounds and furniture were identical on every drawing board. Most important, the scale model was used in choosing interesting angles and composing the shots for the Cinema-Scope process.

Released in 1955, this is the first Disney cartoon feature to use the broad expanse of CinemaScope. Partly as a result of the new technical problems introduced by the wide screen, the picture required four years and cost $4 million to make.

Surrounded by storyboard sketches of the Siamese cat sequence, Peggy Lee sings the "Siamese Cat Song," delighting a trio of the film's artists and directors

From Walt Disney Productions' Motion Picture *The Aristocats,*
based on a story by Tom McGowan and Tom Rowe

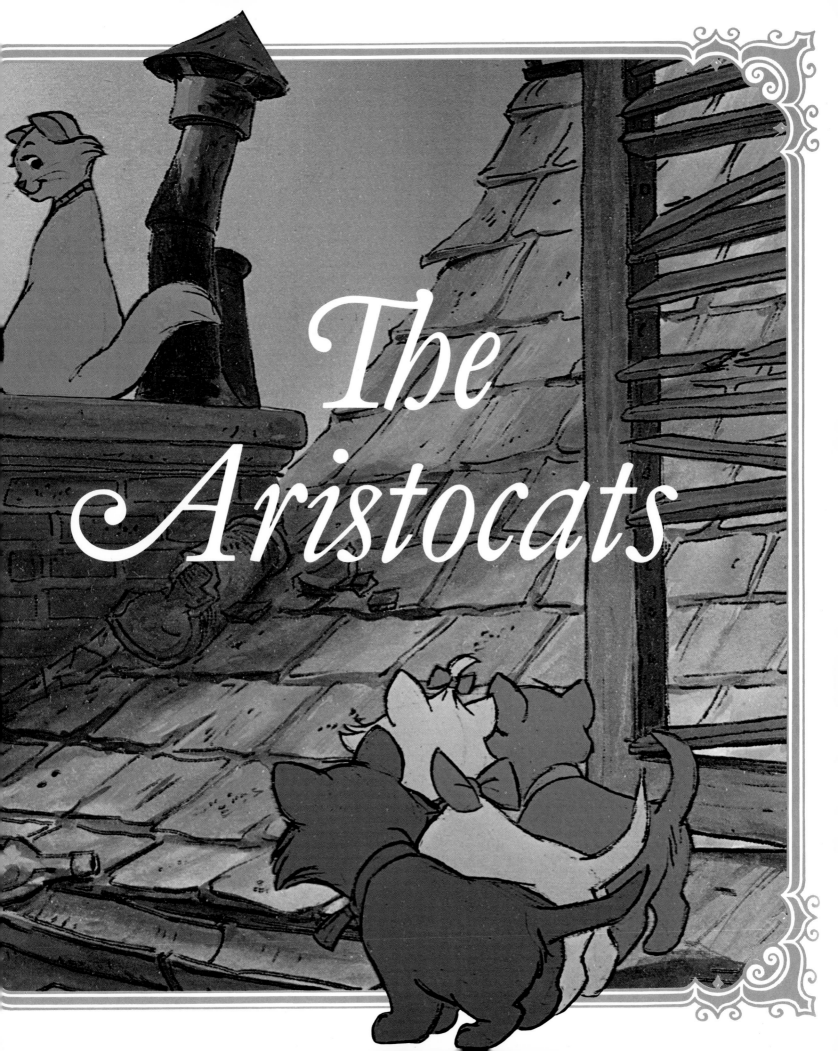

The
Aristocats

n the beautiful city of Paris, quite a long time ago, lived a wealthy old lady and her family of cats. There was Duchess, the mother cat, and her three mischievous kittens, Berlioz, Toulouse, and Marie. On fine spring days Madame Bonfamille would ask her butler, Edgar, to bring around the open carriage so that she and the cats could go for a drive.

At home, on a tree-lined street of elegant mansions, there were wonderful things for Duchess and her kittens to play with: a grand piano, a new-fangled phonograph, balls of fluffy yarn. They were served the very best food on silver trays, and they slept in their own canopied bed in Madame's room. These were no ordinary cats, you may be sure—they were *aristocats*.

Madame loved her cats and she wanted to be certain they would enjoy the good life even after she was gone. So one day she called her lawyer, the oldest in Paris, and asked him to drive right over to help her make her will.

"I want to leave my entire fortune to my cats," she explained after she had greeted the lawyer. "While they live, my faithful servant Edgar will take good care of them."

"Leave everything to your cats, Madame?" asked the lawyer, astonished.

"Yes," Madame Bonfamille said firmly, "that's what I wish. Then, at the end of their lives, everything can go to Edgar."

The butler had been listening to this conversation through the speaking tube in his room. At first he was pleased, but then he thought, "Cats first, and I come after the cats. That's not fair!"

The more Edgar thought about Madame's fortune the greedier he became. He did not want to wait to inherit it from Duchess and the kittens. "Those cats have got to go," he decided, "so I can get the fortune first."

That evening Edgar put a drug in the cats' milk. He waited until it had done its work and the cats were in a deep sleep. Then he sneaked them out of the house in a basket, climbed onto his motorcycle, and sped off to the country, where he planned to drown the cats in the first river he came to.

But two farm dogs spoiled his plans. Aroused by the motorcycle's racket, the dogs chased Edgar, barking and snarling right behind him. In his fright, Edgar dropped the basket of sleeping cats, and he didn't dare turn back for it or stop until he was safely home in Paris.

It was still dark when Duchess and her kittens awoke to find themselves in a very strange place—the country. "Why, we're not home at all," Duchess said. The kittens were frightened by the unfamiliar country

noises, and they thought they had had a bad dream. "We were all riding," said Toulouse. "And bouncing along," Berlioz added. "Yes," said Marie, "and Edgar was in the dream."

Toulouse had a thought. "It wasn't a dream! Edgar really did this to us."

"Oh," Berlioz mewed. "I wish we were home with Madame right now."

"Poor Madame," Duchess sighed, "she'll be so worried when she finds us gone."

When daylight came, Duchess saw that they were under a bridge near a river. And on the opposite bank of the river a large ginger cat was strutting along doing some nifty steps and singing a jolly song. "I'm O'Malley, the alley cat," he caterwauled:

I've got that wanderlust,
Gotta kick up highway dust,
Gotta strut them city streets,
Showin' off my éclat.
I'm O'Malley, the alley cat.

Duchess thought he was quite the handsomest cat she had ever seen. When he finished his song and sat down on a rock near her she applauded. "You are a great talent," she told him. "I liked your song."

"Thanks, Baby," said O'Malley. "I got a million of 'em." He was about to sing her another, but Duchess was worried about finding her way back to Paris with the kittens, and she told him of her troubles.

O'Malley gallantly offered to lead them all back to Paris. "And when we get there," he promised, with a twinkle, "I'll show you the time of your life." The kittens were thrilled, but Duchess explained that her mistress would be worried about them, and they had to return to her as quickly as possible. "You see, she loves us very much. Poor Madame, in that big mansion all alone." And she wiped a tear from her eye with the end of her fluffy white tail.

O'Malley led them to the railroad tracks, which stretched in two long silver lines all the way to Paris. The kittens hopped up on one of the rails. "Let's play train! I'm the engine!" said Berlioz, jumping ahead of Toulouse and Marie. "And Marie has to be the caboose."

With a loud "choo, choo, choo, choo" and a "clickety, clickety, clack, whoo, whoo," the entire family of cats progressed in single file toward Paris, Duchess and O'Malley following the kittens. They were crossing a trestle bridge high above the river when they heard the whistle of a *real* train and the clickety-clack of *real* wheels speeding toward them. "All right now, don't panic," O'Malley ordered, and he showed them how to scramble off the tracks and hang on for dear life underneath the trestle while the train thundered by overhead. It was a narrow escape!

They reached the outskirts of Paris that evening and walked along the rooftops of some old houses. The kittens and Duchess, who were used to being driven in a carriage for even the shortest distances, were weary and footsore. "I'm tired, mama," whined Marie. "Me, too, and my feet hurt," Berlioz complained. "I'll bet we've walked a thousand miles!" said Toulouse.

"Keep your whiskers up, Tiger," O'Malley said cheerfully. "My pad is just beyond that next chimney, and you can stay there tonight." He carried little Marie on his back. "It's not exactly the Ritz," he explained as they approached his window, "but it's peaceful and quiet—" The rest of O'Malley's sentence was drowned out by the sounds of some of the loudest, hottest jazz in all Paris.

"Oh, no!" said O'Malley. "My friend Scat Cat and his gang have dropped by and they're real swingers." Duchess and her kittens forgot how tired they were when they heard the music, and they eagerly climbed through the window to meet the band. Before long all had joined in the bouncy rhythms and were singing with Scat:

Everybody wants to be a cat
Because a cat's the only cat
Who knows where it's at.
I've heard some corny birds
Who tried to sing,
But still a cat's the only cat
Who knows how to swing.
Everybody wants to be a cat. Yeah!
Everybody wants to be a cat.

Later, when the music was over and the kittens were tucked into bed, Duchess and O'Malley sat out on the chimney looking over the rooftops of Paris, under a full moon. They didn't know that the kittens had climbed out of bed and were listening. O'Malley asked Duchess to stay there with him. "You know," he stammered, "the kittens need a—sort of a, kind of a—father around." "Oh, darling," said Duchess, "that would be wonderful, but we can't leave Madame. We just have to go home tomorrow."

"Well, I'm going to miss you, Baby, and those kids," O'Malley said. The listening kittens sighed, and Berlioz whispered to the others, "Gee, we almost had a father," as they tiptoed sadly back to bed.

Early the next morning, when the milk wagons were still rattling

through the streets, O'Malley and Duchess were walking toward Madame's house while the three kittens scampered on ahead. "What a fancy neighborhood! Dig these fancy wigwams!" O'Malley exclaimed. When they reached the gate, Duchess turned. "I'll never forget you, Thomas O'Malley," she said. Then she and the kittens hurried through their own little door into the house, eager to be back with their mistress, where they belonged.

Inside, Edgar was celebrating his cleverness in getting rid of the cats. With his feet on Madame's piano, drinking a bottle of Madame's best wine, he congratulated himself, "Edgar, old chap, some day this will all be yours, you sly old fox." But just at that moment he heard the meowing of kittens. "It can't be them!" Edgar exclaimed. He rushed to the kitchen and grabbed a large sack. When he saw Duchess and the kittens in the hall, he threw the sack over them before Madame could hear them. "You came back," Edgar said. "It isn't fair!" Inside the dark sack Toulouse whispered to the others, "I told you it was Edgar!"

Quickly the butler carried the bag of cats to the coach house and threw it in a trunk. "You're going to travel first class, in your own private compartment, all the way to Timbuktu!" he said as he locked the trunk. "And this time you'll never come back. The baggage truck will be here any minute to pick this up."

But Edgar hadn't counted on the cats' many friends. A little mouse called Roquefort had witnessed the entire homecoming scene. He ran off to warn the carriage horse and then caught up with O'Malley and told him what had happened to Duchess. O'Malley raced to the coach house while Roquefort went to alert the alley cat gang.

Before Edgar knew what was happening, O'Malley had jumped him and, when he got to his feet, the carriage horse kicked him down again. In no time at all the alley cats, with their leader Scat, had joined in the attack. Meanwhile Roquefort unlocked the trunk, and O'Malley tore open the sack, releasing Duchess and her kittens. Edgar lunged after them, but the alley cats and the carriage horse were too much for him. Between them they clawed and kicked the butler into the trunk, slammed the lid closed, and snapped the lock. All was ready when the baggage truck arrived.

The truck men hoisted the heavy trunk. "Heave-ho!" said one of them as they shoved it into the van. "Dis goes all de way to Timbuktu."

Madame Bonfamille was happily reunited with her beloved cats. She never knew why or how they had disappeared for a day and a night, but Duchess seemed to have found a new friend on her outing. "Duchess," said Madame, "I think this young man is very handsome. Shall we keep him in the family?" Then, as she no longer had a butler since Edgar's sudden and mysterious departure, she added, "We need a man around the house."

Madame changed her will to include O'Malley, but more than that, she set up a fund for all the homeless alley cats of Paris. From that time on, it was not only the aristocats who enjoyed the good life.

THE ARISTOCATS

The Story of the Production

Pre-production work was begun in 1963 on this feature, the twenty-third and last of the full-length animated films, starting with *Snow White*, with which Walt Disney himself was at all involved. He had seen Ken Anderson's board of drawings and approved the production plans before he died in December, 1966. But when *The Aristocats* was released in 1970, it was the first film produced in its entirety without him.

The production team was headed by two Disney veterans, Wolfgang (Woolie) Reitherman, who also directed, and Winston Hibler, who is perhaps best known for his nature films in the remarkable *True Life Adventure* series. Reitherman, speaking of his thirty-year association with Disney, said, "I think a little of Walt rubbed off on all of us. That guy was always deeply involved in his work and excited about every project. We make life happen in cartoon form." Hibler worked with Larry Clemmons and the animators on firming the story line in advance, since there would be no Walt Disney to pull everything together in the final stages of filming.

The cast of voices was brilliant: Eva Gabor was Duchess, the fluffy white cat. About her role she said, "It's the first time I've ever done anything like this. It was complicated and difficult, dahling, because to play a cat you have to play it very human. But you have to imagine how this cat is going to react and move, so it needs a lot of thought." Phil Harris (the voice of Baloo the Bear in *The Jungle Book*) was the rough, tough alley cat hero, O'Malley. English character actress Hermione Baddeley created the voice for Madame Bonfamille, the wealthy owner and benefactor of the aristocats. Sterling Holloway spoke for Roquefort the mouse, and Scatman Crothers did the singing and swinging for Scat Cat.

The title song of this picture, set in Paris, was recorded by none other than "Mr. Paris" himself, Maurice Chevalier, who came out of retirement at eighty-two to do it out of respect for Walt Disney. He rehearsed the number once, and recorded a perfect take the first time.

This delightful animated musical comedy, budgeted at over $4 million, is considered to be among the ten best full-length Disney films.

Director Woolie Reitherman runs through an amusing sequence for Vance Gerry, Eric Cleworth, Larry Clemmons, and Ken Anderson

The premiere of *The Aristocats,* at the Westwood Village theater in California, was enlivened by Disney Christmas characters

Authorized Walt Disney Productions' Edition

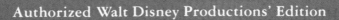

The Rescuers

Featuring characters from the Disney film suggested
by the books by Margery Sharp, *The Rescuers* and *Miss Bianca*,
published in the United States by Little, Brown and Company,
and in the United Kingdom by William Collins Sons and Company

n a dark, moonless night in Devil's Bayou, a little girl clutching her teddy bear tiptoed across the deck of an old riverboat. Quickly she dropped a bottle over the side of the boat, and when she heard it splash she whispered, "Rescue me, somebody. Who will rescue me?" Then, before she could be missed, she hurried back into the boat's cabin. The bottle, with her message inside, floated from the river to the ocean, where currents carried it, many weeks later, into faraway New York Harbor.

In the United Nations Building in New York an important emergency meeting was taking place inside a steamer trunk stored in the basement. This was the headquarters of the International Rescue Aid Society, a group of mice from all over the world who helped people in trouble. They had been summoned because a bottle with a message addressed to the Morningside Orphanage had been found: I AM IN TURIBLE TRUBBLE PLEASE HURRY HELP PENNY. Seawater had washed away the rest of the message, leaving very little information to go on.

But Miss Bianca, a beautiful mouse who was one of the society's special agents, felt sorry for the little girl and was determined to help her. She asked the Chairman of the meeting if she could search for Penny, and she chose Bernard, the janitor, as her co-agent. The Chairman was surprised. "Dear lady, it's absolutely without precedent. A lady? And a janitor? Good heavens!" "Oh, come on," Miss Bianca retorted, "we'll be a great team together." And so they were.

Bianca and Bernard's first stop was at the Morningside Orphanage, where they hoped to find some clues to the missing child. Instead they found the orphanage cat named Rufus, who was too old to chase mice and was terribly grumpy when he saw them. "If folks find out that mice moved in here I'll lose my job," he complained. When Bianca and Bernard explained that they'd leave as soon as they found out what had happened to Penny, Rufus was helpful. "Last time I saw the poor little thing she was sittin' over there on her bed all alone, lookin' awful sad because no one chose her on Adoption Day," he told them. But Rufus didn't believe Penny had run away, because he had cheered her up and she had hugged him and said, "I love you, Rufus."

However, after further questioning by Bianca and Bernard, the cat recalled a weird-looking lady who owned a sleazy pawnshop down the

street, and who had tried to give Penny a ride in her car. "Penny wouldn't have anything to do with scum like her," he reported.

"Miss Bianca," said Bernard, "we must go down there and investigate. We gotta find her and help her."

"Yeah," said Rufus, "but two little mice—what can *you* do?"

That night the two rescuers crawled under the door of Medusa's Pawn Shop and looked around the cluttered interior. On the desk Bianca spied a child's book with a red cover, and when Bernard opened it, there was Penny's name written inside! "She's gotta be here!" Bernard exclaimed.

Just then the telephone rang loudly behind them. The two mice jumped with fright and in a flash both disappeared into a cubbyhole.

Medusa strode angrily into the room and picked up the phone. The mice heard her scolding someone called Snoops because he hadn't found the diamond yet. Then their little pink ears really pricked up when she said, "You caught Penny sending messages in bottles? Can't you even control a little girl? Shut up!" She slammed down the receiver and muttered, "I am taking the next flight down to Devil's Bayou."

While Medusa was packing, Bianca and Bernard managed to hide themselves in her suitcase. But, once they were in the car, Medusa drove like a madwoman, and the suitcase took one great bounce off the back seat and flew out onto the sidewalk, spilling clothes and combs and cosmetics—and the mice—all over, while the car sped off into the distance. Now they would have to get to Devil's Bayou some other way.

Being mice, Bianca and Bernard could not, of course, travel on commercial airlines. By great good fortune they were able to book on Albatross Airlines, a one-bird operation managed and piloted by Captain Orville. Bernard was a little nervous and would have preferred a train, but Bianca and the Captain convinced him that the flight would be safe. "Remember," said Bianca, "we will see Penny tomorrow."

Down at Devil's Bayou, Penny had decided she must escape because, now that Medusa had arrived, life was even more difficult. Carrying her teddy bear, the brave little girl walked off the riverboat and into the scary swamp jungle, hoping that she would find her way to a town. When Medusa discovered that Penny was missing she sent her two pet crocodiles, Nero and Brutus, out into the swamp with the orders, "Bring her back, boys." The great green beasts slithered into the water in pursuit of the little girl. Meanwhile Medusa's partner, Snoops, sent up rocket flares to light up the swamp, and Medusa roared off in her swampmobile to aid in the search for Penny.

Captain Orville was just coming in for his landing approach at Devil's Bayou when the rocket flares burst in the air around him. "Sufferin' Sassafras!" the Albatross exclaimed as his tail feathers caught on fire. "Bail out!" he yelled to his two passengers. Luckily, cautious Bernard never traveled without his umbrella, and the mice used it now for a parachute. Orville, after dousing his tail feathers in the swamp, flew off for repairs.

When Bianca and Bernard landed, they were befriended by two kindly swamp rats, Luke and Ellie Mae. The rats were delighted to help them. "We swamp folks," said Luke, taking a swig from his jug, "would sure like to run that Medusa clean out of our bayou." "Hold it, hold it," Ellie Mae ordered, pushing them all into the reeds. "Somebody's coming this way!"

Horrified, Bianca and Bernard peered up through the leaves at two monstrous crocodiles, one carrying a little girl in his jaws, the other carrying a teddy bear. "It's Penny!" said Bianca. "Oh, how terrible."

"She's tried to run away again," Ellie Mae explained. "They're takin' her back to the ole riverboat, Medusa's hideout."

Luke and Ellie Mae shouted for Evinrude, a dragonfly who had the fastest boat in the swamp, a large leaf that he pushed with a buzzing sound like that of an outboard motor. The mice clambered aboard, and off they zoomed to follow the crocodiles.

When they climbed out of Evinrude's little craft and reached the deck of the riverboat, Bernard called down, "Stick around, Evinrude. We'll signal if we need you." Then, just as the mice were crossing the deck, Bianca shouted, "Look out! Here she comes!" and both mice

ducked for cover. Medusa's swampmobile skidded up the gangplank, bounced on the deck a few times, then came to a screeching stop with a loud explosion of its exhaust.

Medusa stormed into the riverboat, screaming at Snoops, "Where is the little brat?" Bianca and Bernard climbed a rope and peered through the window. They heard Medusa demand, "I want her to find that big diamond, the Devil's Eye. I don't want this junk," as she knocked Snoops's handful of small diamonds to the floor with her cane. "Ouch!" cried Snoops when she struck his hand. Medusa then explained how she planned to lower Penny down the Black Hole into the pirates' cave where the fabulous diamond was hidden. "You didn't leave the child down in the cave long enough, Snoops. Tomorrow she stays down until she finds the Devil's Eye—or else!"

Bianca and Bernard realized there was no time to lose. They had to rescue Penny from this dreadful woman at once. The mice scampered along the deck until they came to the window of Penny's room. The little girl had put Teddy's nightcap on him, and she and her bear were saying their prayers. "And please let someone find my bottle," she sobbed. "There's a message in it."

Bianca and Bernard slipped through the window and onto Penny's pillow. "Penny dear," they whispered, "don't cry. We found your bottle and we're here to help you." Together they planned the escape for that very night. Bernard and Bianca would lure the crocodile guards into a cage. Perhaps Bianca's fancy French perfume could be used as bait. When Nero and Brutus were safely locked away, the rescuers and Penny would make their escape in Medusa's swampmobile. Bernard called down to Evinrude, who had been waiting nearby, and asked him to round up all the swamp folk to help—quickly.

Evinrude buzzed off on his mission, but two hungry bats chased him, their mouths open and ready to devour the little dragonfly, their jaws snapping at his tail. Just in time Evinrude spied a bottle and dived into it while the bats flapped their wings in frustration on the outside.

Before Bianca and Bernard had a chance to put their rescue plan into operation Medusa and Snoops burst into Penny's room. "Hurry and get dressed," Medusa ordered. "We're going to the pirates' cave right away to take advantage of the low tide." The mice quickly slipped into Penny's pocket where, small though they were, their secret presence was a comfort to the little girl.

At the entrance to the Black Hole Penny balked at having to be lowered into the dark and dangerous cave. Medusa snatched Penny's teddy bear. "I'll just keep him up here with me. You get down there and find that big diamond or you'll never see Teddy again!" she shouted. Unhappily, Penny climbed into the bucket and was lowered through the small opening. "Boss," said Snoops in admiration, "you've really got a way with kids."

Down in the damp, echoing cavern Penny, Bernard, and Bianca could hear the sound of the sea booming against the rock. "Way back there is the hole where the water comes in at high tide," Penny told them. "Well, if I were a pirate that's just where I'd hide the Devil's Eye," said Bernard. "I'll ah . . . I'll . . . I'll go over and check it out." While Penny held the lantern, Bernard and Bianca explored deep within

the pirates' cave. The tide was rising, and at the last possible moment the mice found the brilliant diamond embedded in the eye socket of a skull. When they pried it out it was bigger than they were!

"Medusa, I found it!" Penny called. "Hurry and pull me up!" She and the mice jumped into the bucket just as the rising water flooded into the cave. When they reached the surface, greedy Medusa snatched the diamond. She scarcely allowed Snoops to see the prize jewel, though half of it was supposed to be his and, back at her hideout, she secretly concealed the diamond in Penny's teddy bear. When Penny pleaded for the return of Teddy, Medusa laughed cruelly. "Teddy goes with me, my dear. I've grown quite fond of him."

Meanwhile Evinrude had eluded the bats and had buzzed the alarm to the swamp folk. They had joined forces and launched an attack on Medusa's boat. Now was the time for Bernard's escape plan. He and the swamp people tripped Medusa before she could reach her swampmobile. As Medusa went sprawling, the teddy bear flew out of her hands. Penny grabbed it and ran for the swampmobile, while Medusa screamed to the crocodiles, "After her, boys!" Brutus and Nero slithered off in pursuit of Penny, but Bianca and Bernard ran in front of them to divert them.

Using her mouse-sized atomizer, Bianca sprayed perfume in their path. The crocodiles skidded to a stop and sniffed the delicious air, uttering grunts of delight. Spraying perfume as she ran, Bianca led them away from Penny and right into the cage.

Penny, Bianca, and Bernard made their getaway safely while the Swamp Volunteers, an honorary branch of the International Rescue Aid Society, cheered happily.

A few days later, back in New York, Bianca and Bernard watched a television newscast that took place on the steps of the Morningside Orphanage. There was Penny with her new mother and father, who had chosen her from among all the other children in the orphanage. She was not only adopted, she was a heroine! The television reporter announced that the Devil's Eye, the world's largest diamond, had been given to the Smithsonian Institution. "Penny," he added, "you were a brave little girl to do what you did all by yourself."

"Oh," Penny replied, "I didn't do it all by myself. Two little mice, Bernard and Bianca, from the Rescue Aid Society helped me. Could I say hello to them? Hello, Bianca. Hi, Bernard."

The reporter smiled at the television audience and shook his head. "Ah," he said, "the wonderful imagination of a child!"

THE RESCUERS

The Story of the Production

The international success of this full-length cartoon feature, released in July, 1977, is a tribute to the ongoing talents of the Disney creative team forty years after *Snow White and the Seven Dwarfs*. The film was in production for four years, at a cost of more than $6 million. In six months, revenues from foreign distribution alone exceeded $21 million, a record for any Disney film.

Ron Miller was the executive producer and Wolfgang (Woolie) Reitherman produced and co-directed with John Lounsbery and Art Stevens. Between them these men put in 136 years at the Studio! But more significantly for the future, *The Rescuers* also marks the feature-length debut of a remarkable group of young animators. Working under the supervision of veterans Ollie Johnston, Milt Kahl, and Frank Thomas, whose animation has graced every Disney film since the 1930s, the new staff of twenty-five artists came up through the Studio's Talent Development Program.

The Rescuers and *Miss Bianca,* by the British author Margery Sharp, inspired the film's story about two resourceful and courageous mice who rescue a kidnapped orphan from the clutches of a villainess. According to Miss Sharp's publisher, the Disney production helped put *all* the Miss Bianca books on the bestseller list.

A stellar cast lent their voices and talents to the characters. Bob Newhart is heard on the soundtrack as mild but stalwart Bernard, the mouse janitor who embarked on a heroic mission. Eva Gabor's charm and sophistication fit that "minx of a mouse," Miss Bianca, like one of the heroine's tiny suede gloves. The crucial role of the arch-villainess, Madame Medusa, is given its melodramatic yet humorous voice by the fine dramatic actress Geraldine Page. And the weary voice of Captain Orville, the one-bird Albatross Airlines, belongs to none other than Jim Jordan, radio's "Fibber McGee."

In developing the final script, writer Larry Clemmons (who doubled in brass as the voice of Gramps, one of the swamp folks) and his staff spent a year working on rough storyboard sketches, trying to establish the characters. "It doesn't happen overnight," said Clemmons. "The voice and personality of the actors become a major influence, too. We keep making changes until we have the final story and script ready for the animators. They take the characters, situations, and words and make it all come to life."

290

Looking at the animation drawings of the characters they represent, the cast recording the Swamp Folks' voices throw themselves into their parts

The Magic Continues

The Fox and the

From her nest in the oak tree, a plump old owl called Big Mama saw the whole sad affair take place. She was just settling down to a good morning's sleep when a panicky fox, carrying a newborn kit in her mouth, burst out of the woods. She was fleeing from a pack of baying hound dogs. Sensing she might not escape, the fox hid her baby in the grass next to a fence post and then tore across the meadow. Moments later, Big Mama heard rifle shots. She knew that the baby fox was now all alone.

Big Mama flew down to him. "You poor little fella," she said, stroking the shivering kit. "You're gonna need some carin' for." The baby fox snuggled up against Big Mama's soft feathers. "Oh, no, not me, darlin'," Big Mama said, laughing. "But don't you move. Big Mama's gonna be right back."

The owl flew off in search of her two friends, Boomer and Dinky. She found them perched on the branch of an elm tree, trying to prod a caterpillar from its hiding place. Boomer, a woodpecker, was widening a hole in the trunk, while Dinky, a little sparrow, cheered him on.

"Boomer," Big Mama said, "stop that peckin' and listen. I need you and Dinky to help me." She told them about the motherless fox.

"Gosh," said Boomer. "Who'll take care of him?"

Dinky ruffled his feathers and thought. "Hey, I got an idea," he exclaimed. "Widow Tweed's all alone. She'd probably be happy to take care of him. And I'll tell ya how we'll arrange it. . . ."

A few minutes later, Boomer tapped on the door to Widow Tweed's farmhouse.

"Yes?" Widow Tweed answered, looking around bewildered. Just as she was about to close the door, Big Mama and Dinky flew down and yanked her pink bloomers from the clothesline. "My word!" she cried. "You come back with those!"

The birds flew to the edge of the garden and dropped the bloomers near the fence post. Widow Tweed hurried out of her house to retrieve them. When she picked them up, she was surprised to find a little furry ball huddled on the ground.

"Why, it's a baby fox," she said. As she bent down low, the tiny creature tottered over to her. "You're such a little toddler," she said, laughing. "I think I'll call you Tod." She wrapped him in her apron and brought him inside.

That afternoon, Widow Tweed's neighbor, Amos Slade, drove his rattletrap truck past her farm and pulled up to his shabby house down the road. His old gray hunting dog yawned and ambled over to greet him.

"Looky here, Chief," Amos said to the dog, who was busy scratching himself. He grabbed a small sack from the truck. "I've got a surprise—someone for you to look after." Chief sniffed the bag and a brown spotted puppy poked out his head.

"Whaddya think of our new huntin' dog?" asked Amos. "His name's Copper. Just a little runt now, but he'll grow." Chief raised one eye and grumbled. But when Copper licked him on the nose, he decided the little hound might not be so bad after all.

Early in the morning, Widow Tweed put on her rubber boots and trudged out to the barn. Tod followed along curiously. As Widow Tweed milked the cow, Tod wandered in and out of the cow's legs and batted at her switching tail with his paw.

"You're going to have to be patient with Tod," Widow Tweed told the cow. "He's one of the family now." But after Tod chased the pigs through the mud, upset the hens, and knocked over the milk bucket, even Widow Tweed became flustered. "I'll never get my chores done. Run along, dear, and play somewhere else. And try to stay out of mischief."

As Tod trotted past the elm tree, he saw Boomer and Dinky, still trying to catch the same caterpillar. He wandered across the meadow toward Amos Slade's house, where Copper and Chief lay stretched out in the yard.

Copper raised his head and sniffed the air. "I smell somethin' funny," he said to Chief. "I'd better go check it out." Sniffing his way across the meadow, he bumped straight into Tod.

"What are you smelling?" Tod asked.

"Don't know yet," answered Copper. He took another sniff. "Why, it's . . . you!" He raised his head and let out a hoarse little howl.

"Why're you doing that?" asked Tod.

"Us hound dogs are supposed to do that when we find what we've been trackin'," explained Copper.

"I see," said Tod, not exactly sure what tracking was. "I'm a fox, and my name is Tod. What's yours?"

"Mine's Copper."

Tod smiled. "I bet you'd be great at hide-and-seek. Wanna play?"

"Can I use my nose?" asked Copper.

"Sure," said Tod. And from that moment on, they became the best of friends.

Copper and Tod spent the summer playing together all day long. They splashed around in the swimming hole, chased butterflies through the meadow, and played endless games of hide-and-seek. By dinnertime they were always exhausted, but every night they'd drift off to sleep dreaming of the next day's fun.

Big Mama often watched the two of them from her oak tree. "Imagine that! A fox and a hound playin' together! Those little darlin's think life's just one big happy game." She shook her head and sighed. "Too bad nothin' lasts forever."

One fall day, Tod and Copper were playing tag near the swimming hole when they heard a loud whistle.

"Dagnabit, Copper!" Amos shouted from the house. "Get over here!"

"He sounds mad," Copper said. "I gotta go home."

"Do you have to?" asked Tod.

"Sure do," said Copper. "See ya here tomorrow."

But the next morning, Copper didn't show up. So Tod wandered over to Amos Slade's yard, where he found Copper tied to a barrel.

"My master says I gotta stay home from now on," explained Copper.

"Well, we can play around here then," suggested Tod.

"No, we can't," said Copper. "Not with Chief around." He pointed his nose behind the barrel, where Chief lay fast asleep. "Chief's supposed to keep his eye on me."

Tod inched closer and took a good close look at the snoozing dog. Carefully, he peeled down Chief's lower lip. "Look at those teeth!" he exclaimed with wide eyes.

Copper gulped. "You'd better go!" he warned. "Chief's a great guy, but he can get pretty cranky."

Dreaming he was chasing rabbits, Chief took a big sniff. One of his eyes popped open, then the other. "It's . . . it's a fox!" he yowled, and charged after Tod.

"Run, Tod! Run!" shouted Copper. Tod scooted across the yard, squeezed under the chicken coop fence and, with Chief nipping at his heels, raced into the coop. The chickens squawked, and feathers flew everywhere.

Hearing the commotion, Amos grabbed his shotgun and burst out of his shack. "Goldang it!" he cried, firing a shot into the air. "It sounds like a fox is after my chickens!"

Tod squeezed out the back of the coop and started down the road. At that moment, Widow Tweed just happened to drive by with a truckload of milk cans. As she slammed on her brakes and jumped out, Tod leaped inside the truck. "Gimme that, you trigger-happy lunatic!" she scolded, grabbing the gun away from Amos.

"Dagnabit, woman," Amos cried. "Your thievin' fox was after my chickens. If I ever catch him on my property again, I'll blast him. And next time there'll be no warning shot."

Widow Tweed decided it was best to keep Tod inside. "It's getting cold anyway," she told him. "I know you weren't out to harm those chickens. But you caused a lot of trouble and Amos is really upset."

In the morning the smell of the approaching winter filled the air. Boomer and Dinky had already flown south, and the caterpillar they had been stalking all summer was settling down to winter in one of the widow's flowerpots. Widow Tweed watched Amos load his truck with hunting gear, lock up the house, and whistle for his dogs.

"He's going on his winter hunting trip," she explained to Tod. "And good riddance!" Before she could stop him, Tod dashed through the open door to go and say good-bye to Copper.

Big Mama flew down from her nest. "He's gone, Tod, honey. But what are you doin' over here? And what did you expect to do if you ran into Chief?"

"I can outfox that old dog," Tod boasted, sticking out his chest.

"Now hold on one minute," Big Mama said. "Didn't you learn anythin' yesterday?" She flew toward a small shed. "Come here, I want to show you somethin'."

Tod nudged open the creaky door and peered inside. The floor was covered with rusty traps, and rows of animal skins hung tacked to the walls.

"That's awful!" gasped Tod. "Those poor things!" He looked up at Big Mama, who sat perched on top of the door.

"You're gonna be one of 'em, darlin'," she warned, "if you don't keep away from Copper when he gets back!"

Tod's mouth dropped open. "You mean he's gonna become a huntin' dog? He's gonna be my enemy?" Big Mama nodded. "But he's my friend," insisted Tod. "We'll keep on being friends forever."

"Darlin'," said Big Mama, "forever is a long, long time, and time has a way of changin' things."

The winter months passed very slowly. Every morning, Tod looked down the icy road, hoping to see Amos Slade's truck bouncing along and bringing Copper home. It seemed forever, but little by little, the days grew warmer.

Big Mama was cleaning out her nest one fine morning when she spotted Boomer and Dinky flying back from down south.

"Welcome home, boys," she said. "It's been kind of lonesome around here without you rascals."

Tod trotted up to greet them. "Hi, fellas." Boomer blinked hard and stared.

"Say, this can't be the scrawny little squirt we found by the fence post, can it?" asked Dinky.

"He's gotten so big," said Boomer. "Look at that bushy tail!"

A butterfly fluttered past, brushing Boomer's nose.

Big Mama chuckled to herself. "I wonder if they know that was the caterpillar they were after."

"Someone's comin'," Boomer said, cocking his head. They all turned and saw a truck jounce around the bend in the muddy road.

"Big Mama," cried Tod. "Copper's back!"

As Amos drove past, they saw Copper sitting in the front seat.

"He's gotten *real* big," said Tod.

"Uh-huh," agreed Big Mama, catching a glimpse of the backseat. "And look at that pile of skins he helped track down. Your friend Copper's an honest-to-goodness huntin' dog now. Just remember that you're a fox."

"Aw, that won't make any difference," said Tod. "Copper's gonna be glad to see me. I'll go over tonight when Chief and Amos are sound asleep."

As soon as it grew dark, Tod went to look for Copper. He spotted him lying next to the doghouse, with Chief by his side.

"Hey, Copper," Tod whispered, "Over here. It's me, Tod."

"I thought so," Copper said, trotting up to greet him. "It's good to see you, Tod, but you shouldn't be here. You're gonna get us both into a lot of trouble."

Tod's heart sank. Maybe Big Mama was right after all. "We're . . . we're still friends, aren't we?" he asked.

Copper sadly shook his head. "Those days are over. This winter Chief taught me how to track rabbit and other stuff. I was kinda clumsy at first, but I got good at it—real good. I've become a huntin' dog, Tod. In fact, my master says he's got the two best dogs there are!"

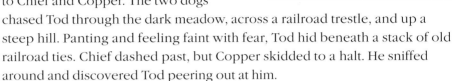

A sudden yowl startled them both. Turning around, Tod saw Chief charging straight at him. Right behind was Amos toting his gun. "It's that durn fox again!" he cried. "Well, now I've gotcha!" He fired at Tod. Tod streaked out of the yard and disappeared under the fence.

"Track 'im down, boys!" Amos shouted to Chief and Copper. The two dogs chased Tod through the dark meadow, across a railroad trestle, and up a steep hill. Panting and feeling faint with fear, Tod hid beneath a stack of old railroad ties. Chief dashed past, but Copper skidded to a halt. He sniffed around and discovered Tod peering out at him.

"Tod," Copper whispered, "I don't want to see you get killed." He could hear his master lumbering up the hill. "I'll let you go this one time." He ran off after Chief.

Tod held his breath until Amos wheezed by. Scrambling from his hiding place, he raced back down the hill and headed for the moonlit trestle. Just as he began to feel safe, Chief sprang out from the shadows.

Tod ran for his life. Halfway across the trestle, he heard a shrill whistle. As a train thundered onto the trestle, Tod squeezed himself flat. But Chief stood frozen in the engine's blinding headlight.

"Jump, Chief!" yelled Amos, running down the hill. At the last second, the old hound dog jumped out of the way. He fell from the trestle, tumbled down some rocks, and landed in the water below. Copper raced down to help but saw that Chief's leg was broken. Looking up, he glared at Tod. "If it's the last thing I do," he growled, "I'll get you for this!"

Amos lugged his injured dog back home and immediately stormed over to Widow Tweed's house. "I know he's in there!" he roared, banging on the door. "That fox of yours almost killed Chief. And I'm gonna get 'im!"

"Amos Slade, you're an old friend," Widow Tweed hollered through the window, "but you can't come barging onto my property!" Still she knew the time had come. She'd have to do something to save Tod.

As soon as the sun came up, Widow Tweed got dressed, put on her coat and flowered hat, and carried Tod to her truck. She drove past Amos Slade's house, past Big Mama's oak tree, and past Dinky and Boomer's favorite elm tree. Tod gazed silently out the back window, watching it all slowly disappear. After driving several miles, Widow Tweed pulled onto a road that led to the local game preserve.

"You'll be protected here and free to run," she said. "It's much too dangerous for you to stay with me. But you'll always be in my heart." Blinking back tears, Widow Tweed gave Tod a farewell hug. "Now, dear, don't you follow me." She gently placed him on the ground and then drove away.

It started to rain, then it poured. For a long time, Tod just sat in a puddle, shivering and watching the empty road.

It was dark when Amos saw Widow Tweed pull into her yard. "She's been gone all day," he said to Copper. "And she's come back alone. I'll bet she's dropped that fox off at the game preserve. But we'll get 'im. We'll get 'im!"

The next morning Big Mama flew to the preserve. "I'm gonna see how that little darlin's doin'," she said to herself. She thought she saw Tod sitting at the edge of a pond, but when she got closer, she saw that it was another fox that she knew. Her name was Vixey.

"Hi, Big Mama," said Vixey. "What brings you way out here?"

Big Mama settled down next to her. "I'm lookin' for a fox called Tod," she said. "He's new here—about your age and very handsome."

Vixey smiled. "Well, I'm not doing anything. I'll help you find him."

After a while, they found Tod sitting slumped in a ditch. "He seems so downhearted," said Vixey.

"Well," Big Mama sighed, "you can't blame him. He was dropped off here and left all alone. Honey, he needs cheerin' up. I'll tell you what we'll do. . . ." She whispered her plan in Vixey's ear.

A few moments later, Big Mama landed next to Tod. "Morning, Tod," she said brightly.

"Oh, hello, Big Mama," Tod said, trying to be cheerful but sounding very sad.

"Last night was pretty miserable for you, wasn't it," Big Mama said.

"It was terrible," Tod answered. "I couldn't find a dry spot to sleep in." Big Mama glanced over at Vixey, who was sitting by the pond, minding her own business. Tod followed her glance.

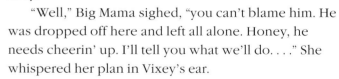

"Who . . . who . . . is . . . that?" he asked. "She's *really* pretty."

"Why don't you ask her her name?" suggested Big Mama.

"Good idea," Tod said, jumping up. He ambled down to the pond.

"Hi, there," he said to the fox, who became prettier the closer he came. "My name's Tod. What's yours?"

"Vixey," the other fox answered. "Did you know this pond is filled with fish?"

Tod's eyes lit up. "I'll catch some for you," he boasted. But it was the first time he'd ever fished, and he ended up falling in the water.

"That's the funniest thing I ever saw!" Vixey giggled.

Tod heaved himself out of the pond. "Go ahead and laugh," he sputtered. "You're just a silly female."

"You've got a lot of nerve," Vixey snapped. "Why don't you just grow up?"

Big Mama, who'd been watching from a tree, flew down to them. "Now look, you two, you like each other, so why not get along?" She shook her head at Tod. "That was no way to talk to Vixey. Just be natural and stop showing off, darlin'."

Tod looked ashamed. "Yeah, you're right," he said to Big Mama.

Vixey smiled prettily at him. "I just know you're going to love the forest. Come on, I'll show you around." They played together all day and by evening they were good friends.

Bright and early the following day, Amos Slade took Copper and drove up to the game preserve. He parked next to a tree with a sign that read NO HUNTING. "We're not doin' any of that," he grinned. "We're just gonna get us a no-good fox." He pointed toward the woods. "Now, get trackin', boy," he yelled to Copper. Copper sniffed his way into the forest, while Amos set traps. Soon he found the trail leading up to the pond.

"Good boy," said Amos. "That fox'll be comin' this way for water—only he won't be drinkin' any!" Carefully, he laid several traps on the ground. "Now we'll just relax and wait for him to show up."

A little later, Tod and Vixey appeared. "I sure am thirsty after all that walking," said Tod, heading toward the pond.

"Wait a minute!" Vixey warned, catching her breath. "Something's not right. It's too quiet." As Tod stopped short, he kicked a stone, which landed on one of the traps. It snapped shut, just missing Tod's foot. Instantly, Amos and Copper sprang from their hiding places.

"Quick, Vixey, run!" cried Tod. With Copper snapping at their heels, they headed into an open field and squeezed into an abandoned burrow. Copper clawed furiously at the entrance, but he was too big to fit inside.

"We can get out through the other end!" Vixey shouted. But Amos was already there. He lit a wad of dried grass on fire and shoved the flaming weeds into the narrow opening. Smoke poured into the burrow and choked the foxes. "Run through the fire," Tod gasped. "Run really fast. Maybe we won't get burned." They tore from the burrow and darted past Amos.

"I don't believe it," the old hunter growled. "Get 'em, Copper!" he yelled.

Tod and Vixey raced through the woods to the top of a rocky hill. Pausing to catch their breath, they looked back and saw an enormous bear lunge from the bushes. It attacked Amos just as he was loading his gun. The gun went flying in the air. Amos fell over backward and yowled—his foot

was caught in one of his own traps! Howling, Copper jumped between the bear and Amos. But with one swipe of his paw, the bear lifted Copper off his feet and sent him sailing through the air. He hit the ground so hard, he could barely get up.

Tod tore back down the hill. Copper saved my life once, he thought. Now I can pay him back. He sprang forward, landed square on the bear's back, and bit his ear. The enraged bear shook him off and chased Tod up a nearby cliff. With nowhere else to go, Tod backed out onto a fallen tree spanning a roaring waterfall. As the bear approached him, the tree suddenly gave way, sending them both crashing into the churning water below.

The bear was swept downstream. Tod managed to heave himself onto a floating log and push toward shore. Copper, shaking with fright, was waiting for him.

"Tod?" he asked. "Are you all right?" Amos limped forward, aiming his shotgun at Tod. At once, Copper stood over Tod and shielded him.

"Come on, Copper," said Amos. "Get out of the way."

Amos stared at Copper. Copper stared back at Amos—and slowly, Amos lowered his gun. "Well, all right, boy," he said, at last, "let's go home."

Tod watched his old friend head back toward the road. Then Vixey gently nudged him. "Let's go home, too," she said. And, together, the two foxes trotted into the forest.

The next day, just as Big Mama was settling down to sleep, Boomer and Dinky landed in the tree and began to search for another caterpillar. Then she heard somebody yell "*Ouch!*" Over on the farmhouse porch, Copper and Chief were watching Widow Tweed bandage Amos's foot.

"Well, well," Big Mama said, grinning. "Everythin's back to normal." Looking toward the woods, she saw that Tod and Vixey, side by side, were watching, too. "Yes, indeedy," said Big Mama, ruffling her feathers. "It surely is one fine mornin'!"

THE FOX AND THE HOUND
Behind the Scenes

Based on a book by Daniel P. Mannix, *The Fox and the Hound* began production in 1977 and was released in the summer of 1981. Veteran animator and producer-director Wolfgang "Woolie" Reitherman encountered the book while looking for new ideas for a movie. Remembering that his own son had once brought home a fox cub as a pet, Reitherman was so intrigued by the tale that he decided to bring it to the screen. The talented actors whose voices characterized the creatures in the film include Mickey Rooney as Tod, the fox whose best friend is a dog, and Kurt Russell as Copper, the dog who at first befriends and then nearly betrays Tod. Pearl Bailey lent her robust voice to Big Mama, and Tod's love interest, Vixey, was articulated by Sandy Duncan. With its pastoral backgrounds and muted color styling, the visual look of the picture was influenced by story sketches and impressionistic pastel drawings by Mel Shaw, an artist whose first project for Disney was *Bambi* and whose drawings influenced many of the Disney films made in the 1970s.

Copper and Tod meet for the first time in this pastel story sketch by artist Mel Shaw.

This story of a dog and a fox who did not know they were meant to be enemies was the final picture to feature the talents of Frank Thomas and Ollie Johnston. The last of the group of Disney artists known as the "Nine Old Men," these animators had worked with Walt Disney on the Studio's earliest feature films and were undisputed masters of their craft. The renowned pair left the film midway to work on their classic book about animation, *The Illusion of Life*. *The Fox and the Hound* was also the last film for Woolie Reitherman, who had worked on nearly every Disney animated film from *Snow White and the Seven Dwarfs* to *The Rescuers*, and who was Walt's hand-chosen successor as producer and director of all the Studio's animated features.

Legendary animators Ollie Johnston and Frank Thomas at work on the production of The Fox and the Hound.

With that last bow of the first generation of Disney artists, a group of untried young animators took the stage. Most of the work on *The Fox and the Hound* was completed by artists drawn from a recruitment program established by the Studio in the late 1970s at California Institute of the Arts. The roster of raw talent working on the movie was formidable. Don Hahn, who would go on to produce the modern·classics *The Lion King*, *Beauty and the Beast*, and *The Hunchback of Notre Dame*, served as assistant director. The dramatic bear fight sequence at the end of the film was animated by Glen Keane, who would later create the Beast, Aladdin, and Pocahontas. Tim Burton, the creator of *Edward Scissorhands*, *Beetlejuice*, and *The Nightmare Before Christmas*, animated Vixey. Henry Selick, who went on to direct *James and the Giant Peach*, also worked on the movie, as did the directors of *The Little Mermaid*,

Frank Thomas and Ron Clements discussing the animation of Tod.

Aladdin, and *Hercules*, Ron Clements and John Musker. Mostly in their early twenties during the making of this film, these talented people were, in many cases, just acquiring command of their crafts. At the fingertips of these developing artists, a new era in Disney animation was quietly dawning.

313

THE

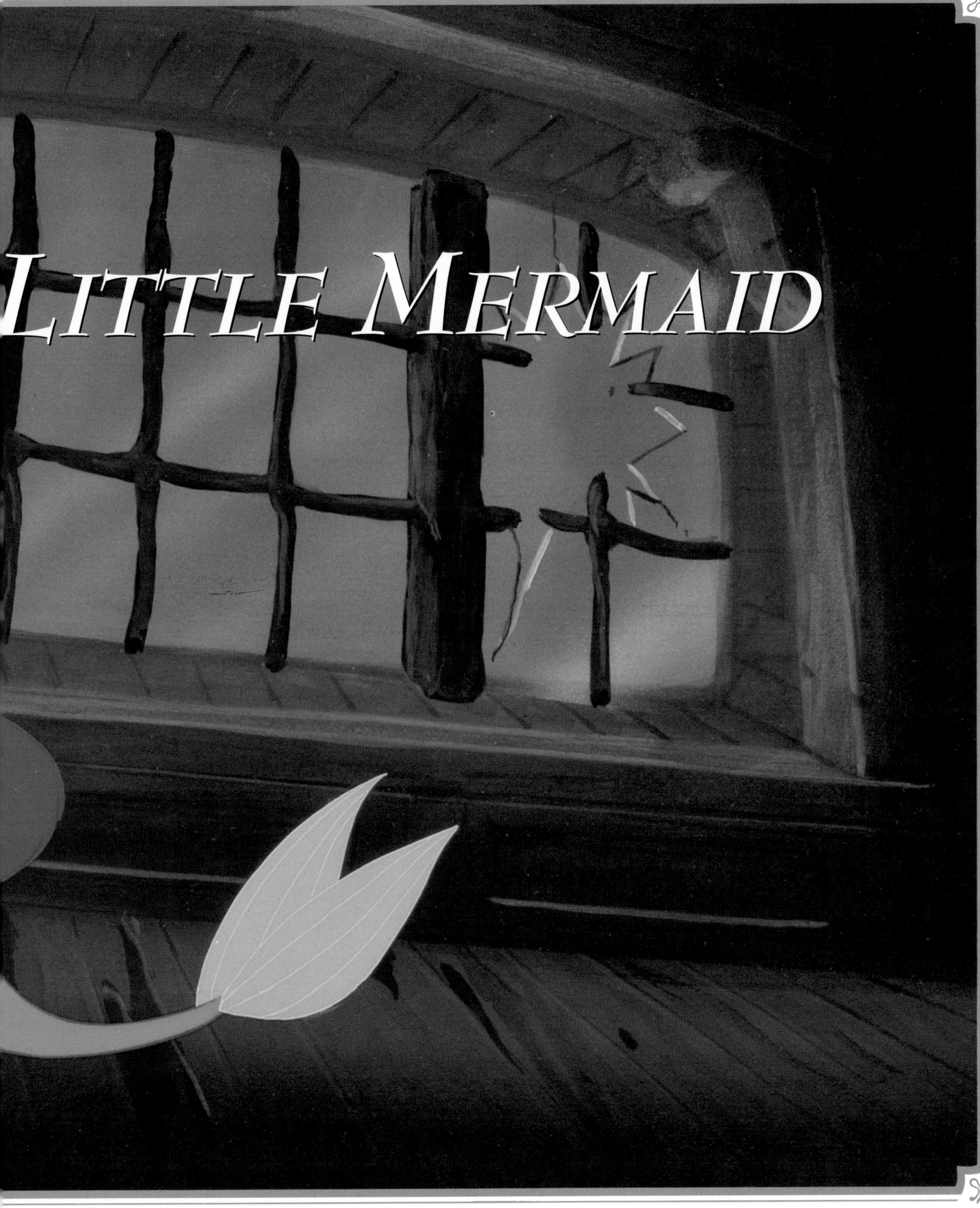
LITTLE MERMAID

The enchanting merpeople, half fish and half human, dwelled in a shimmering kingdom at the bottom of the sea. Their ruler, King Triton, was the father of seven daughters. The youngest was named Ariel. She had a beautiful voice and loved to sing. Although Ariel disobeyed her father now and then, he loved her with all his heart.

Ariel and her best friend, a fish called Flounder, spent most of their time exploring sunken shipwrecks. Whenever they found a human treasure, like a worn belt buckle or rusty oil lamp, Ariel would add it to her collection, which she kept hidden in a cave.

One day Ariel came across two objects she'd never seen before—a silver fork and a pipe. "Flounder, look!" she said. "Maybe Scuttle can tell us what these are." They swam to the water's surface to find the seagull. Spotting them from his rocky perch, Scuttle gave out a cheerful squawk.

Ariel showed Scuttle her new treasures. "Hmmm," he said, examining the fork. "I do believe this is a dinglehopper. Humans use it to comb their hair. Here, I'll show ya." He twirled the feathers on his head into a fluffy hairdo. "And this," the gull continued, pointing to the pipe, "is a snarfblatt, which humans blow in to make music."

"Music!" Ariel cried. "I completely forgot. I'm supposed to sing at the royal concert today! Sorry, Scuttle, but I've got to go."

Flounder trailed after Ariel as she dove down to her father's palace. "What am I going to do with you, Ariel?" asked King Triton. "You have the most beautiful voice in the kingdom yet you missed the concert." He gestured toward a disappointed-looking crab. "Poor Sebastian was beside himself when you didn't appear."

Sebastian, the court composer, scurried up to her. "Princess Ariel," he said, shaking his claw at her, "because of your forgetfulness, the entire program was ruined."

"It wasn't Ariel's fault," Flounder said. "It took Scuttle forever to figure out about the dinglehopper and the snarfblatt."

"You visited that seagull?" King Triton asked, glaring at Ariel. "How many times have I told you not to travel to the surface! You might have been seen by one of those horrible humans. Do you think I want my youngest daughter snared by some fish eater's hook?" Knowing it was no use arguing, Ariel apologized and swam off with Flounder.

Sebastian edged forward and cleared his throat. "Your Majesty, if I may suggest something. I think Ariel needs constant supervision. You know, someone to watch over her."

Triton beamed. "A fine idea, Sebastian," he declared. "And you're just the one to do it."

Sebastian followed Ariel into her cave of treasures. "How do I get myself in these situations?" he crabbed. "I should be writing symphonies." Sebastian's eyes goggled. Piled high along the walls were pocket watches, mirrors, eyeglasses, vases, telescopes, paintings, and pots—human treasures of every kind! Ariel carefully placed the fork and pipe among them.

"Father must be mistaken," she told Flounder. "How could humans be bad when they make such wonderful things?"

She held up an old teapot. "I'd like to meet these humans. I'd like to trade in my fins for a couple of . . . feet! If I could only have one day on land, I'd run around and—oh, Sebastian!"

"Ariel!" he scolded. "If your father heard you talking that way, he'd flip out."

Suddenly, a large form floating on the surface cast a dark shadow on the sea floor. "What do you suppose that is?" Ariel said. Before Sebastian could stop her, she rose to the surface.

Ariel had never seen such a sight! Silhouetted against the full moon was a huge ship. The night sky thundered with bursts and cascades of brilliant color.

KABOOM!

"Jumping jellyfish!" exclaimed Sebastian.

Scuttle came flying over. "What's all the racket?"

Ariel swam to the side of the ship and pulled herself up to the edge of the deck. The crew was having a rousing party, dancing and shooting fireworks. A shaggy dog, barking happily, bounded among the men's prancing feet.

"Calm down, Max," an elderly gentleman called to him. "It's time for Prince Eric's surprise." With a flourish, he unveiled a life-size statue of the prince, bravely drawing his sword. "Prince Eric," he said, "may I, as your humble valet, wish you a most happy birthday."

Eric grinned in embarrassment. "Thank you, Grimsby, but, er, you really shouldn't have."

Ariel stared dreamily at the prince. "He's so handsome," she whispered.

Sebastian gave Ariel's tail a little pinch. "Will you please get your head out of the clouds and back in the water where it belongs."

A black misty curtain drifted across the moon.

"Hurricane a-comin'!" a sailor shouted down from the crow's nest. "Secure the rigging!"

The ship began to pitch and roll in the whistling winds. With an ear-splitting crack, a bolt of lightning struck the mast, setting the ship afire. "Abandon ship!" ordered Eric, and, at once, the men lowered the lifeboats over the sides.

As Eric rowed away, he realized Max was missing. He dove back into the water and, climbing aboard the flaming ship, tossed Max to safety. Before he could leap from the deck, the ship's powder kegs blew up, and Eric was thrown, unconscious, into the sea.

Ariel dove into the fiery debris to save Eric. Using all her strength, she swam with him toward shore and pulled him onto the sand. She pushed back his damp hair and sang softly to him. With the first light of dawn, Eric weakly opened his eyes and smiled. When Ariel heard voices approaching, she vanished back into the water.

"Prince Eric!" cried Grimsby. "Thank heavens you're safe!" Max waggled over and happily licked his master's face.

"A girl rescued me," Eric murmured, as if in a dream. "She held me in her arms and sang with the most beautiful voice I've ever heard."

"I think you swallowed too much water," Grimsby said, picking seaweed from Eric's jacket.

On some nearby rocks, Sebastian scolded Ariel. "We're going to forget this ever happened," he said. "Your father must never know." But all Ariel could do was gaze at the prince in the distance, limping away with Grimsby toward his castle.

"Ariel," said Flounder, bobbing up next to her. "Come see what I just found."

Ariel followed her friend along the coral-covered sea floor. As they approached her secret cave, she saw a tall form shining in the sun's slanted rays.

"It's Eric's statue!" cried Ariel. "This is the greatest treasure of all!"

Meanwhile, in a dark grotto close by, Ursula, the cruel sea witch and enemy of King Triton, gleefully watched Ariel through her shimmering magic bubble.

"So little Ariel's in love with a human prince," she said to her underlings—a pair of snickering moray eels called Flotsam and Jetsam. "Triton's daughter would make a fine addition to my little garden." With her long, black tentacles she gestured down toward the shriveled gray souls of her merpeople victims ensnared in the weeds.

"Who knows?" she continued. "The little mermaid's disobedience may be the key to my defeating Triton."

A few days later, King Triton called for Sebastian. "Ariel's been acting very peculiar," he said. "You know, mooning about and singing to herself. I suspect she's in love. Have you been keeping something from me?"

"I tried to stop her," Sebastian cried. "I *told* her to stay away from humans."

"Humans?" Triton gasped. "What about humans?"

"Uh, who said anything about humans?" Sebastian asked sheepishly.

Triton glared. "Maybe you'd better tell me what's going on."

When King Triton heard everything Sebastian had to tell, he stormed over to Ariel's cave. He found her inside, singing softly to Eric's statue.

"I consider myself a reasonable merman," Triton thundered, "but contact between the merworld and the human world is strictly forbidden. Why did you disobey me and rescue that human?"

"I had to—he would have died," protested Ariel.

"One less fish eater to worry about," her father roared.

Ariel admitted the truth at last. "Daddy, I love him."

Triton was stunned. "I'm going to get through to you," he said, raising his trident, "and if this is the only way—so be it!"

"Daddy, no!" begged Ariel.

Bolts of lightning shot from the trident, shattering all of Ariel's treasures one by one. Finally, Triton leveled the staff at the statue and completely destroyed it. Ariel fell to the cave floor and sobbed.

After Triton had gone, Flotsam and Jetsam slithered out from behind a rock. "Poor, sweet child," said Flotsam. "You have a serious problem."

"But we know someone who can help," added Jetsam. "Someone who can make all your dreams come true."

Ariel looked up at the eels uneasily. "I don't understand."

"Ursula . . . has great powers," Flotsam said slyly.

"The sea witch?" Ariel asked, horrified. "No, I couldn't possibly . . ." Ariel paused when she looked down and saw what remained of Eric's statue. Flotsam and Jetsam crept closer.

"Imagine," they said, "you and your prince . . . together . . . forever!"

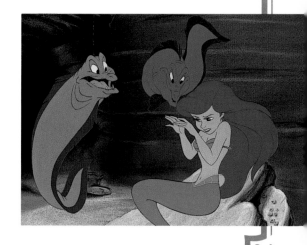

Outside the cave, Flounder and Sebastian were startled to see the eels swim past followed by Ariel.

"What are you doing with this riffraff?" Sebastian demanded.

"I'm going to see Ursula," Ariel replied. "Why don't you tell my father? You're good at that!"

Tagging along fearfully, they followed Ariel to the dark grotto and were revolted by the sight of the gray wormy creatures reaching out to them for help.

"Come right in, angelfish," said Ursula, ushering Ariel into her lair. "I hear you're in love with a human. Well, dearie, the solution to your problem is simple. *You* must become human, too!"

Ariel gasped. "Can you do that?"

"Of course," Ursula chuckled. "It's what I do. I confess I've been nasty in the past, but now I live to help poor needy merfolk—like you."

Ursula wrapped Ariel in one of her long tentacles and squeezed her close. "Here's the deal. I'll make you a potion that will turn you into a human for three days. If dear old Princie kisses you before sunset on the third day, you will be human forever. But if he doesn't," she said, squeezing tighter, "then you'll turn back into a mermaid and belong to *me*!"

"But if I become human," Ariel realized with alarm, "I'll never be with my father or sisters again."

"That's right, but you'll have your man," Ursula persisted. "Life is full of tough choices, isn't it? And there's one more thing, sweet cakes. We haven't discussed payment."

"But I don't have anything," Ariel protested.

"Oh, it's just a token, a trifle. You'll never even miss it. What I want . . . is your voice!" Ursula whipped out a golden scroll. "Just sign here."

Ariel wavered with the fish bone quill in her hand. Then she cringed and quickly signed her name.

"A wise decision!" said Ursula.

She bent over a black cauldron and, stirring the potion, recited a magic spell. A great cloud rose and enveloped Ariel. The little mermaid's voice was sucked from her throat in a swirling golden mist, which floated straight into a shell necklace hanging around Ursula's flabby neck. Laughing maniacally, the sea witch waved her arms over the cauldron. A bright light flashed and suddenly Ariel's tail was transformed into two legs.

Ursula gestured toward the entrance. "Now you are free to go to your prince!" she said.

Ariel found she could barely swim, so Sebastian and Flounder helped push her to the surface.

"Oh, what a soft shell I'm getting to be," muttered Sebastian. "I know I should report this to King Triton at once, but little Ariel is so happy."

Every day since the storm, Prince Eric had wandered along the shore searching for the beautiful girl who had rescued him.

"Be reasonable," Grimsby told him again and again. "You must have imagined her."

"I tell you she's real," the prince replied. "And when I find her, I'll marry her."

One morning, as Eric strolled along the beach, Max ran ahead, bounding right up to a girl relaxing on the sand.

"I hope he didn't scare you," Eric said to Ariel. "Say, you seem very familiar to me." He peered into her eyes. "Haven't we met?" Ariel smiled. "I knew it!" he cried. "You're the one I've been looking for. What's your name?"

Ariel's smile faded as she tried to talk. She put her hand to her throat and shook her head sadly. Eric was crestfallen. "You couldn't be who I thought you were," he said. "She had a beautiful voice." Believing Ariel had been washed ashore from a shipwreck, he took her to the castle to rest.

Instead of resting, the little mermaid spent the day wandering around the castle, marveling at all the treasures. That evening, one of the servants showed Ariel to her chamber and gave her a gown to wear to dinner. It fit her perfectly and, as she entered the dining room, the prince smiled at her.

Grimsby leaned forward and whispered, "Isn't she a vision? And she's *real*!"

Ariel sat down and noticed a dinglehopper next to her plate. She picked it up and started to comb her hair. Eric burst out laughing. "What a funny girl," he commented to Grimsby. "Combing her hair with a fork!" But he thought she was charming and enjoyed her company very much.

Eric and Ariel spent the next day exploring the village together. Ariel had never imagined life on land could be so wonderful. And Eric began to forget all about the girl with the beautiful voice.

Late in the afternoon, they went rowing and floated into a sparkling lagoon turning gold in the late sun. Sebastian, Scuttle, and Flounder hid among the tall reeds and watched closely.

"If only you could speak," Eric said, gazing fondly at Ariel. "I'd love to know your name." He closed his eyes and tried to think of a name to suit her. As they passed by, Sebastian perched on a cattail and whispered to the prince: "Her name is Ariel."

Eric opened his eyes. "I know. It's Ariel!" She nodded. "What a lovely name," murmured Eric. Slowly, he leaned forward to kiss her. But just as their lips were about to touch—*SPLASH!* The rowboat tipped over.

Peeking out from behind the overturned boat, Flotsam and Jetsam snickered and swam off. From her shadowy lair, Ursula watched through the magic bubble.

"Nice work, boys," she chortled.

By the time Flotsam and Jetsam slithered back into the cave, Ursula was beside herself with rage.

"The little tramp! At this rate he'll kiss her before sunset tomorrow for sure," she screamed at them. She reached into a large clamshell containing her potions. "It's time Ursula took matters into her own tentacles. Triton's daughter will be mine, and then I'll make him writhe."

Before the eels' eyes, the sea witch transformed herself into a beautiful young woman with shiny, black hair. The shell around her neck began to glow, and she sang in Ariel's clear, melodious voice. "Call me Vanessa," said Ursula, winking slyly at her two lackeys.

Eric stood on his balcony watching the moon rise. He was thinking about Ariel and their wonderful day together when he became aware of the sound of someone singing. He could hardly believe his ears. It was the girl who had rescued him! He ran downstairs and out toward the garden where Ursula, disguised as Vanessa, was waiting for him. Prince Eric was so swept away by the sound of her voice that all thoughts of Ariel vanished. At dawn, he woke Grimsby to tell him he planned to marry Vanessa that very day.

When Ariel heard the news, she was brokenhearted. She sat by the water's edge thinking of her father and regretting the deal she'd made with Ursula. She looked up sadly as the wedding ship sailed away toward the setting sun.

"This is terrible," Sebastian whispered to Flounder. "I wonder who the prince is marrying so suddenly."

Out of the blue, Scuttle landed next to them all in a dither. "Listen to this," he said, panting for breath. "I just peeked in the porthole and saw the bride in her cabin. She's really Ursula, the sea witch, in disguise. And she's singing with a stolen set of pipes."

Sebastian sprang into action. "Ariel," he said, knocking a barrel, with a rope attached to it, into the water. "Tie the rope around Flounder and hold on to the barrel. He'll tow you out to the ship." He turned to Scuttle. "You must stall the wedding. I'll go and warn the king that something terrible is about to happen."

Swimming as fast as his fins could carry him, Flounder finally reached the ship. As Ariel climbed over the rail, she saw that the ceremony had already begun. Vanessa and Prince Eric were standing side by side before the Royal Minister.

"Do you, Eric," he asked, "take Vanessa to be your—"

Without any warning, a group of squawking birds, led by Scuttle, flew in from all directions. The alarmed guests scattered, covering their heads, as Max barked at their feet. Flapping wildly, Scuttle dove at Vanessa. He snatched away the shell necklace and it dropped to the deck. The sea witch let out a shriek. A golden mist streamed from the broken shell into Ariel's throat. Overwhelmed with joy, she began to sing. Hearing her, Eric rushed to take her in his arms. "It was you all the time," he said. Then he kissed her.

"Too late!" Vanessa declared triumphantly and pointed to the horizon. "The sun has already set. Ariel's mine!"

The terrified guests recoiled in horror as Vanessa changed back to her true hideous self. Ariel tried to run but fell—she was a mermaid once again. Helpless, she was dragged by Ursula back into the sea.

King Triton emerged from the depths and confronted the sea witch. "Let her go!" he demanded.

"Not a chance, Triton. She made a deal," Ursula explained, showing him the golden scroll. "It's legal, binding, and watertight. But," she added, "I might be willing to make an exchange . . . for you!"

Knowing the decision he must make, King Triton pointed his glowing trident at the scroll. With a blinding bolt, Ariel's name changed to his own.

"At last!" Ursula cried, grabbing the trident and placing his golden crown upon her head. "I'm the ruler of all the seas!" Triton fell at her feet and slowly began to shrivel up.

"Daddy!" Ariel screamed. As she leaped at Ursula, she saw Eric swimming underwater toward them, aiming a harpoon. Before Ursula could react, he struck her in the arm.

"You little fool!" she yelled. With a roaring gush, Ursula grew to an enormous size and burst through the water's surface. She stirred the sea with the trident into a raging whirlpool that swept Eric away and sucked Ariel to the bottom. Above, a violent storm broke out and the sky turned black.

The swirling water caught Eric's sunken ship and spun it toward the surface. Like a drawn dagger, the broken mast surged upward. Eric grabbed hold of a rope dangling over the ship's side and pulled himself aboard.

Ariel clung to a rock at the bottom of the whirlpool. "Good-bye, sweet cakes," Ursula said, aiming the trident at her.

Throwing his weight against the wheel, Eric steered straight at the sea witch looming before him. The ship lurched forward on a great wave, impaling her on the mast. At the same instant, flashes of lightning struck the golden crown on her head. There was a blinding explosion. In seconds all that was left of Ursula was a charred tentacle floating on the water.

The sea witch's spell was broken. All of her captives turned back into mermen and mermaids. As the trident settled down near Ursula's cave, Triton snatched it up. Once again he took his place as ruler of the underwater world.

The following day, King Triton summoned Sebastian to his throne room. "I see now that Ariel and Prince Eric truly love one another," he said. "I've decided to make her human and let her go."

"A good choice, Your Majesty," said Sebastian. "I always say children have to be free to live their own lives."

Triton laughed. "Oh, is that what you say? The only trouble," he added sadly, "is how much I'm going to miss her."

At sunset, before the wedding ship sailed, Ariel said good-bye to Flounder, Sebastian, and Scuttle. "I'll never forget you," she told them. One by one, she hugged her six sisters. King Triton blinked back tears and smiled. Ariel threw her arms around his neck and kissed him. "I love you, Daddy," she whispered.

As all the merpeople waved farewell, Ariel felt truly happy. She would miss them all, but now she would hold their memories in her heart and treasure them forever.

THE LITTLE MERMAID
Behind the Scenes

Roger Allers was finishing up the detail work on some storyboards for *Oliver & Company* when he found himself being distracted by music wafting through the walls of his Flower Street office. Right next door, Howard Ashman and Alan Menken were working on the songs for an upcoming animated feature based on Hans Christian Andersen's "The Little Mermaid." Allers was so taken by the infectious energy of those songs that, upon reading the story treatment, he volunteered to work on *The Little Mermaid*.

The engaging songwriting and delightful score for *The Little Mermaid*, Disney's 1989 release, inspired nearly all the artists who came to work on the film. Lyricist Ashman and his partner, composer Menken, brought the spirit, craft, and form of a classic Broadway musical, along with boundless talent, energy, and ideas, to the world of animation. Early in the production, Ashman, who coproduced the film with John Musker, spoke to the Disney artists about the relationship between the forms of the animated film and the classic musical comedy. Ashman talked about the significance of different kinds of songs and how they could be used to drive the action. Menken studied the scores of earlier animated classics to get a better feel for how the music worked with the animation. The result was a score full of memorable and integrated musical numbers ranging from mermaid Ariel's longing to be "Part of Your World" to Sebastian's Calypso-influenced counsel to stay "Under the Sea," and from villainous Ursula's sarcastic lament "Poor Unfortunate Souls" to the playfully animated love song "Kiss the Girl." The close collaboration among songwriters, directors, and story artists harked back to the early days at Disney, when the director's office was known as the "Music Room" and songs were sometimes written before storyboarding began.

The idea for the first animated classic fairy tale since *Sleeping Beauty* released thirty years earlier, came from director Ron Clements, who had found the story while browsing in a bookstore, hunting for projects. He and John Musker share both the directing and writing credits for the film. Among the many people who contributed to the early visual development of *The Little Mermaid* were cartoonist Rowland B. Wilson, two-time Caldecott medal winner Chris Van Allsburg, and Disney layout artist Ken O'Connor. Pastel drawings created by sketch artist Kay Nielsen in the 1940s for a treatment of the classic tale, which was never made, also helped inspire the contemporary group.

The unforgettable songs created by lyricist Howard Ashman (left) and composer Alan Menken inspired all who worked on The Little Mermaid.

The artists worked to create both a convincing illusion of underwater reality and an emotionally believable set of characters. For inspiration in creating the fantastic undersea world, an aquarium was installed in the animation building. To emulate the movements of mermaids, a larger tank was built for live-action model Sherri Stoner to swim in. "Watching seals was helpful, since they are mammals with definite spines and bone structure," says Mark Henn, the supervising animator for Ariel. Yet the difficulty of creating believable underwater animation paled compared to the task of bringing life to Ariel on dry land. "During the second half of the picture she's not speaking," explains Henn. "She has to communicate her feelings without saying a word, which for an animator is the greatest challenge."

Codirectors Ron Clements and John Musker led *The Little Mermaid* team to produce a film with a strong story and values yet modern appeal. The immediacy of the central theme, that we have to let children grow up and be who they are, resonated with audiences, and *The Little Mermaid* became the most successful animated film made to that point. It attracted both children and adults for repeat viewings with its combination of a memorable classic tale, playfully witty story-telling, and unforgettable songs. People could feel, emanating from the screen, the energy that began in the room next door to Roger Allers's office.

Ariel and Sebastian in a development piece by artist Rowland B. Wilson.

BEAUTY AND THE BEAST

Once upon a time, in a faraway land, a young prince lived in a splendid castle deep in the forest. He had everything his heart desired. But despite his wealth and possessions, he was spoiled, selfish, and unkind.

One bitter winter night, an enchantress, disguised as an old beggar woman, appeared at the castle gate and asked for shelter from the cold. In return, she offered the prince a single beautiful rose. Repulsed by her haggard appearance, the prince told her to go away. "Do not be deceived by appearances," she told him, but he refused to let her in. As punishment for his selfishness, the enchantress transformed him into a hideous beast and placed a powerful spell on the castle and all who lived there.

Before leaving, the enchantress handed the rose to the prince. "This rose will bloom until your twenty-first year," she said. "During that time, you must learn to love another. If you also earn her love by the time the last petal falls, the spell will be broken. If not, you will remain a beast forever!"

The prince concealed himself in his castle, hiding his ugliness from those outside. Alone and friendless, his only means of seeing the world around him was through a magic mirror.

As the years passed, the prince fell into despair. For who could ever learn to love a beast?

One morning, in a village beyond the forest, a beautiful girl named Belle skipped down her cottage steps and strolled into town to the bookseller's shop. "Do you have any new books?" she inquired.

The shopkeeper laughed. "Not since you asked me yesterday," he said, taking a book from the shelf. "But you may have this one to keep. I believe it's your favorite."

"Oh, thank you!" Belle said. "It's a wonderful story about far-off places, magical spells, and a prince in disguise."

As Belle walked down the street with her nose buried in her new book, the townspeople gossiped. "Belle is very nice," said the butcher. "And she certainly is a beauty," whispered the fishmonger. But everyone agreed that she was very odd. "But what can you expect—with a crazy father like Maurice!" the baker explained.

Belle heard them talking but she didn't care. "They're right," she thought. "But I'm glad I'm different."

"Hello there, Belle," said a tall, handsome young man with a deep voice.

"Oh, hello, Gaston," Belle said, trying to ignore him.

Gaston snatched the book from her. "How can you read this?" he asked. "There are no pictures!" Belle grabbed the book back. "You should get your head out of books," he said, patting her shoulder, "and pay attention to important things—like me. Think about becoming my wife. After all, I am the strongest, most handsome—"

"Vainest man around," interrupted Belle. "Please go away, Gaston. I have to get home to help my father. He's getting one of his inventions ready to show at the fair."

"That crazy old loon," Gaston said, laughing. "Your father needs all the help he can get!"

KABAAAM! Clouds of smoke billowed from Belle's cottage.

"Papa!" she called, rushing home and peering into her father's workshop. "Are you all right?"

Maurice climbed out from beneath a strange contraption with a shiny hatchet attached on top. "I've done it, Belle!" he declared. "Watch." He flicked a switch, and the hatchet began chopping up and down in a frenzy. Splinters and wood chips flew everywhere as the machine tossed neatly cut logs into a stack nearby.

"It works, Papa!" cried Belle. "You're sure to win first prize."

She helped her father lug the wood chopper outside and strap it to their wagon. Maurice hitched the cart to Phillipe, their devoted horse, and climbed into the saddle. "This invention will bring a new life for us, Belle," he said, leaning down and kissing her good-bye.

"Good luck, Papa," she called out as he rode away.

Maurice traveled through the forest for hours before he realized he was lost. "Dear, dear," the old man muttered, glancing about nervously. "This doesn't look right to me." All of a sudden, Phillipe stopped short.

"What is it?" asked Maurice. Out of the darkness crept a pack of snarling wolves. They rushed at the frightened horse and snapped at his flanks. Whinnying, Phillipe reared and charged forward. "Whoa!" Maurice shouted, but he was thrown and landed sprawling in the mud. Phillipe galloped off with the wolves close behind.

Scrambling to his feet, Maurice fled through the forest. With several wolves at his heels, he came upon an iron gate and, squeezing through, found himself in the courtyard of a great castle. As he stumbled toward the entrance, it began to pour. Shivering, Maurice pulled his soaked cape around him and began pounding on the door. To his surprise, it opened a crack.

Maurice poked his head inside. "Hello?" he called in a shaky voice. "I don't mean to intrude, but I've lost my horse and I need a place to stay for the night." As he wandered about the gloomy chamber, a candelabrum and a wooden mantel-clock watched from the shadows.

"Not a word, Lumiere," the clock whispered. "Maybe he'll go away."

But the candelabrum, ignoring the clock, called out to Maurice. "Over here!"

"Incredible," Maurice said, squinting across the room. "A talking candelabrum!"

The clock, known as Cogsworth, stepped forward. "I am sorry," he announced to the dumbfounded Maurice, "but you'll have to leave. The master doesn't like uninvited guests."

Lumiere pushed past Cogsworth. "Of course you are welcome to stay," he said. "Cogsworth can be a bit stuffy." He led

Maurice to an armchair in front of a crackling fire. "Please, sit down and relax. Mrs. Potts will be here in a moment with some hot tea."

"Not the master's chair!" Cogsworth sputtered. A footstool scurried over and tucked itself under Maurice's feet.

"Thank you," Maurice said. He leaned back and sighed. "You are most kind."

Cogsworth tried to head off Mrs. Potts, a teapot, in the hall. "No tea!" he ordered. "This has gone far enough. Remember who's in charge of the household."

Mrs. Potts bustled right past him, with a little teacup at her side. "Would you like some tea?" she offered Maurice.

"It will make you feel warm and cozy," the teacup piped up. "Won't it, Mama?"

Mrs. Potts smiled at him as she poured from her spout. "Yes, Chip," she answered. "A spot of tea will fix him right up."

Just as Maurice raised the cup to his lips, he heard pounding footsteps.

"It's the master!" Cogsworth gasped.

Maurice stared in horror: a fearsome beast, more terrifying than any creature he had ever seen, stood snarling in the doorway. "Who's this stranger?" the Beast roared.

"I-I-I," Maurice babbled, "was lost and—"

"Are you staring at me?" the Beast demanded. Maurice shook his head frantically, but he couldn't take his eyes off the hideous figure before him. The Beast yanked him out of the chair, dragged him to the castle tower, and locked him in a dark cell.

In the forest, Phillipe barely managed to outrun the wolves. He raced back to the cottage yard.

"Phillipe! Where's Papa?" Belle cried out anxiously. She unhitched the wagon and mounted the exhausted horse. "You must take me to him, at once!"

Phillipe cautiously retraced his steps through the forest. They came up to the castle, where they found a hat lying near the gate. "It's Papa's!" Belle gasped. She dismounted and, leaving Phillipe in the yard, entered the castle.

"Hello?" she called softly. "Papa, are you here?" Not even Lumiere dared to answer this time. Hearing a faint cry, Belle climbed a winding staircase that led up to the tower. "Papa?"

"Belle? Is that you?" her father called. Shaking with fever, he reached out to her.

"Papa!" Belle sobbed, grasping his cold hands through a barred window. "Who did this to you?"

"No time to explain," said Maurice. "You must get out of here!"

The Beast came storming down the hall. Belle recoiled at the sight of him. "Who are you?" the Beast growled.

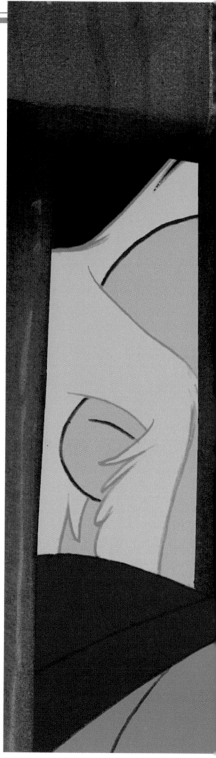

"I'm Belle, and I-I've come for my father," she said, trying to keep her voice steady. "Please, let him out. Can't you see that he's ill?"

"He never should have trespassed!" the Beast replied.

"Please! I'll do anything," pleaded Belle.

"There's nothing you can do. He's my prisoner," said the Beast, turning away.

Belle held his arm. The touch of her hand startled him. "Wait, take me instead."

The Beast was astounded. "You? You would take his place? You wouldn't run away?"

"No, Belle! Don't do it!" pleaded her father. Belle only nodded. "You have my word."

"Please, let me stay," the old man begged as the Beast carried him down the stairs. "I've lived my life. Spare my daughter!"

Out in the courtyard, the Beast shoved Maurice into a carriage. "Take him home," he commanded. Obediently, the enchanted carriage sped through the gate and was gone.

The Beast stormed back into the castle and was met by Lumiere. "Your Grace," he said nervously, "since the girl is here to stay, you might want to offer her a comfortable room."

The Beast growled in response and returned to the tower. There, he found Belle sobbing.

"You didn't even let me say good-bye," she cried.

"Come," said the Beast. "I'll show you to . . . your room."

"My room?" Belle asked surprised.

"The castle's your home now," he said, leading her to a spacious room. "You may go anywhere you please, but . . . you must never set foot in the west wing." He paused at the door. "You will join me for dinner tonight. It's not a request. You'll come!"

Belle threw herself on the bed and sobbed into a pillow. Soon she heard a gentle knock on the door. Mrs. Potts, with Chip behind her, stepped in. "I thought you might like some tea," she said softly.

"A talking teapot!" Belle exclaimed.

Chip giggled. "She's pretty, Mama."

Mrs. Potts poured tea into Chip. "That was a very brave thing you did," she said.

At that, the wardrobe spoke up. "We all think so."

Belle stared back in amazement.

"Here, let me help you dress for dinner," continued the wardrobe, opening her doors. "I have lots of ravishing gowns from which you may choose."

Belle gently closed the doors. "You're very kind," she said, "but I'm not going to dinner."

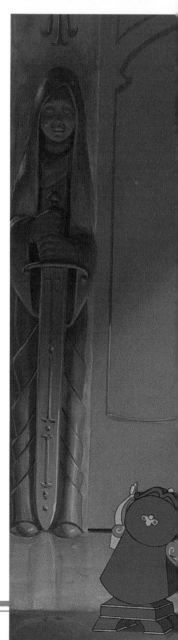

In the royal dining room, the Beast paced back and forth. "What's keeping her so long?" he shouted at the servants.

"Be patient with her," urged Mrs. Potts. "And try to act polite. She's lost her father and her freedom all in one day."

"Have you thought that if you and this girl fall in love, the spell will be broken?" Lumiere asked.

"Of course I have," the Beast snapped. "But look at me! She'll never see me as anything but a monster."

"But, Your Eminence, the rose—" Lumiere began.

Cogsworth appeared at the door. "Your Highness," he said nervously. "Don't get upset, but . . . uh . . . she's not coming."

"WHAT?" ranted the Beast. He charged up the stairs to Belle's room. "Come down to dinner NOW!" he bellowed at her closed door. Then, remembering Mrs. Potts's suggestion, he lowered his voice. "Please. It would give me . . . great pleasure."

But Belle refused to leave her room.

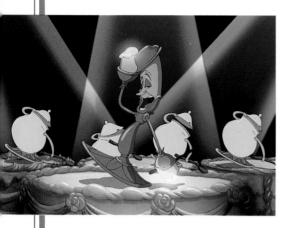

Later that night, having grown quite hungry, Belle cautiously found her way down to the kitchen.

"Splendid to see you," said Cogsworth. "You must be famished."

"Why, yes," replied Belle. The servants immediately began rushing about, grabbing pots and pans and setting the table. In no time at all, they presented Belle with a sumptuous dinner. She had never eaten such wonderful food.

"That was quite a feast," she said, patting her mouth with an embroidered napkin. "You certainly are generous to your guests." She rose from the table. "And now I'd like to see the castle, if you don't mind."

Cogsworth spoke right up. "Lumiere and I will show you around." They escorted her on a tour, pointing out the tapestries and furnishings. After a while, Belle was unable to contain her curiosity. She slipped away and ventured straight to the west wing. Reaching the end of a dark hall, she opened a door and found a room in shambles. A painting that had been clawed to shreds hung crookedly over the mantel. Looking closely, Belle saw it was a portrait of a young prince. His blue eyes were the color of the summer sky.

On a table in the center of the room, a single rose bloomed beneath a crystal dome. Enchanted by its brilliant glow, Belle reached out to touch it.

"NO!" roared the Beast, coming up behind her suddenly. "I ordered you to stay away from here. Now, get out!"

Belle fled down the stairs and out the door. "I don't care if I gave my word," she said to herself. "I'm not staying here another minute." She found Phillipe waiting patiently in the courtyard. She leaped on his back and rode off into the night.

It was snowing hard, and Phillipe stumbled in the deep drifts. Four hungry wolves appeared from behind a thicket. Belle's heart filled with terror. Their fangs bared, the animals sprang at Phillipe. The terrified horse slipped, throwing Belle to the ground. Just as a wolf was about to spring at her throat, the Beast appeared in the blinding storm. He snatched the wolf away while several others attacked him. They fought fiercely until the wolves slunk off, defeated. Exhausted, the Beast collapsed.

Belle rushed to his side. "You . . . saved my life," she said shyly.

Helping the Beast onto Phillipe, Belle led them back to the castle.

All the following days, while Belle cared for the wounded Beast, she worried about her father and wondered if he was safe at home. Back in the village, Maurice was growing frantic. He begged the townspeople to help him rescue his daughter, but they all laughed at his fantastic story about a great hairy beast in a castle. "Maurice, the old loon," they chuckled. "He really is crazy!"

But Maurice was determined to rescue his daughter, even without their help. "Poor child," he thought. "She must be miserable."

Oddly, Belle came to like living in the castle. The Beast gradually changed as well. He didn't lose his temper as often. At times, he was even gentle and sweet. "It's so strange," thought Belle. "I'm beginning to grow fond of him."

One morning at breakfast, the Beast told Belle that he had a surprise for her. He led her deep into the castle to a room she'd never visited before.

"A library!" Belle exclaimed in delight. "I've never seen so many books."

"They're all yours," the Beast said, but he was surprised to see her eyes suddenly fill with tears.

"Is anything wrong?" he asked.

"Everything would be so nice if only I could see Papa again, just for a moment," she said. "I miss him so."

The Beast smiled. "You can see him," he told her, taking her hand and leading her to the forbidden room in the west wing. He held up the magic mirror. "This will show you anything you wish to see."

But Belle gasped when she looked into it and saw her father wandering lost in the forest, calling her name. Suddenly, he collapsed on the ground.

"Oh, Papa!" Belle sobbed. "He's in trouble. He may be dying. I must go to him."

The Beast studied the rose on the table. It had begun to droop, and he sighed as one more petal fell. Then he turned to Belle and gently stroked her hair.

"I will set you free," the Beast said. He handed her the magic mirror. "Take it with you so you'll always have a way to look back and remember me."

Blinking back tears of joy, Belle hugged him. "I will never forget you," she said.

The Beast and his servants watched Belle ride away on Phillipe. "How could you let her go?" Cogsworth asked in amazement.

"Because . . . I love her," the Beast said simply and walked away.

"He's fallen in love!" Lumiere shouted. "The spell will be broken!"

"That's not enough," Mrs. Potts reminded him. "She has to love him in return."

Belle found her father lying unconscious. Using all her strength, she managed to lift him onto Phillipe. When they reached home, she put him to bed.

"I thought I'd never see you again," Maurice murmured, opening his eyes. "How did you escape?"

"I didn't escape, Papa," Belle said. "The Beast is different now. He let me go. Look what he gave me."

As she took the mirror out of her bag, Chip tumbled into her lap. "A stowaway!" Belle exclaimed.

"Did you leave because you don't like us?" Chip asked.

Belle set the little teacup on the night table. "Of course not—"

There was a knock at the door. Belle found Gaston standing outside.

"Hello, Belle," said Gaston. "I'm here to take your crazy father to the asylum. He thinks he's seen a beast."

"My father isn't crazy," Belle said angrily.

"Of course he is," said Gaston. "But I can save him from the asylum—*if* you'll marry me!"

Belle pushed past him and found a crowd of people in the yard. "To the asylum!" they shouted.

"My father's telling the truth," Belle declared. "Look!" She held up the magic mirror. When the Beast's image appeared, everyone drew back in horror. He was standing on the balcony, roaring in anguish.

"He's a monster!" cried a woman. "Our children won't be safe."

"I say let's kill the Beast!" shouted Gaston.

"But he's not dangerous," Belle pleaded. "He's kind and gentle."

Gaston pushed Belle into the cottage and locked her and Maurice in the workshop. "Now you can't warn your beast friend," he said. Riding in front of the angry mob and using the magic mirror to guide him, Gaston led the way to the castle. "Kill the Beast!" they chanted.

After they'd gone, Chip tumbled down from the night table and peered outside. "Ah!" he said when he saw the shining hatchet on top of Maurice's wood-chopping machine. He toddled across the yard, climbed up, and flipped the switch. It rattled forward and—chop, chop, chop—right through the workshop wall. Belle and Maurice rushed out to find Phillipe.

Outside the castle, Gaston dismounted and boldly thrust his way through the door. He rushed to the tower and found the Beast gazing sadly out the window. Gaston slipped an arrow into his bow and aimed carefully. He struck the Beast in the shoulder and then shoved him out onto the balcony. "What's the matter, Beast?" jeered Gaston. "Too kind and gentle to fight back?"

The Beast, despite his pain, was silent. Since Belle had gone, he no longer cared what happened to him. Gaston broke off a chunk of stone railing and raised it over his head.

"No!" screamed Belle from the courtyard below. She rushed through the door and up the stairs. The sound of Belle's voice aroused the Beast from his despair. He grabbed Gaston and pinned him against the wall.

"Let me go," begged Gaston. "Don't hurt me!"

The Beast glared at him. "Leave!" he ordered.

But as soon as the Beast's back was turned, Gaston pulled out a dagger and stabbed him. The Beast swung around in agony and knocked Gaston off balance. Screaming, Gaston plummeted to the courtyard far below. The Beast fell back mortally wounded.

Belle took the Beast in her arms. He managed a smile. "You came back," he whispered. Then he closed his eyes. Inside the room, the last remaining rose petal trembled, ready to fall.

"Oh, please don't leave me." Belle pleaded. She rested her head on his chest and sobbed. "I love you."

Suddenly, as if by magic, a glowing light swirled about the Beast's body, gradually transforming him from a beast into a man. When the light faded away, a handsome young prince lay in the Beast's place. When he opened his eyes, Belle saw they were as blue as a summer sky.

"Belle," he said, rising to his feet, "it's me."

She gazed into his eyes. "It *is* you," she said. Behind her, glowing magically, the rose was in full bloom.

Belle and the prince embraced and kissed. The delighted servants cheered, and then they, too, were transformed back into people. Mrs. Potts brushed off her apron and hugged her little boy.

"Mama," asked Chip, "are they going to live happily ever after?"

"Of course, my dear." She smiled. "Of course."

BEAUTY AND THE BEAST
Behind the Scenes

ABOVE: Rough animation of the Beast by Glen Keane.

On January 18, 1992, *Beauty and the Beast* was awarded the Golden Globe for best comedy/musical of 1991. The film, which was the first animated feature directed by Kirk Wise and Gary Trousdale, was also the first animated feature ever to be nominated for best picture by the Academy of Motion Picture Arts and Sciences. *Beauty and the Beast* was admired for its artistic achievement and its impeccable crafting as a piece of entertainment, but even more, the film was and continues to be beloved for its heart.

Asked to explain its appeal, producer Don Hahn points to the movie's sincerity. "*Beauty and the Beast* strikes an emotional chord with people," says Hahn. "People relate to the Beast's character, they want to know more about him. The enchanted objects are charming, and people want to know more about *them*, and the settings—the French farmyard, the enchanted castle, and the forest—are extremely appealing and inviting."

At the emotional core of *Beauty and the Beast* is the wonderfully conceived cast of characters, led by the magnificent Beast. Supervising animator Glen Keane built a Beast of disparate parts—taking from the lion his mane, from the buffalo his beard and head structure, from the boar his tusks and nose bridge, and from the gorilla his brow. The animator placed this frightening countenance atop the body of a bear and the legs and tail of a wolf to create the Beast's singularly imposing physical appearance.

Interpreting the Beast involved far more than developing a set of external characteristics; Keane needed to show the Beast's nature both inside and out. "The eyes are the windows of the soul," says Keane. "When Belle looks into the Beast's eyes, she must see his human heart and soul. She must see sincerity and believe that she can truly love this creature. This had to come across in our animation."

Beauty and the Beast has no external evil for the hero to overcome. Asserts Don Hahn, "The Beast's greatest obstacle is his own nature, and his success depends not on his conquering a villain but on dealing with negative aspects of himself."

The *Beauty and the Beast* team relished the chance to devise a story line that would turn some well-worn clichés inside out. The Beast is clearly, in Belle's words, "no Prince Charming," yet Gaston, the nominal villain of the piece, has the look of a typical leading man. If the Beast is a transformation of the traditional Disney hero, Belle is a departure from the classic heroine and a far cry from the passive girl in the fairy tale. In the original tale, the young woman simply follows her father's instructions to go to the Beast's castle. In the animated film, Belle's own decision to find and rescue her father sets the story in motion. The original character evolved in the artists' minds to become the independent, smart, courageous Belle, strong enough emotionally to give up her own world in order to save her father.

The strength of the characters extends beyond the major players. It was executive producer and lyricist Howard Ashman's inspiration to present the enchanted objects in the castle as animated characters with unique personalities. His practical need for a set of characters that could further the story in song resulted in a cast of animated objects truly compelling and fascinating to watch.

Supervising animators for the enchanted characters (left to right): Will Finn (Cogsworth), Nik Ranieri (Lumiere), and Dave Pruiksma (Mrs. Potts and Chip).

"No one really knows how an enchanted object moves," asserts Nik Ranieri, supervising animator of Lumiere, so the animators had a great deal of freedom in their drawing. "You can get away with anything as long as the character has weight and volume," adds Ranieri. Yet getting away with *anything* was not really the intention of the animators. The challenge and fun in animating Cogsworth, Lumiere, Mrs. Potts, Chip, and the rest was to allow each personality to come through distinctly while preserving the integrity of the objects. Cogsworth's affectation and stuffiness are personified in the limitations of his enchanted state as a wooden clock, while Lumiere's suave and devil-may-care manner shines through his incarnation as a candelabrum. Mrs. Potts's transformation into a teakettle seems to embody her nurturing personality.

As Belle's supervising animator Mark Henn explains: "The goal was to create strong performances. We tried to understand each character's situation or predicament and create a believable personality that would come across, so people would forget that they were looking at drawings and painted backgrounds. We wanted the audience to be as caught up in the drama as the characters themselves seemed to be."

ALADDIN

Agrabah was an enchanting city—a lush, tree-filled oasis in the desert, where date palms grew and waters flowed like silver in the twilight. It was also a place of mystery and danger, where knives flashed in the dark and blinding sandstorms choked one's breath.

One chilly night under a bright crescent moon, a lone man sat astride his steed. The man's name was Jafar—Royal Advisor to the Sultan. Perched quietly on his shoulder was a red-and-blue parrot, called Iago. Together, they waited in silence for the thief. At last, a panting horse bearing a man in rags galloped up to them.

"A thousand apologies for my lateness," the thief said, "but I have found the treasure you seek." He held up a piece of a golden ornament, decorated with a scarab, the sacred beetle.

Jafar reached inside his robe and pulled out the other half of the ornament. The instant he joined the halves together, a crash of thunder shook the still air. The scarab glowed and leaped from Jafar's hand. Surrounded by a blinding light, it streaked across the dunes.

"Give chase!" Jafar shouted, spurring his horse. "It will lead us to the Cave of Wonders . . . and the LAMP!" Jafar and the thief raced after the magical scarab, which split apart and lodged into the sand. With a roar, the huge head of a tiger-god rose from the trembling dune, its scarab eyes burning like coals. It opened its cavernous mouth to reveal a stairway winding endlessly downward.

7

"At last!" breathed Jafar. "After all my years of searching—I have found the Cave of Wonders!" He pushed the thief toward the tiger-god's gaping maw. "Now, bring me the lamp," he charged, "and the rest of the treasure is yours. But remember, the lamp . . . is mine."

"WHO DISTURBS MY SLUMBER?" demanded the tiger-god.

"Er . . . it is I, your most humble Gazeem," replied the thief.

"KNOW THIS! ONLY ONE MAY ENTER HERE. ONE WHOSE WORTH LIES FAR WITHIN. THE DIAMOND IN THE ROUGH!"

The thief hesitated. "Go on!" Jafar urged him. "What are you waiting for?" Fearing the worst, the thief approached the stairway and peered into the unknown depths. The instant the thief shakily trod on the first step, the tiger-god let out an earsplitting roar. The thief vanished, his cry cut off in midscream. And then there was silence.

The Cave of Wonders began to dissolve back into sand. Its voice fading, the tiger-god spoke once again: "SEEK THEE OUT . . . THE DIAMOND IN THE ROUGH."

Jafar stared in bewilderment—the Cave of Wonders was gone! Iago poked at the scarab halves, lying dull in the sand. "We're never going to get hold of that stupid lamp," he squawked. "We got a problem here, a big—"

"Patience, Iago," mused Jafar. "The thief was obviously less than worthy. It seems only one may enter. Now I must find this one . . . this diamond in the rough."

Late one afternoon in the marketplace, a poor peasant named Aladdin was running for his life. The royal guards were after him again. "All this for stealing a loaf of bread?" he asked himself as he scrambled up a wall. He leaped from the rooftop, grabbing hold of a clothesline, and tumbled down right in front of Razoul, the Sultan's head guard.

"Gotcha!" cried Razoul, seizing Aladdin. But, at that moment, a scrappy little monkey jumped from an awning and pulled the guard's turban over his eyes.

"Perfect timing, Abu!" said Aladdin. "C'mon, let's get out of here." They darted through the city, dodging the guards at every turn. At last, they dropped to safety behind a high wall. "And now," Aladdin said to Abu, taking the bread from inside his shirt, "we feast!"

Two little street urchins stood watching him with hungry eyes. Aladdin sighed and held out the bread to the children. "Here, go on," he told them. "Take it."

As the children ran off to eat, they crossed in front of a richly dressed man on horseback, heading toward the Royal Palace. "Out of my way, you filthy brats," he barked.

"Look at that, Abu," said Aladdin, shaking his head in disgust. "Another worthless prince has come to town, seeking Princess Jasmine's hand in marriage." He shivered and rubbed his arms. "Wind's blowing in from the east. We'd better go home."

Keeping to the shadows, they made their way to the edge of Agrabah. They climbed into an old burned-out building, where Aladdin lived with all his possessions—two straw mats, a small stove, and a tin cup. He pushed back a ragged curtain and watched the twilight settle over the city.

"Someday, Abu," said Aladdin, "we'll be rich and live in a palace. . . ."

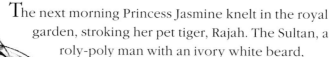

The next morning Princess Jasmine knelt in the royal garden, stroking her pet tiger, Rajah. The Sultan, a roly-poly man with an ivory white beard, watched his daughter in dismay. "Rajah has frightened away another suitor," he said. "This must stop."

Jasmine smiled sweetly. "He was just playing with him, Father. Weren't you, Rajah?" The tiger nuzzled her and purred with a low rumble.

"You've got to stop rejecting every suitor who comes to call," the Sultan scolded her. "The law says you must be married to a prince by your next birthday—merely three days away!"

"Father, I'm not going to be forced into marriage," protested Jasmine. "If I ever do marry, it will be to a man I love. I know you want to protect me, but try to understand. You've never let me do a thing on my own. I've never even been outside the palace walls!"

The Sultan rolled his eyes toward the heavens and waddled back into the throne room. Jafar stepped from the shadows. He was carrying his staff, adorned with the head of a serpent.

"Ah, Jafar, my most trusted advisor, what am I to do?" asked the Sultan, wringing his hands. "Jasmine refuses to choose a husband."

Jafar smiled. "Perhaps there's a solution to this thorny problem. But it would require the use of a mystic blue diamond. . . ."

"You mean, my ring?" asked the Sultan, looking at his hand. "But it's been in the family for years. . . ."

Jafar held up his staff and slowly waved it back and forth before the Sultan. The serpent's eyes glowed bright. Transfixed, the Sultan slowly removed his ring. "Take . . . it . . . Jafar," he said in a dazed voice. "Whatever you need . . . will be fine."

The Royal Advisor, bowing low, backed out of the throne room. Quickly, he stepped into a hidden passage and climbed a staircase to a secret chamber.

"Now we shall see!" Jafar murmured to Iago. He hastened across the room to a brass hourglass. Holding his breath, Jafar inserted the Sultan's ring into a groove on top.

"Sands of time!" Jafar intoned, as he turned the hourglass over. "Reveal to me the one who can enter the cave!" Before his eyes, a sandstorm whirled

within the glass and the image of a young man appeared. It was Aladdin.

"There he is!" Jafar exclaimed to Iago. "My diamond in the rough! Let's have Razoul extend this boy an invitation to the palace, shall we?"

Out in the royal garden, Jasmine, concealed in a hooded cloak, was saying good-bye to Rajah. "I'll miss you," she said, stroking his neck. "But I can't stay here and have my life lived for me." Without looking back, she climbed a tree next to the wall and dropped down on the other side. She hurried from the palace grounds and found herself, for the first time in her life, wandering about the crowded streets of Agrabah.

"Sugared dates! Pistachios!" the merchants in the marketplace called out, hawking their wares. "Would the lady like a silver necklace?" "Try this melon—your taste buds will dance and sing!"

Jasmine saw a little boy staring at a mound of ruby red fruit. "You must be hungry," she said and chose the ripest apple for him. When she started to turn away, the vendor was furious. "You'd better pay for that!" he cried.

"Pay?" Jasmine said, surprised at his anger. "But I don't have any money. Please, if you let me go to the palace, I'll get some money from the Sultan."

"Do you know what the penalty for stealing is?" the vendor threatened, grabbing her hand and unsheathing his dagger.

Aladdin, who had been watching from nearby, leaped forward. "I've been looking all over for you!" he said loudly to Jasmine. Then he whispered in her ear. "Trust me!" He shook the merchant's hand. "I'm so glad you found her. My sister's a little crazy."

The vendor was suspicious. "She says she knows the Sultan," he told Aladdin.

"She thinks this monkey is the Sultan," said Aladdin, pointing to Abu.

Jasmine knelt before Abu. "O wise Sultan," she said, trying not to giggle. "How may I serve you?"

"Get her out of here," the vendor told Aladdin.

Aladdin led Jasmine through the market up to his dwelling. "Is this where you live?" she asked.

Aladdin gestured to a gaping hole in the wall. "It's not much, but it's got a great view." He gazed over the rooftops at the palace, shimmering in the hot sun. "I wonder what it's like to live there?"

Jasmine murmured to herself. "People tell you what to do and when . . ."

"Where're you from?" Aladdin asked. "I've never seen you in the marketplace before."

Jasmine shrugged. "It doesn't matter. I ran away and I'm not going back. My father is forcing me to get married."

Without warning, Razoul and his guards burst into the room. "Run!" Aladdin yelled, but the guards were too quick.

Jasmine threw back her hood. "Unhand him!" she commanded. "By order of the Princess."

Aladdin was stunned. She was dressed in the finest silks and a gleaming jewel adorned her hair.

"P-P-Princess Jasmine," Razoul stammered. "What are you doing outside the palace?"

"That's not your concern," she replied. "Release him at once."

"My orders come from Jafar," Razoul explained, dragging Aladdin away. "You'll have to take it up with him."

When they reached the palace, Jasmine summoned Jafar. It was several moments before he arrived. "I cannot honor your request to release this boy," he lied. "He was convicted of kidnapping you. The sentence was carried out immediately—death by beheading."

It was cold and dark in the palace dungeon. Aladdin sat slumped with his wrists shackled to the damp wall. "I can't believe she was the Princess. I must have sounded so stupid to her," he said aloud.

As soon as it was night, Abu peeked through the bars of the window high above Aladdin's head.

"Abu," Aladdin whispered. "See if you can get me out of here." Abu swung down by his tail and, in a few minutes, managed to undo the locks.

"Wait," wheezed a shaky voice. Jafar, disguised as a crippled beggar, limped out of the shadows. "There is a Cave of Wonders filled with treasures beyond your wildest dreams," he said. "If you want to impress your princess, you'd be wise to listen."

"But she has to marry a prince," Aladdin said, warily. "What good would a treasure be to *me*?"

"You've heard of the golden rule," said Jafar. "Whoever has the gold . . . makes the rules."

Aladdin's eyes widened. "So why would you share all this treasure with me?"

"I need a pair of strong young legs to get it," said Jafar, extending his bony hand. "Do we have a deal?" Aladdin looked uneasily at Abu as he shook hands with the beggar. Jafar pushed against a stone in the wall and it slid back, revealing a staircase. "Let us go!"

Late that night, out in the chilly desert, Aladdin stood amazed as the Cave of Wonders emerged from the sands. "Fetch the lamp," Jafar urged, pushing him forward, "and you shall have your reward."

"WHO DISTURBS MY SLUMBER?" demanded the tiger-god.

Aladdin gulped. "Uh, it is I, Aladdin," he answered.

"PROCEED. TOUCH NOTHING BUT THE LAMP."

Aladdin made his way down the winding steps and found himself in an enormous cavern piled high with mountains of gold coins and sparkling emeralds, rubies, and sapphires.

"Look at this place, Abu!" Aladdin said. As he began to search about, he felt Abu yank his trousers. Chattering wildly, the monkey pointed to a gold-tasseled carpet. It was sneaking up behind them.

"A Magic Carpet!" gasped Aladdin. "Maybe you can help us," he said to the little rug. "We're looking for a lamp."

The Magic Carpet rose, spun in a circle above their heads, and soared across the cavern. Aladdin and Abu chased after it and ended up in a shadowy chamber. Rising from the center, a huge pillar of rock stood in a shaft of light, filtering through a crack in the ceiling. Aladdin spied a small object resting on the very top—it was the lamp!

"Wait here, Abu," Aladdin said. "Whatever you do, don't touch anything!" He climbed the pillar and grabbed the lamp. As he stuck it under his shirt, he saw Abu pick up a shining jewel. "No, Abu!" yelled Aladdin.

At once, the tiger-god's voice echoed throughout the chamber. "YOU HAVE TOUCHED THE FORBIDDEN TREASURES. NOW YOU SHALL NEVER AGAIN SEE THE LIGHT OF DAY."

The cavern walls began to rumble and shake. Molten lava flowed from cracks in the stone floor and bubbled up in a boiling pool beneath Aladdin. Clutching the pillar, Aladdin slipped toward the fiery liquid. At the last second, the Magic Carpet swept beneath him. Zooming down, they plucked up Abu and rose toward the opening of the cave. Jafar was waiting for them with outstretched arms.

"Give me the lamp!" he ordered, snatching it from Aladdin and hiding it under his cape. He pulled a sharp dagger from his sleeve. "Now for your reward!"

Abu shrieked and sprang at Jafar, who cried out as the monkey, baring his teeth, bit him hard on the hand. Writhing in pain, Jafar struggled to free himself. He shoved Aladdin and Abu backward down into the depths. When they landed, the ground quaked and the cave sealed shut.

"We're trapped!" cried Aladdin. "Whoever that no-good beggar was, he's long gone with that lamp." Abu grinned and revealed the lamp hidden under his vest.

"You hairy little thief!" Aladdin said with delight. Squinting in the dim light, he examined the lamp. "I wonder why he wanted it so much. It's just a beat-up worthless piece of junk. There's something written here . . . but it's hard to make out." He rubbed it with his sleeve.

POOF! Blue smoke poured from the spout, swirling and billowing, and finally taking shape in the form of a towering blue man. His body trailed behind him into a thin stream, trapped within the lamp.

"Hello, there," he said. "Nice to be out for a change. I've been cooped up in here for ten thousand years. Say, you're a lot smaller than my last master. What's your name?"

"A-A-Aladdin," he stammered. "Wait a minute—I'm your master?"
The blue man nodded. "Hey, what you rub is what you get! I'm the Genie of the Lamp—all set to grant you three wishes."

Aladdin scratched his head. "I must be dreaming. . . ."

"So, what'll it be?" the Genie asked him. "Remember, though, a few no-can-dos: You can't wish for more wishes. I can't kill anybody. I can't make anybody fall in love. And I can't bring people back from the dead. That's it. Anything else—it's yours!"

Aladdin turned his head and winked at Abu. "Some all-powerful Genie," he said. "I don't know, Abu, he probably can't even get us out of this cave."

"Did you listen to me?" asked the Genie. "You're getting your wishes—so have a seat!" He grabbed Aladdin and Abu and leaped onto the Magic Carpet. "Yo, Rugman! Gimme some tassel!" In a blinding flash, the cavern ceiling cracked open wide and the Magic Carpet rose into the early morning sky. They floated across the hot desert and landed in a shady oasis. "Doubt me, will you?" said the Genie with a big smile. "Now, you've got two wishes left. What'll they be?"

"Three wishes," Aladdin corrected him. "I never actually wished to get out of the cave. You did that on your own."

The Genie rubbed his chin. "All right, you baaaad boy! But no more freebies."

"I want these wishes to be good," said Aladdin. "Give me an idea. What would *you* wish for?"

"Freedom!" said the Genie.

"You're a prisoner?" Aladdin asked surprised.

"It's part of the whole Genie gig," he explained. "Phenomenal cosmic powers, itty-bitty living space. The only way for me to be free is for my master to wish me out. But let's get real. It's not gonna happen."

"I'll do it," promised Aladdin. "After I make two wishes, I'll use my third one to set you free."

The Genie looked doubtful. "Well, here's hoping. Now! Let's make some magic! What is it you want most?"

"Well, there's a girl I like a lot," Aladdin told him, "but she's the Princess. So, for my first wish, Genie, I wish to become a prince!"

"No problem," said the Genie. With a double *POOF!* and a twist of smoke, he transformed Aladdin into a prince, garbed in a white turban and elegant robes.

"Ooh, I like it! But now you'll need to make a grand entrance." With a snap of his fingers, he changed Abu into an elephant. "Talk about your trunk space! But we're not through yet. Hang on to your turban, kid. We're gonna make you a STAR!"

That afternoon, Jafar rushed up to the Sultan. "O Great Ruler," he announced, unrolling a long scroll, "there's a solution to your problem. It says right here . . . if the Princess hasn't chosen a husband by her sixteenth birthday, the Sultan shall choose for her."

"But," stammered the Sultan, "how can I choose for her? She's hated all the suitors so far."

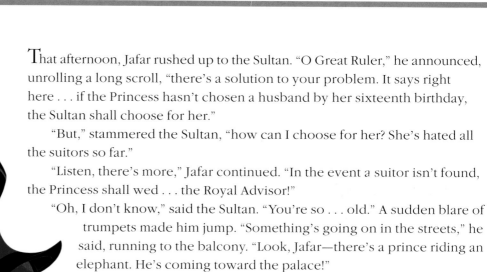

"Listen, there's more," Jafar continued. "In the event a suitor isn't found, the Princess shall wed . . . the Royal Advisor!"

"Oh, I don't know," said the Sultan. "You're so . . . old." A sudden blare of trumpets made him jump. "Something's going on in the streets," he said, running to the balcony. "Look, Jafar—there's a prince riding an elephant. He's coming toward the palace!"

"Make way!" shouted the Genie, darting through the excited crowd. "Make way for Prince Ali Ababwa!" The whole city welcomed the mysterious prince as he rode through the palace gates in front of a grand procession.

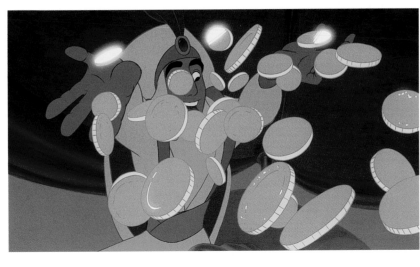

"Your Majesty," Aladdin said to the Sultan, "I, Prince Ali Ababwa, wish to seek your daughter's hand in marriage."

"I'm delighted to meet you," replied the Sultan. "May I present Jafar, my Royal Advisor. We both agree you've made a most impressive entrance." He nudged Jafar. "You might not have to marry Jasmine after all."

"No, no," cautioned Jafar, eyeing the Prince suspiciously. "I must advise against this. This man is not for the Princess."

"Oh, I'm sure I'll like her," insisted Aladdin, wondering where he'd seen Jafar before. "Just let me meet her. I'll win her over."

Unnoticed, Jasmine entered the throne room. "How dare you! All of you," she cried. "I'm not a prize to be won." Turning on her heels, she stormed out to the royal garden.

Day passed into night. Aladdin watched Jasmine as she stood on her balcony gazing at the stars. The Genie floated behind him. "What'll I do?" Aladdin asked.

"Just be yourself," advised the Genie. "Tell her the truth."

Aladdin frowned. "That's the worst thing I could do. She'd never marry a street rat like me." Clutching his turban in his hands, Aladdin called up to her: "Princess Jasmine, please give me another chance."

"Just leave me alone," she replied coldly. At that moment, the moon, emerging from behind a cloud, revealed his face. "Wait! Do I know you? You remind me of someone I met in the marketplace."

"Oh, no," said Aladdin. "I'm a prince. My servants go to the marketplace for me."

"Well," said Jasmine. "I'm not interested in marrying you. Now, please go."

Aladdin's shoulders slumped. "Before I leave," he added, "I want to tell you something." He stepped onto the Magic Carpet and floated up to the balcony. "I don't think you're a prize to be won. You should be free to make your own choice."

Jasmine blinked. "Your carpet . . . floats?"

"Want a ride?" asked Aladdin, holding out his hand.

Jasmine carefully stepped onto the Magic Carpet and knelt beside him. Together, they floated out across the sleeping city of Agrabah.

"This is really fun!" said Jasmine, looking over the edge of the carpet. "Too bad Abu's not here to enjoy it."

"Oh, he doesn't like flying much—" Aladdin began. He realized too late that he'd been tricked.

"I thought so!" exclaimed Jasmine. "You *are* the boy from the marketplace. Why did you lie to me?" And why, she wondered, had Jafar told her he was dead?

Aladdin gulped. "Well, it may sound strange, but I sometimes dress as a commoner to escape the pressures of palace life. I really *am* a prince."

Remembering her own little escapade in the marketplace, Jasmine smiled and took his hand. Aladdin smiled back. For the first time in my life, he thought, things are starting to go right.

When they returned to the palace, they hovered for a moment outside Jasmine's balcony and kissed in the moonlight.

Aladdin's good fortune would not last for long. As he was returning to his guest chamber, the royal guards grabbed him from behind and dragged him away. The last thing he heard was Jafar's voice: "Make sure he's never found."

The following morning Jasmine rushed into her father's throne room.

"Oh, Father, I had the most wonderful time last night," she said. "I'm so happy—"

The Sultan stared at her with glassy eyes. "I have chosen a husband for you," he mumbled. "You . . . will . . . wed . . . Jafar."

The Royal Advisor stepped out from behind a pillar and grinned.

"You? Never!" protested Jasmine. "I choose Prince Ali."

"Prince Ali has left, like all the rest," Jafar informed her.

A voice interrupted him. "Better check your crystal ball again, Jafar."

When he saw Aladdin appear in the doorway, Jafar staggered backward. "Prince Ali!"

"Tell them the truth, Jafar," said Aladdin, holding the lamp. "Last night, you tried to have me killed. If I hadn't wished for my Genie to save me—"

"You're lying!" Jafar hissed.

"Yes . . . you're . . . lying," echoed the Sultan.

"Father, what's wrong?" Jasmine cried. "You're acting so strange!"

Aladdin wrested the snake-head staff from Jafar's grip and smashed it on the marble floor. The Sultan rubbed his eyes, coming to his senses.

"You traitor, Jafar!" He called for the guards. Jafar made a lunge for the lamp, but Aladdin was too fast for him. As the guards rushed into the room, Jafar threw down an exploding smoke pellet and, in the confusion, escaped.

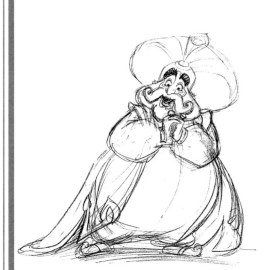

"Find him!" the Sultan ordered. He turned to Aladdin and beamed. "So, Prince Ali, my daughter has finally chosen! You will be wed at once. You will be happy and prosperous, and one day, my boy, you will become Sultan!"

Aladdin was stunned. Later, as he returned to his palace suite, the Genie floated up to him with open arms. "Congratulations, you've won Jasmine's heart. But don't forget your third wish—free the Genie!"

Aladdin looked a little guilty. "The only reason anyone thinks I'm worth anything is because of you. What if they find out I'm not a prince? Sorry, Genie, but I can't free you."

"I understand," replied the Genie. "You lied to everybody else—why not me?" Downcast, he disappeared back into the lamp.

"Go ahead and be like that," Aladdin grumbled, tossing the lamp on a cushion. He stopped himself. "What am I doing? Genie's right. I've got to tell Jasmine the truth."

At that moment, Aladdin heard Jasmine call from the garden. "Prince Ali, come quickly!" Aladdin hurried outside—but she wasn't there.

In the evening, a huge throng gathered in the palace courtyard to celebrate Jasmine's birthday and await the announcement of her engagement. The Sultan, with Jasmine at his side, stood proudly before them.

"People of Agrabah," he announced, "the day has come at last. Princess Jasmine will be wed—to Prince Ali Ababwa." With a flourish, he pulled back a curtain and gestured to Aladdin to step forward.

"Jasmine, listen," Aladdin whispered, smiling weakly. "There's something I've got to tell you about myself—"

Before he could finish, a fierce wind sprang up. Billowing clouds formed and swirled down from the sky. Before everyone's astonished eyes, the Genie appeared, grown to an immense size. He ripped the palace from its foundation and set it down hard on a nearby mountaintop.

"What's going on?" sputtered the Sultan, trying to regain his balance. "And Jafar, what are you doing here? And how dare you wear my turban!"

"I'm Sultan now," Jafar proclaimed, holding up the lamp. "You see, Aladdin, you were careless to leave this lying about. Like all parrots, my clever Iago imitates voices. It was he, not Jasmine, who called you to the royal garden. While you were looking for her, Iago stole the lamp for me!"

Jafar briskly rubbed it with his sleeve. The Genie appeared instantly and smiled sadly at Aladdin. "Sorry, kid. I have a new master now."

"Genie," Jafar ordered, "for my second wish, I wish to be the most powerful sorcerer in the world! And with my new power, I'll reveal Prince Ali for what he really is."

The Genie sighed and snapped his fingers. Jafar laughed wickedly and waved his staff at Aladdin. In a flash, he was once more a peasant in rags. He looked imploringly at Jasmine. "I tried to tell you. . . ."

"And now," Jafar roared at Aladdin, "I banish you to the ends of the earth!"

Knocked off his feet, Aladdin was whirled up into a high palace tower. With an enormous blast, the tower rocketed into the sky and disappeared.

As the days passed, Jasmine and her father, both bound in chains, watched in disgust as Jafar whiled away his time polishing the crown jewels.

"What do you say, my dear Jasmine," Jafar would ask her, "with you as my queen, we could—"

"Never!" Jasmine replied each time.

Then, late one afternoon, an unexpected visitor slipped through an open window. Quietly, he crept up behind Jafar, but Jafar heard him and spun around. Aladdin stood smiling at him.

"You!" Jafar roared. "How many times do I have to kill you!"

Aladdin raised his dagger. "Come and fight me yourself, you cowardly snake." He winked at Jasmine.

"Cowardly snake, am I?" hissed Jafar. Furious, he conjured up his newly granted powers and changed himself into an enormous snake. As he squeezed his coils tight around Aladdin, the Genie looked on, helpless.

"The Genie has more power than you'll ever have," Aladdin grunted.

"What are you saying?" asked the Genie. "Why are you bringing me into this?"

Aladdin continued. "The Genie gave you your power—he could take it away. Face it, Jafar, you're still second best!"

"Yes . . . you're right. His power does exceed my own. . . ." Jafar stopped to think. "But not for long!"

He uncoiled himself from Aladdin and transformed back into a man. Rubbing the lamp, he made his third and final wish: "I wish to be an all-powerful Genie!"

Jafar cried out in triumph as he rose from his lamp. "I'm a Genie! I have absolute power! I can control the universe!"

Aladdin grabbed Jafar's lamp. "You wanted to be a Genie," he told him. "Now you must put up with everything that goes with it! Unless someone summons you, you must stay inside your lamp."

Jafar, realizing his fate, let out a terrible scream. "NOOO!" In a swirl of black smoke, he was sucked down into the darkness of the lamp.

"You've still got one wish left, Master," the Genie said, patting Aladdin on the back. "Just say the word and you're a prince again."

Aladdin put his arm around Jasmine. "I love you," he said, "but I have to stop pretending to be something I'm not."

"I understand," said Jasmine, trying not to cry. "I just wish we didn't have such a stupid law."

Aladdin turned to the Genie. "I wish for your freedom."

The Genie was stunned. "Really? I'm free?" He flew out from his lamp and somersaulted about the room. "I'm FREE!" He hugged and kissed Aladdin. "You'll always be a prince to me!"

The Sultan spoke up. "And to me, too! You've certainly proven your worth as far as I'm concerned. As Sultan, I will change the law—Jasmine shall marry whomever she pleases!"

Jasmine threw her arms around Aladdin and kissed him. "Tell me something," she asked, "how did you ever get back from the ends of the earth?"

Aladdin grinned. "Jafar forgot the Magic Carpet was up in the tower. Want a ride?"

Jasmine laughed and stepped onto the Magic Carpet. Holding hands, they floated through the starry sky back to the enchanting city of Agrabah.

ALADDIN
Behind the Scenes

ABOVE: *Eric Goldberg animates the Genie.*

Disney's 1992 release *Aladdin* broke away from the fairy-tale, heightened realism of the Oscar-nominated *Beauty and the Beast* to define a fresh and winning new style. The wacky improvisations of Robin Williams as both the voice of the Genie and as the narrator who opens the movie helped give the animators license to make *Aladdin* an all-out comedic turn, pushing the boundaries of visual and verbal humor as far as possible. For the narrator's scene at the beginning of the movie, the filmmakers put together a box full of odds and ends, covered it, and brought Robin Williams and the box into a recording studio. The resulting hilarious stream of ideas was translated into visual madness by the animators. "I've always loved animation that has a sense of enjoying itself on-screen," says Eric Goldberg, supervising animator of the Genie. This character provided a perfect opportunity for "animation that looked like the characters were having a good time."

Directed by Ron Clements and John Musker, *Aladdin* not only stretched the boundaries of the Disney animated film with the humorous tone of its story-telling, it conquered new ground in terms of artistic style. One of the first artists to work on the film was production designer R. S. Vander Wende, who brought to the project very clear ideas about the look and style of the environment he wished to create. Recalls background artist Natalie Franscioni-Karp, "Our mission was to take something unreal and give it reality—to make a fantasy environment that looked believable." Goldberg, who was the first animator to work on the film, and whose background in commercials gave him a keen eye for distinct graphic styles, recalls that Vander Wende's original concepts for the environments inspired him to take an equally stylized approach to the characters. Goldberg created a Genie "simplified and curvy, with not a lot of anatomy—a character that seemed to belong to the 'Hollywood Arabian' world Vander Wende was envisioning."

Aladdin set a standard for a unified approach to the filmmaking that has been a part of the creative process on Disney animated features ever since. Explains Goldberg, "It was the first time in this generation that the Studio had got together all the lead animators, the art director, and the directors and designed the character and backgrounds to exist in the same universe." The integrated design process permitted the artists to create a world in which the backgrounds make as strong a statement about the personality of a character as the animation itself. Jasmine's room resembles a birdcage, reflecting her trapped situation. The egg motif in the columns, throne, and oil lamps in the Sultan's throne room mirror his rounded shape and soft-boiled character. When Jafar takes over as Sultan, the shapes in the throne room are reorganized to echo the far more angular silhouette of the elegant and sinister villain.

As a natural jumping-off point, the artists drew on the art and culture they were representing for visual inspiration. In early 1991, layout supervisor Rasoul Azadani returned to his hometown of Esfahān in Iran to photograph buildings and interiors from the Islamic world of the fifteenth century. The artists drew for style and color ideas on Arabian calligraphy and on Persian miniature paintings from about A.D. 1000 to 1500 Background supervisor Kathy Altieri notes, "We used the colors that appear in those miniatures—very specific shades of red, blue, green, and antiqued gold—punched up to a high degree of saturation and brightness."

A color key for the magic carpet ride suggests the influence of Persian miniature paintings.

The starry African night had passed. As the morning mist rose with the sun, eager birds, flying from every nest, filled the sky with the sound of wings. Below, the ground trembled as thousands of elephants, hippos, antelopes, and giraffes hurried across the land. By the time creatures of every size and sort arrived at the foot of Pride Rock, the sun shone hot on their backs.

A hornbill named Zazu flew down from his perch and circled above the patient, waiting animals. He reported back to the king. "All is ready, Sire," he said. King Mufasa nodded. The ceremony would begin.

Rafiki, the wise old baboon, made his way forward through the crowd. Leaning on his walking stick, he hobbled to the top of the rock. There, King Mufasa and Queen Sarabi proudly presented their newborn son to him. Rafiki smiled at little Simba. He cracked open a ripe gourd and smeared its fragrant juices over Simba's brow. Then he sprinkled a handful of earth over the tiny cub. Taking Simba in his arms, he stood on the pinnacle of Pride Rock and held him high for all to see. At once, the animals fell to their knees to honor their new prince.

One member of the royal family wasn't there. The king's brother, Scar, stayed away and sulked. "I was first in line for the throne until that little hair ball was born," he muttered to himself. "Now Simba's to be the next lion king." He smiled thinly. "But not if I can help it!"

The months passed quickly for Simba, and just about every day he learned something new. Early one morning when the mist was still rising, Mufasa took Simba for a walk around the plain. As they strolled, the sun broke through the haze.

"Look, Simba." Mufasa said. "Everything the light touches is our kingdom—the Pride Lands." Simba looked wide-eyed across the brightening plain. "A king's time as ruler rises and falls like the sun," his father continued. "One day, Simba, the sun will set on my time and will rise with you as the new king."

Simba stood quietly and watched a line of zebras approach the water hole. Several tiny gazelles, already drinking, raised their heads as a flock of chattering birds landed and hungrily poked about the reeds for insects.

"Everything you see," said Mufasa, "lives together in a delicate balance. As king you must respect this."

"Dad," Simba interrupted, "don't we eat animals?"

"Yes, we do, Simba," Mufasa answered, "but let me explain. When we die, our bodies nourish the grass. Many other animals eat grass to stay alive. And so, in a way, we are feeding them. You see, we're all connected in the great Circle of Life."

As Simba thought about all his father had told him, he noticed a distant shadowy place, untouched by the sun's warm rays. "That land is beyond our domain," Mufasa warned him. "You must never go there."

At that moment, Zazu flew in with the morning report. "Well, the buzz from the bees," he began, "is that the leopards are in a bit of a spot, and the baboons are going ape—"

An anxious mole suddenly popped up from a hole in the ground. "Sire," the mole said in a raspy voice, "bad news from the underground. Hyenas are in the Pride Lands!"

"Zazu, take Simba home," Mufasa ordered and bounded off.

"I never get to go anywhere," Simba complained.

"Oh, young master," Zazu replied, "when you are king, you can chase those mangy scavengers from dawn till dusk."

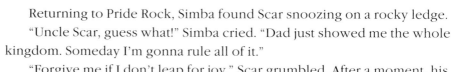

Returning to Pride Rock, Simba found Scar snoozing on a rocky ledge. "Uncle Scar, guess what!" Simba cried. "Dad just showed me the whole kingdom. Someday I'm gonna rule all of it."

"Forgive me if I don't leap for joy," Scar grumbled. After a moment, his eyes popped open. "Did he show you . . . everything?"

Simba scuffed his paw in the dust. "Well, no," he answered. "Not that place to the north. Dad says I can't go there. What's out there, anyway?"

Scar shook his head. "Sorry, Simba, I just can't tell you. Besides, an elephant graveyard is—"

Simba brightened up. "An elephant what?"

"Whoops! I've said too much. Just do me one favor." Scar grinned at his nephew. "Promise me you'll never visit that dreadful place. Only the bravest lions go there."

"Sure, Uncle Scar," Simba replied. "See ya—gotta go now."

"Remember," Scar whispered, "it's our little secret."

Simba dashed off to find his best friend, Nala. "Wait'll she hears about this!" he said to himself.

He found Nala with the rest of the pride behind the Rock. "Hi, Nala," he said. "Want to come out and play?"

"Not until my daughter is finished with her bath," Sarafina told him.

"What do you want to do?" Nala asked. "Wrestle, climb trees?"

Simba paused a second. "Uh . . . just go to the water hole."

Sarafina looked at Simba's mother. "What do you think, Sarabi?"

"It's all right with me," Sarabi answered, "as long as Zazu goes with them."

Simba frowned. "Oh, all right," he agreed. "Come on, Nala, let's go."

Simba and Nala raced across the plain with Zazu flapping madly to keep up. They headed toward a patch of tall grasses. "Run in there," Simba said, panting. "We have to ditch the dodo." They plunged into the thicket and hid. Giggling, they peeked up at Zazu as he circled in confusion. Finally, he flew off to look elsewhere.

Nala grinned at Simba. "Where're we really going?"

"Follow me!" he yelled. Nala charged after him, leaped on his back, and flipped him over.

"Pinned ya!" she said. "Now—where're we *going*?"

Simba laughed and scrambled to his feet. "To an elephant graveyard! And we'd better hurry before Zazu shows up!"

Simba led Nala toward the far border. "It's getting foggy," said Nala, peering through the gloom. "I can hardly see."

WHOOOOSH! A geyser of steam erupted inches away, spinning them both off their feet. "Nala! This is it!" hooted Simba. "The elephant graveyard!"

A field of huge gray bones lay strewn before them. "This is really creepy," Nala breathed. "Look at that giant skull! I wonder if its brains are still in there."

"There's only one way to find out," Simba answered. He started to climb into the eye socket.

"There you are!" squawked Zazu, fluttering down through the mist and shaking off his damp feathers. "We're way beyond the Pride Lands. And right now we're all in very real danger. We must leave before it's too late."

"It's already too late," chuckled a voice, followed by whoops of laughter. Shenzi, a foul-smelling creature, stepped from the shadows accompanied by her two comrades, Banzai and Ed.

Zazu fluttered backward. "Hyenas!" he gasped to the cubs. "Run!"

Shenzi cut them off. "Well, well, well. What have we got here? A trio of trespassers?" The hyenas all giggled.

"Quite b-b-by accident," stuttered Zazu. "A simple navigational error, I assure you."

Shenzi sniffed around Zazu. "I know this one," she said. "You're Mufasa's little stooge."

Banzai circled Simba. "And that would make you . . ."

"The future king!" Simba announced, standing as tall as he could. "So, you'd better watch out!"

The hyenas fell to the ground, laughing hysterically and kicking their feet in the air. Simba and Nala made a break for it.

"Not so fast!" Shenzi snickered, grabbing Simba. "Didn't you know it's dinnertime?" She gave him a good pinch. "And you'd make the perfect cub sandwich."

"r-r-r . . ." Simba tried to roar.

"Was that a roar?" Banzai inquired. "Or a squeak?"

"*ROARRRRR!!*"

The hyenas whipped around to find Mufasa glaring down at them. "Your Majesty," Shenzi sputtered. "We were just—"

With a sweep of his paw, Mufasa swatted Shenzi and sent her flying. "Silence!" he commanded. "If you ever come near my son again . . ."

Giggling, the trio slunk off into the fog.

Zazu took Nala home, leaving Mufasa alone with Simba. "You could have been killed," he said to his son. "You deliberately disobeyed me. And what's worse, you put Nala in danger."

"I'm sorry, Dad," Simba sobbed.

Mufasa's voice shook. "I was afraid I'd lost you."

Simba looked up in surprise. "Dad, I didn't think kings were ever afraid."

"Even kings get scared," Mufasa replied. "Like everybody else." He gave his son a playful cuff.

"Say, Dad? We'll always be pals, right?"

Mufasa paused and looked up at the twinkling stars. "Simba, let me tell you something my father told me. The great kings of the past look down on us from those stars."

"Really?" Simba asked, staring up at the boundless night sky.

Mufasa nodded. "Remember, whenever you feel alone, those kings will always be there to guide you. And so will I."

Simba rubbed his head against his father's side. "I'll remember," he promised.

Meanwhile, in a musty cave not far away, Shenzi, Ed, and Banzai stood cowering before Scar. "I'm disgusted with you three," Scar snarled. "I practically gift wrapped those cubs for you—and you let them get away!"

"Well, ya know, boss," Shenzi told him, "it wasn't like they were exactly alone."

"Yeah," Banzai agreed. "What were we supposed to do? Kill Mufasa?"

Scar grinned. "Precisely."

"Hey, great idea—no king!" the hyenas yipped.

"*I* will be king, you giggling fools!" Scar snapped. "Stick with me and you'll never go hungry again."

The next day, Scar led Simba down to the bottom of a deep gorge. "Wait here on this rock," he said. "Your father has a marvelous surprise for you."

Simba hopped onto the rock and eagerly looked around.

"Now, don't run off," instructed Scar. "You don't want to end up in a mess like you did with the hyenas, do you?"

Simba gulped. "You know about that?"

"Simba, my boy," he replied, "everybody knows about that." He loped away and left his nephew all alone.

Standing at the top of the gorge, Scar narrowed his eyes and observed the massive herd of wildebeests browsing along the rim. In the distance, he spied Mufasa with Zazu, making their usual morning rounds. "Excellent," he murmured to himself. "Everything is working out perfectly." Anxiously, Scar scanned the bluff for the hyenas. They were ready and waiting.

"There's the signal!" yelled Shenzi. "Let's go!" Whooping crazily, the hyenas dashed among the peaceful wildebeests. Confused and frightened, the herd stampeded down into the gorge.

Simba jumped from the rock and ran for his life. He was about to be trampled when he scrambled up a dead tree. He clung to a limb as the wildebeests thundered past.

Scar dashed up to Mufasa. "Brother!" he shouted. "There's a stampede! Simba's down there!"

Mufasa lunged down into the gorge. Zazu flew ahead, frantically searching for Simba. "He's over there, Your Majesty!" he cried. Mufasa hurled himself into the frantic herd and snatched Simba from the limb. Thrashing his way to the side of the gorge, he spotted an overhanging ledge and tossed his son to safety. A charging beast knocked Mufasa back down, and he was swept away in the flow. Gravely wounded, Mufasa made a valiant leap and clung to a steep incline. He clawed his way up toward a ledge, where he found Scar peering down at him.

"Brother," gasped Mufasa, hanging onto the jagged rock. "Please . . . help me."

Scar looked deep into Mufasa's eyes. "Long live the King," he hissed and pushed Mufasa backward into the gorge.

Simba clambered up onto a ledge, just in time to see his father vanish into the stampede. Choking back tears, Simba searched the dust-filled gorge. Then he felt his heart drop. Mufasa's broken body was lying on the ground.

"NOOO!" Simba screamed. When he rushed to his father's side, he realized he was dead. Sobbing, he buried his face in Mufasa's tangled mane.

Scar ambled over to him. "Now see what you've done," he said.

Tears streamed down Simba's face. "It was an accident," he wailed. "There were wildebeests . . . and Dad tried to save me. I didn't mean for it to happen."

"Of course you didn't mean it," replied Scar. "No one ever means for these things to happen. But the king is dead, and if it weren't for you, he'd still be alive. Oh, what will your mother think?"

"What'll I do?" asked Simba.

"Run away," Scar answered. "Run away and never return."

Simba looked out across the shimmering plain toward the desert. He nodded. With his head cast down, he turned his back on Pride Rock and trudged away.

The hyenas sidled up to Scar. "We did it, boss," Shenzi bragged.

Scar shook his head. "The job's only half done." He gestured toward the tiny cub disappearing over a rise. "Finish it!"

Yipping, the hyenas chased after Simba, and Scar returned to Pride Rock. Looking sorrowful, he delivered the sad news to the pride.

"Mufasa's death is a terrible tragedy," he lamented. "But to lose Simba as well is, for me, a deep personal loss."

The other lionesses nuzzled Sarabi in sympathy.

"So it is with a heavy heart," Scar announced, "that I assume the throne. . . ."

The hyenas squatted on the rise, watching Simba make his way into the desert.

Shenzi shook her head. "There ain't no way I'm going out there."

"Yeah, I hate it when the sun burns you to a crisp," Banzai said. "But we gotta finish the job."

"He'll never make it," Shenzi replied. "He's as good as dead."

The hot afternoon sun bore down on Simba. Buzzards circled overhead, waiting. But he didn't care. He collapsed on the sandy ground and passed out cold. The buzzards flocked to the ground and prodded him.

"YEEEEE-HAAAAAAAA!" Out of nowhere, a meerkat astride a warthog came galloping in and scattered the buzzards in all directions.

"Aw, Timon," said the warthog. "Look, it's just a little lion. He's so cute and all alone. Let's keep him."

"Pumbaa, old buddy, are you nuts?" cried the meerkat. "Lions eat guys like us!"

Pumbaa thought it over. "But maybe he'll be on our side."

"That's the stupidest thing I ever heard," Timon said. "But, hey! I've got it! Maybe he'll be on our side."

"So, we're keeping him?"

"Of course! Who's the brains in this outfit anyway?"

Pumbaa gently picked up Simba with his tusks and carried him to their shady forest home. Soon, Simba opened his eyes.

"You okay, kid?" Timon asked. "You were that close to being dessert for some buzzards."

"Who cares?" Simba responded.

Pumbaa was curious. "So, where're ya from?"

"It doesn't matter. I can't go back—I did something terrible."

"Look," Timon told him, "when the world turns its back on you, you turn your back on the world, right?"

Simba shook his head. "That's not what I was taught."

"Then maybe you need a new lesson," said Timon. "Repeat after me: *Hakuna matata*. It's the rule we follow. It means no worries, no responsibilities."

"Hakuna matata," repeated Simba, liking the sound of it. Simba decided to stay with his new friends. "Maybe they're right," he said to himself. "I gotta put my past behind me. No more worries!"

Days became weeks and weeks became months. Years slipped by and Simba grew from a cub into a lion. The brown spots on his coat faded and a bushy golden mane covered his head and shoulders.

One night Simba, Timon, and Pumbaa were lying on the grass, gazing up at the twinkling sky.

"Ever wonder," said Pumbaa to his friends, "what those sparkly dots are?"

"Someone once told me the great kings of the past are up there—watching over us," replied Simba.

"Ya mean a bunch of royal dead guys are watching us?" Timon scoffed. "Who told you that?"

Simba wandered away to be alone. He wondered what would his father think of him now. He flopped down on the ground and sighed. His breath carried a wispy puff of milkweed into the treetops. A fresh breeze picked it up and blew the milkweed all the way across the desert to the Pride Lands, and into the waiting, outstretched hand of Rafiki.

Pulling the milkweed apart, the old baboon examined the seeds. His eyes filled with tears of joy. "Simba," he murmured, "you're alive!" He nodded slowly to himself and began to prepare for his journey.

The next day, Simba was strolling about looking for something to eat when he heard Timon cry out: "Help! She's going to eat us!"

Simba tore through the underbrush and saw Pumbaa hiding in an old log. Nearby, a lioness, crouching in the grass, was about to spring at Timon. Simba leaped out and tackled her. As they wrestled, the lioness flipped him on his back and pinned him with her paw. Simba looked up at her in surprise. "Nala?"

The lioness peered down at him. "Simba?"

Timon watched in shock as the two lions roared in delight and hugged each other. "Hey, what's goin' on here?" he yelled. Simba introduced Nala to his friends.

But Nala couldn't keep her eyes off Simba. "I can't believe you're alive. Why did Scar tell us you were dead?"

Simba shrugged. "It doesn't matter," he answered.

"Of course, it matters," she insisted. "You're alive! And that means you're the king!"

Pumbaa dropped to his knees and stretched out flat. "Your Majesty," he said. "I gravel at your feet."

Timon yanked him up. "It's not *gravel*," he corrected him. "It's *grovel*—and don't! He's not the king."

Simba made a face. "Well, actually, she's right."

Timon's mouth dropped open.

Nala smiled at him. "Could you and Pumbaa excuse us for a little while?" she asked. "I'd like to talk to Simba."

"Sure," Timon responded in a huff. "Come on, Pumbaa. Let's give them a little privacy." He muttered as they walked away. "This is one big surprise—you think you know a guy . . ."

Nala's eyes welled up with tears. "I really missed you, Simba. It's like you're back from the dead. You don't know how much this will mean to everyone."

Simba nuzzled her. "I missed you, too."

"Then you'll come home?" she asked, smiling.

Simba looked away. "I can't. I live by new rules now. Hakuna matata—no worries, no cares."

"Listen to me," pleaded Nala. "You have to come back to the Pride Lands. Scar's in power now. He's let the hyenas take over and everything's destroyed. There's no food, no water—Simba, it's your responsibility. Your father would want you to come home."

Simba blinked back his tears. "My father's dead," he told her. To himself he added, "and it's all my fault."

That night Simba couldn't sleep. He wandered down and stretched out beside a weedy stream. "Nala's wrong," he thought. "I can't go back. It wouldn't change anything." He looked up at the stars. "You said you'd always be there for me—but you're not." Gradually, he became aware of a faint sound—the sound of someone singing a little tune:

"*Asante sana, squash banana, we we nugu, mi mi apana.*"

PLOP! A stone dropped into the water, almost hitting him on the head. Startled and annoyed, Simba looked up to find an old baboon squatting by the side of the stream.

"Who are you?" asked Simba.

Rafiki looked him in the eye. "The question is," he asked in return, "who are *you*?"

Simba blew out his breath. "I thought I knew, but now I'm not so sure."

"Well, I know who you are," Rafiki said, hopping to his feet. "You're Mufasa's boy." He scampered into the underbrush.

"Wait!" Simba called out, charging after him. "You knew my father?"

Rafiki paused. "I *know* your father," he said.

Simba felt sorry he had to tell the old baboon the sad truth. "I hate to tell you this," he said, "but my father died a long time ago."

"Wrong!" Rafiki corrected him. "Your father's alive. Follow me."

Simba thought his heart would burst with joy. He dashed after Rafiki, following him through the underbrush toward a deep pool.

Rafiki pushed some tall reeds aside. "Look down there," he whispered.

Simba gazed into the starlit water. But all he saw was his own reflection staring back at him. "It's not my father," he said, disappointed. "It's just me."

"Look harder," Rafiki urged him and touched the surface with his finger.

Simba peered into the water again. His reflection began to shimmer. Suddenly, he was staring into his father's eyes.

"You see?" said Rafiki. "He lives in you."

"*Simba.*"

Simba leaped to his feet. It was his father's voice coming from somewhere above. "Father, where are you?" he called, looking up at the night sky. The shadowy clouds parted, and Mufasa's image emerged among the stars.

"*You have forgotten who you are,*" said Mufasa. "*And so, you have forgotten me.*"

"Oh, no, Father," Simba cried out. He felt a sob rising in his throat. "I'd never forget you."

Mufasa continued in a softer voice. "*Look inside yourself, my son. You are more than what you have become. You must take your place in the Circle of Life.*" His voice faded away. "*Remember who you are. You are my son and the one true king. Remember who you are.*"

"Please don't leave me, Father," Simba pleaded. But Mufasa had vanished.

"Most peculiar weather, eh?" remarked Rafiki.

"I know what I should do," replied Simba, "but going back means facing my past. And I've been running away from it so long."

Without any warning, Rafiki whacked him hard on the back with his walking stick.

"Ow!" exclaimed Simba. "What's that for?"

"It doesn't matter now," Rafiki replied with a twinkle in his eye. "It's in the past."

Simba stretched his stinging back. "Even so," he said, "it still hurts."

Rafiki scratched his head, pretending to think. "Yes," he agreed, "the past can hurt. But the way I see it, you can run from it or you can learn from it." He waved his walking stick over Simba's head. Simba ducked. "You see? So what are you going to do?"

"First, I'm going to take your stick!" Simba kidded. "And then I'm going back home!"

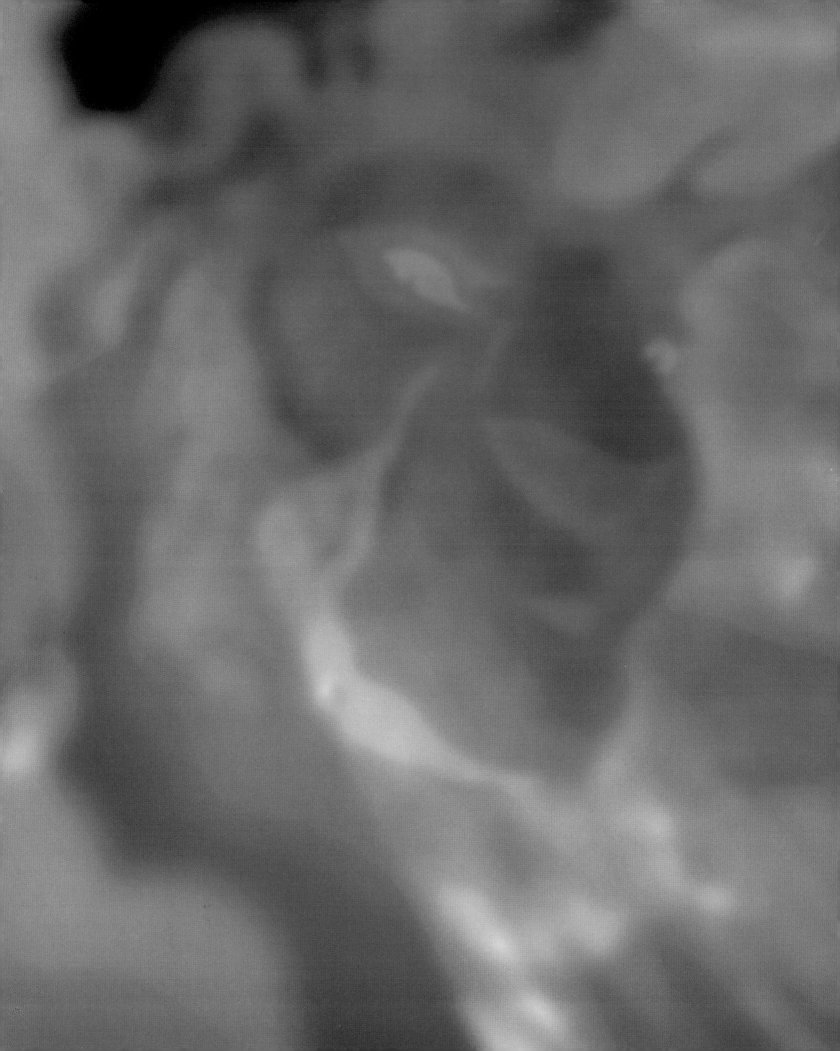

In the forest, Pumbaa and Timon were snoring loudly when Nala shook them awake. "Where's Simba?" she asked. "I've looked everywhere."

Timon rubbed his eyes. "We thought he was with you."

Just then Rafiki swung down from a tree limb. "You won't find him here," he chuckled. "The king has returned."

Simba didn't stop running until he saw Pride Rock against the pale morning sky. But it was nothing like the home he remembered. No animals were left, the earth lay parched, and the only signs of past life were wildebeest bones, lying near the dry water hole.

For a long time he gazed at the ruined kingdom. Nala appeared and quietly stood at his side. "It's awful, isn't it," she said. "What made you come?"

Simba choked back his tears. "I finally got some sense knocked into me. And I've got the lump on my back to prove it."

"We're gonna fight your uncle for this?" asked a familiar voice.

"Timon?" asked Simba, turning around. Pumbaa trotted up with Timon on his back. "What are you guys doing here?"

Timon squared his shoulders. "Well, Simba," he said, "if this is important to you, we're with you to the end."

Simba smiled at his friends. "Thanks, fellas, I can use all the help I can get!"

In the distance they could hear the hyenas whooping with laughter.

"Pumbaa, Timon," Simba ordered calmly, "you'll have to divert the hyenas. Nala, you find my mother and rally the lionesses. I'll look for Scar."

Scar waited impatiently for Sarabi outside his cave on Pride Rock. A storm was brewing, and as he paced back and forth, his mane blew in the hot wind.

"You called?" Sarabi asked.

"Where's your hunting party?" he demanded. "The hyenas need food."

"It's over, Scar," she told him. "There is no food. The herds have moved on. Our only choice is to leave the Pride Lands."

"We're not going anywhere," Scar snarled.

Sarabi was stunned. "Then you are sentencing us to death," she said. Scar looked away but Sarabi stood firm. "If you were half the king Mufasa was, you would never—"

Scar whirled around and swatted her hard. "I AM TEN TIMES THE KING MUFASA WAS!" he roared. Out on the plain, lightning flashed and thunder shook the air. Quietly, the figure of a lion stepped out of the shadows.

"M-M-Mufasa?" stammered Scar. "It can't be. You're dead!"

Sarabi raised her head. "Mufasa?" she asked groggily.

Simba went to her side and nuzzled her. "No, Mother, it's me."

"Simba?" Scar said, nervously. "I'm a little surprised to see you . . . alive."

"Give me one good reason why I shouldn't rip you apart," Simba demanded.

"Y-You know," began Scar, "the pressures of ruling a kingdom—"

Simba cut him short. "—are no longer yours," he finished. "I'm back to take my place as king. Step down or fight!"

Scar was growing panicky. Out of the corner of his eye, he saw Nala and the lionesses assembling, ready to defend Simba. Lurking behind them, the hyenas silently gathered.

"I'd hate to be responsible for the death of a family member, wouldn't you agree?" Scar asked, raising his voice for all to hear. "Go on, Simba. Tell everyone who's responsible for your father's death!"

Simba bowed his head, ashamed. "I am," he answered. Sarabi gasped. Simba sadly turned to her. "It's true, Mother," he said, "but it was an accident."

"Murderer!" roared Scar.

"No!" protested Simba, backing out of the cave. He stumbled over the ledge. Barely able to hang on to the jagged rock, he desperately looked up at Scar.

"This looks familiar," Scar said in Simba's ear. "You look just the way your father did—*before I killed him*."

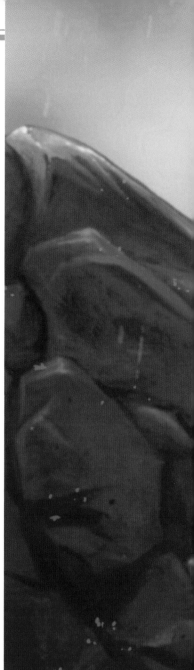

The words filled Simba with rage, and a new strength surged through his body. Letting out a deafening roar, he sprang at Scar and gripped him by the throat. "Tell them what you just said!" he commanded. "Tell them!"

Scar could hardly breathe. "I did it," he wheezed.

"Louder!" ordered Simba. "So everyone can hear you."

"I KILLED MUFASA!" Scar yelled.

Furiously, the lionesses attacked him. Nala sprang to Simba's side, and a fearsome fight followed as the howling hyenas descended from all sides to defend their leader.

Like a huge wailing animal, the wind moaned around Pride Rock. A lightning bolt flashed, setting the dead grasses ablaze. In seconds, the air was blanketed in thick black smoke. Fleeing the flames, Scar dashed on to a ledge. Simba was right at his heels.

"Nephew, I am family!" Scar begged. He didn't notice Shenzi, Banzai, and Ed creeping up behind Simba. "It was the hyenas' fault. They're the real enemy. Please, I'll do anything." When they heard this, the hyenas slunk back off the ledge.

Simba thought for a moment. "Run away, Scar," he said. "Run away and never return."

"Yes, of course, Your Majesty," replied Scar. He started to turn away, but all of a sudden, he spun around and kicked red-hot embers into Simba's face. Simba staggered, and Scar flung himself upon him. They fought on the charred ground. In the struggle, Scar fell backward off the ledge, hitting the ground below. The betrayed hyenas closed in on him.

Simba stood in the refreshing rain. Its cool water would soon bring life back to the land. Sarabi and Nala rushed forward to greet him. Then they

stepped back and let him pass. Slowly, Simba climbed to the top of Pride Rock. He gazed up at the sky and heard his father's voice. "*Remember. . . .*"

Simba threw back his head and let out a triumphant roar.

Years later, all the animals gathered, once again, at Pride Rock. As they waited on the soft grassy plain, Zazu flew down and circled the crowd.

"Sire," he reported back to the king, "everyone is here."

While Timon and Pumbaa watched proudly, King Simba and Queen Nala presented their new son to Rafiki. Gently, the old baboon took the cub in his arms and held him high. All across the Pride Lands, the animals bowed low to welcome their future Lion King.

THE LION KING
Behind the Scenes

ABOVE: *Elton John and Tim Rice work on music for* The Lion King.

In the beginning of *The Lion King*'s journey from idea to finished film, back when it was known as *King of the Jungle*, the only certainties were that it would be a story about growing from childhood to adulthood; that it would feature animals, probably lions; and that it would be set in Africa. The making of *The Lion King* was a journey of discovery; it was a film that revealed itself to its creators as their ideas unfolded. "We weren't basing the movie on a fairy tale or an existing story," explains director Roger Allers, who, along with director Rob Minkoff and producer Don Hahn, led the creative team on Disney's 1994 summer blockbuster. "We developed the story visually and verbally at the same time. Ideas flowed back and forth among the writers and the story people in a great creative swirl."

The development of the opening song, "The Circle of Life," was, for many members of *The Lion King*'s creative team, one of the things that helped define what the movie would ultimately become. "Music is a great way to tell a story when words don't quite reach you," says Hans Zimmer, composer of the award-winning score. Elton John and Tim Rice developed the memorable tune and simple lyrics for "The Circle of Life." The piece then passed to Zimmer who, with African-born musician Lebo M, reinterpreted the original song, adding African rhythms and Zulu chants. As producer Hahn recalls: "We went over to Hans's studio to listen to his arrangement for 'The Circle of Life.' It was just thrilling. We said we needed some sort of cry in the wilderness at the beginning because the sun is rising and all the animals are going to see the newborn king. We needed some sort of call to worship. And Lebo M said, 'Oh, I think I can do something.' The first thing that came out of his mouth is the piece that ended up in the film. It was just so great, we never changed it."

Sketches by artist Jean Gillmore.

Art director Andy Gaskill calls Africa "the unspoken character in this film," and the artists worked to evoke the same depth in visual storytelling as the song-writing team had revealed through music. The artists created subtle atmospheric conditions—leaves rustling in the trees, lions' manes blowing, and moving clouds that cast shadows on the ground. The background artists painted loosely, drawing on their knowledge of African terrain. The result was an organic environment, with no architectural details to speak of, and a majority of scenes with a realistic color scheme. Dramatic weather conditions such as wind and lightning helped the film come alive, and the drama unfolded against a symbolic cycle of seasons and weather, as drought and fires gave way to rain and rejuvenation.

The Lion King was for many of the animators the first opportunity to draw four-legged creatures realistically since *Oliver & Company* in 1988. Wildlife expert Jim Fowler from *Wild Kingdom* visited the Studio on several occasions with lions and other creatures native to Africa to discuss behavior and give the animators some firsthand knowledge of their subjects. Anatomy consultant Stuart Sumida gave lectures on comparative anatomy, skeletal structure, and action analysis. Artist Jean Gillmore made dozens of sketches of animals for the animators to draw from. Ruben Aquino, who animated the adult Simba, was the first artist assigned to *The Lion King*, and his earliest assignment was to research forms of animal locomotion. "Animating four-legged creatures from certain angles can be very difficult," says Aquino. "The more we understood the anatomy of these creatures, the easier it was to animate them."

The challenge to the animators was not merely to animate realistically but to create personalities within the confines of believable animal behavior. "With *The Lion King*, we had less to work with than on other films. There are no props, no hands—it's a pretty sparse environment," says producer Don Hahn. "The artists had to be inventive at every turn." The animators learned to concentrate on overall body attitude, using angles of the head and subtle facial expressions. For example, the raising of an eyebrow might be their sole means to express a particular emotion.

The animators worked with the voice actors to create a cast of distinct and winning personalities. The range of acting styles runs the gamut from the subtle Shakespearean shadings of Jeremy Irons as Scar to the sonorous tones of James Earl Jones as Mufasa. And from the wildly comedic talents of Whoopi Goldberg and Cheech Marin as two malevolent hyenas and Ernie Sabella and Nathan Lane as Pumbaa and Timon to the sincerity of Matthew Broderick as the adult Simba. That same range is reflected in the style of different parts of the film. "We were going from crazy, comic shtick to big, stirring drama. We took a lot of care with transitions to help the audience move in and out of these sequences," says Roger Allers. With the emotional content of the film ranging from the death of a parent to a flatulent warthog, the filmmakers took their cue from the message of their opening number: there's a place in the world for all these different expressions of life.

POCAHONTAS

One foggy morn in 1607 the harbor dock in old London town was
crowded with families and friends bidding farewell to the good
ship *Susan Constant* and its crew of adventurers—all set to sail far
across the ocean to the New World.

One young fortune-seeker, named Thomas, kissed his worried-looking
mother. "I'll be fine, Mum," he assured her. He stepped back to let a tall, fair-
haired man, armed with a musket and shiny sword, pass by.

"That's Captain John Smith," pointed out Thomas. "I'll be safe with him
along. They say you can't fight Indians without John Smith!"

A carriage, drawn by four prancing horses, pulled up and Governor
Ratcliffe, the leader of the expedition, climbed out. He wore a thin black
mustache, a plumed hat, and two pigtails, neatly tied with little scarlet ribbons.

Ratcliffe climbed out of the coach, followed by his servant, who was
carrying his pug dog Percy on a tassled satin pillow. He strode haughtily
onto the boat.

The ship's bell clanged. "Cast off!" shouted a sailor. The Union Jack
snapped in the freshening wind and the ship was underway.

Two days out a fearsome storm tossed the sleeping men from their berths. Up on deck, sailors scrambled up and down the rigging furling the sails. The wind, roaring like a wild animal, ripped the Union Jack to shreds. As the swamped ship listed far to one side, a wave exploded over the rail.

"Man overboard!" shouted a sailor. "It's young Thomas!"

Without hesitating, John Smith tied a rope around his waist and dove off the stern. The salt water stinging his eyes, he battled the waves, searching for Thomas. Finally, he found him, and three brawny sailors hoisted the exhausted men aboard. As Thomas lay gasping for breath on the deck, Governor Ratcliffe strutted out from his dry cabin.

"Don't lose heart, men," said Ratcliffe. Smiling, he reassured the crew. "This little storm will be a mere memory in no time. Remember what awaits us in the New World—freedom, prosperity, the adventure of our lives!" As he returned to his cabin, he mumbled under his breath, "And the mountains of gold you witless peasants will dig up for me!"

Late that afternoon, Smith and Thomas leaned on the rail and watched the setting sun.

"Yes, sir," Thomas exclaimed. "I'm gonna get me a pile of gold, build a big house, and if any Indian tries to stop me . . . I'll blast him. So," he said turning to John, "what do you think the New World will be like?"

"Like all the others, I suppose," answered John. "I've seen hundreds of New Worlds. What could possibly be different about this one?"

Over the horizon, far to the west, a river wound its way through the forest and met the sea. Long ago, people built a village along its shore and were provided with all the riches they needed from the abundant waters and fertile land.

Early one morning, a young woman named Pocahontas paddled her canoe along a forest stream. As always, a raccoon named Meeko was with her. Hovering close to her shoulder was another friend, a rosy-throated hummingbird called Flit.

"I need some advice from Grandmother Willow," Pocahontas told them. She floated into a sunny glade and quietly sat before an ancient willow tree. The bark on the tree gradually changed into the face of a kindly old woman.

"Good morning, child," Grandmother Willow greeted her. "I was hoping you'd be coming to see me."

"Good morning, Grandmother Willow," Pocahontas said. "I need to talk to you. Father wishes me to marry the young warrior Kocoum."

Grandmother Willow wrinkled her nose. "Kocoum? He's so serious!"

"I know," agreed Pocahontas. "But Father thinks I'm not serious enough! He says a chief's daughter should accept more responsibility and that marrying Kocoum is the right path for me." She fingered a smooth white shell hanging from a necklace around her neck. "Father even gave me Mother's necklace—the one she wore on the day of her marriage."

Grandmother Willow thought for a moment. "You do have a bit of a problem," she admitted.

"But there's something else," Pocahontas went on. "I keep having a strange dream: I'm running through the woods and I see a spinning arrow. It spins faster and faster until it suddenly stops. Then I wake up."

"Hmmm . . . I think this spinning arrow," observed Grandmother Willow, "is pointing you to the right path."

"But, Grandmother Willow," asked Pocahontas, "what *is* my path? How am I ever going to find it?"

Grandmother Willow smiled. "As I told your mother when she was young, listen to the spirits. They are all around you—in the Earth, the Water, and Sky. If you listen with your heart, they will guide you."

A sudden breeze rustled Grandmother Willow's branches. "Listen to it, Pocahontas," she said. "Listen to the wind."

Pocahontas closed her eyes as the wind blew though her hair. "It's speaking to me," she murmured. "It's saying something's coming. Strange clouds?"

She climbed to the top of Grandmother Willow. There, above the tree-tops, she saw the towering sails of the *Susan Constant* billowing in the wind.

"What do you see?" asked Grandmother Willow.

"Clouds," answered Pocahontas. "Strange clouds."

"Better go see," Grandmother Willow advised.

By the time Pocahontas reached a ledge overlooking the river, the ship had anchored and the crew was rowing ashore. Pocahontas had never seen such strange-looking men! They had pale skin and odd clothes and some had bushy hair growing from their cheeks and chins—like animals! When the last boat reached the shore, the men stood in a circle, and their leader, a fat man in brightly colored clothes, jammed a flagpole in the ground.

"I hereby claim this land and all its riches in the name of His Majesty, King James the First of England," he boomed. "And I name this settlement: Jamestown."

One man wandered away from the group and climbed a tall tree that rose next to the ledge where Pocahontas was hiding. She backed away and, crouching behind a shrub, stared at him in wonder. His yellow hair glinted like sunlight and his eyes were as blue as a robin's egg! To Pocahontas's horror, Meeko squealed and scrambled over to him.

"Well, you're a strange-looking fellow," the man remarked and gave Meeko a biscuit from his pocket. Before gobbling it up, Meeko proudly held it up to show Pocahontas.

"You've got a friend back there?" asked the man, climbing onto the ledge. Just as he was about to discover Pocahontas, Flit zoomed straight at him. While the man tried to bat Flit away, a settler called, "Smith! The governor wants you!"

When Pocahontas went home, she found the whole village astir. By now, everyone had heard about the ship carrying people from a strange land. In the evening, her father, Chief Powhatan, called a meeting in the longhouse.

"I saw the strangers chopping down many trees," a brave reported. "They seem to be building a village of their own."

Another raised his voice. "They are digging holes in the earth . . . but what do they expect to find?"

Powhatan spoke to the wise medicine man at his side. "We must know more about these visitors. What do you see, Kekata?"

Kekata poured a handful of powder on the blazing fire. The coals hissed and a plume of smoke twisted upward in ghostly shapes. In silence, the elderly man observed them. "The white men are not like us," he said, at last. "They prowl like wolves, consuming all they find. Their weapons spout fire and thunder!"

Kocoum jumped to his feet. "I will lead our warriors to the river and attack. We will destroy these invaders the way we have destroyed foes in the past!"

Powhatan motioned for him to be still. "In past battles we knew how to fight an enemy," he cautioned Kocoum, "but these pale visitors are strange to us. Take some men to the river and observe them. Let us hope they do not intend to stay."

The next afternoon, John Smith knelt beside an icy stream. As he cupped his hands to drink, he saw, in the reflection, some movement behind him. In a flash, he picked up his rifle and spun around. A young woman with dark eyes and long black hair stood watching him. For a long moment, they gazed into each other's eyes. But as soon as John took a step forward, she fled.

John raced after her. "No, wait! Please, don't run away." Finally, she stopped and turned. "What's your name?" asked John.

"*Mat-ta-que-nat-u-roth*, I do not understand," she answered. But then a sudden breeze, like a loud whisper, stirred throughout the forest. It was carrying Grandmother Willow's words.

Listen with your heart, then you will understand.

"My name . . . is Pocahontas," she said, pointing to herself.

John tapped his chest. "Mine is John Smith."

She introduced him to Flit and Meeko. When John shook Meeko's paw, Pocahontas looked confused. "Shaking hands is how we say hello," explained John.

Pocahontas held up her hand and, with her palm facing him, moved it in a circle. "*Wing-gap-o*—it's how we say hello."

Just then Meeko plucked a shiny object from John's pouch and scampered off with it.

"Meeko, stop!" cried Pocahontas, embarrassed.

"He can have it," said John. "It's just a compass. It tells which direction you're going. I can get another one when I'm back in London."

"London?" asked Pocahontas. "Is that your village?"

John nodded. "It's a very big village—with streets filled with carriages, bridges over the rivers, buildings as tall as trees. . . ."

"I'd like to see these things," said Pocahontas.

"Oh, you will," John told her. "We're going to build them right here. We'll show your people how to use the land properly, and make roads and decent houses.

"Our houses are fine!" Pocahontas said, annoyed.

"But there's so much we can teach you," he continued. "We've already improved the lives of savages all over the world."

"Savages?!" Pocahontas cried out. Furious, she glared at him.

"It's just a word," John explained. "You know, a term for people who are uncivilized."

"You mean people who are *not like you*." Pocahontas led John to a rise overlooking the river and trees. "Your people do not understand the world as we do. The creatures of the forest, each rock and every bird, the fish in the rivers—they are our brothers and sisters. We are all one—with the sun, the moon, and the stars."

Flit hovered, protectively, above her shoulder. "You, me, Meeko, the raindrops and mountaintops," Pocahontas continued, "we are all a part of our Mother, the Earth." She formed a circle with her arms. "My people say life is like a giant hoop—with no beginning and no end."

As they wandered through the forest and Pocahontas spoke about the land and her people, John began to understand.

"You know, Pocahontas, what you're saying is beginning to—"

They were interrupted by the sudden beating of signal drums.

"Something's happened," said Pocahontas. "I have to go."

John called after her. "Will I see you again?" But she'd gone.

Pocahontas found a hushed crowd gathered outside the village longhouse.

"What is it?" she asked her friend, Nakoma, whose eyes were big with fright.

"Kocoum and Namontack went to spy on the white men," Nakoma informed her. "One of them shot Namontack."

Pocahontas hurried inside and found her father and Kekata beside the wounded brave. "These beasts invade our shores," Powhatan muttered to her, "and now *this*!"

"Chief Powhatan," Kekata observed, "this wound is beyond my power to heal. The white men have used one of their terrible weapons."

Powhatan's eyes narrowed with rage. He turned to Kocoum. "We'll fight this enemy," he vowed. "But we cannot do it alone. Send messengers to every village in our nation. We will call on our brothers to help." Powhatan strode from the longhouse and shouted to his people. "The white men are dangerous! No one is to go near them!"

The next afternoon, Pocahontas and Nakoma were gathering corn in a sunny field outside the village.

"We'd better pick a lot," said Nakoma, tossing ripened ears into her basket. "The warriors will probably be starving when they arrive." Looking up, she drew in her breath. "A white man is coming from the forest!"

Pocahontas whipped around. It was John! Before Nakoma could call for help, Pocahontas covered her friend's mouth. "Quiet!" she whispered. "What are you doing here?" she asked John.

He took Pocahontas by the hand. "I didn't have a chance to say good-bye."

"Pocahontas?" shouted a voice from across the field.

"It's Kocoum!" Pocahontas gasped. "Nakoma, please don't say anything." Taking John's hand, she ran with him into the forest.

"Where is Pocahontas?" Kocoum asked, approaching. Nakoma lied for her friend, but she wondered. Should she have told him the truth?

Pocahontas led John into the heart of the forest. "You took a great risk," she said, "but now that you've come, I'd like you to meet someone." Puzzled, John followed her up to a huge weeping willow.

"This place is pretty," said John, glancing around. "And to think we came all this way just to dig it up for gold."

"Gold?" Pocahontas asked, raising her eyebrows.

"Gold! It's yellow and shiny and comes from the ground," John tried to explain. "It's very valuable."

Smiling, Pocahontas pulled an ear of yellow corn from a woven basket slung over her shoulder. "Oh, here's gold," she said, handing it to him. "There's lots of it."

"No," John said, laughing. He took a coin from the deerskin pouch tied to his belt. "*This* is gold."

Pocahontas examined it and shrugged. "There's nothing like that here."

John was surprised. "Are you sure?" he asked. Pocahontas nodded. "The men aren't going to like this," he murmured. "They may just pick up and leave."

Pocahontas brightened up but then asked shyly, "What about you? Will you go home, too?"

John looked at the ground. "Well, it's not like I have much of a home to go to," he answered. "I've never really belonged anywhere."

"You could belong here," suggested Pocahontas. As she spoke, Grandmother Willow's face appeared on the side of the tree.

"Did you see that??" John cried, stumbling backward.

"Hello, John Smith," said Grandmother Willow. "Come closer." She squinted at him for a minute. "He has a good soul, Pocahontas," she decided. "And he's handsome, too."

John chuckled to Pocahontas. "Oh, I like her!"

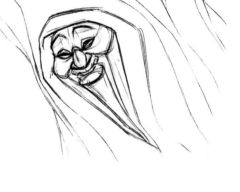

From across the glade, they heard men's voices approaching. "Smith, where are ya, mate? Ratcliffe's lookin' for ya!"

"I'd better go before they find us," said John. He took Pocahontas's hand. "Will you meet me here tonight?"

Pocahontas nodded. "When the moon rises," she answered.

She watched him disappear and slowly shook her head. "Grandmother Willow," she said. "I know I shouldn't be seeing him again. But something's telling me inside that it's the right thing."

"Perhaps it's your dream," mused Grandmother Willow.

"My dream!" Pocahontas cried. "Do you think he's the one my spinning arrow's pointing to?"

Grandmother Willow smiled.

Pocahontas found the villagers crowded along the riverbank. They cheered as painted warriors paddled long war canoes ashore.

Kocoum's eyes shone bright. "Everything will be fine," he told her, "now that our brothers are here. Chief Powhatan will hold a war council, and then together we shall destroy the white savages!"

As Powhatan and Kekata approached the longhouse, Pocahontas reached out and held her father's arm. "Father," she pleaded, "there must be a better path to follow. Why don't you talk to the white men?"

Powhatan scowled. "They do not wish to talk."

"But if one of them wanted to talk," Pocahontas persisted, "you would listen, wouldn't you?"

Powhatan sighed wearily. "Of course," he responded. "But it is not that simple. Nothing is simple anymore."

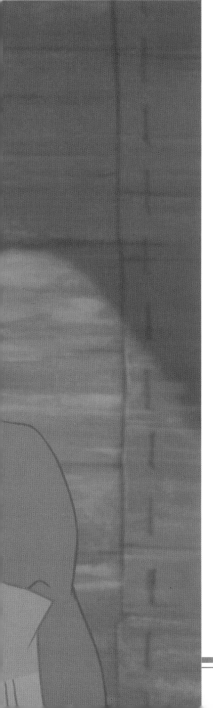

When John emerged from the woods in Jamestown, Thomas aimed his musket at him. "Easy, Thomas! It's me!" shouted John.

Thomas looked stricken. "I-I could have killed you!" he stammered.

"Not aiming like that," John instructed him. "Don't close one eye when you aim. Keep both eyes open."

Governor Ratcliffe stormed from his tent, gnawing on a chicken wing. "Smith, where have you been?" he roared. "I figured out why we're not finding any gold—even with all our digging. The Indians have already dug it up and will do anything to keep it. They're hiding—"

John interrupted him. "They have no gold."

Ratcliffe wiped his greasy mouth with his hand. "Who told you that?"

"I met one of them," replied John.

Thomas's jaw dropped. "You met a savage?"

"They're not savages," John said angrily. "And we don't have to fight them. They can help us. They know the land and how to navigate the rivers." He pulled the ear of corn from his pouch. "Best of all, they can show us how to grow food!"

"They don't want to feed us!" Ratcliffe shouted, shaking his fist. "They want to kill us! And I say that anyone who so much as looks at an Indian will be tried for treason!"

At moonrise, Pocahontas left the village and headed toward the cornfield.

"Pocahontas, don't go," Nakoma pleaded, catching up to her. "You're turning your back on our people."

"I'm trying to help our people," she replied. "I know what I'm doing."

Nakoma watched her friend disappear into the night. In a panic, she decided she had to tell Kocoum. She found him outside his hut, sharpening his stone knife. He looked up at her as she approached.

"It's Pocahontas," Nakoma said. "I think she's in trouble."

While Pocahontas was hurrying through the cornfield, John slipped past the guards and through the fort gate. Young Thomas, who saw him go, was worried. He felt a rough hand on his shoulder.

"Follow him!" Ratcliffe hissed in Thomas's ear. "I want to know where he's sneaking off to. And remember, if you happen to see any Indians— shoot them!"

"Pocahontas," said Grandmother Willow, as they waited for John to come. "The Earth is trembling with fear. . . ."

"The warriors are here," began Pocahontas.

John came charging up to her. "My men are planning to attack your people. You've got to warn them!"

"Maybe it's not too late to stop this," insisted Pocahontas. "You have to come and talk to my father."

"I don't think talking will do much good," said John.

Grandmother Willow dipped one of her long trailing branches into the water. "Watch the ripples," she said in her gentle voice. "So small at first. Then look how they grow." She nudged John with the branch. "But someone has to start them."

John studied the widening rings of water. "All right," he said at last. "Pocahontas, let's go talk to your father." Pocahontas threw her arms around John and kissed him.

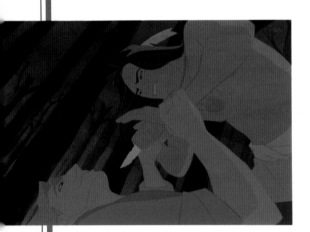

Without any warning, Kocoum sprang out from behind a bush. With a ferocious cry, he slammed John down and held a knife to his throat.

"Kocoum! Stop!" pleaded Pocahontas.

Thomas stepped out from the bushes, raised his musket, and carefully aimed. "Both eyes open," he reminded himself. Then he fired. Kocoum cried out in surprise and pain. He was dead before he hit the ground.

"You killed him!" Pocahontas screamed at Thomas.

The glade was suddenly filled with war cries, drawing closer and closer. Thomas stood dazed.

"Run!" John ordered. "RUN!"

No sooner had Thomas vanished into the forest than a group of warriors swarmed into the glade and surrounded John. Heartbroken, Pocahontas watched as John was taken away and the grieving men carried Kocoum home.

Powhatan trembled with rage and sorrow as they laid Kocoum's body before him. "Who did this?" he demanded.

"Pocahontas ran into the woods and Kocoum went out to find her," a brave explained. He gestured to John. "And then this white man attacked him."

"Your weapons are strong, but now our anger is stronger," Powhatan said to John through clenched teeth. "At sunrise, you will be the first to die." He raised his hand. "Take the white man away!"

"But, Father—," began Pocahontas. Powhatan spun around.

"I told you to stay in the village and you disobeyed me. You have shamed your father."

"I was just trying to help," Pocahontas tried to explain.

"Because of your foolishness, Kocoum is dead," said Powhatan. He turned from her while Pocahontas buried her face in her hands.

Nakoma stepped from the shadows. "Pocahontas, I sent Kocoum after you. I was so worried about you. I thought I was doing the right thing."

"All this happened because of me," Pocahontas said with tears streaming down her face. "And now I'll never see John Smith again."

"Come with me," said Nakoma. She led Pocahontas to a tiny hut guarded by two stern-looking warriors.

"Pocahontas wants to look into the eyes of the man who killed Kocoum," Nakoma told them.

"Be quick," they said, stepping aside.

Pocahontas found John kneeling with his hands tied to a post.

"I'm so sorry," she whispered. "It would have been better if we'd never met. None of this would have happened."

"Pocahontas, you must listen," John told her. "I'd rather die tomorrow than live one hundred years without knowing you."

Nakoma poked her head inside. "We'd better go."

"I can't leave you," sobbed Pocahontas.

"You never will," John said softly. "No matter what happens to me, I'll always be with you. Forever."

When Thomas ran yelling into Jamestown, the men grabbed their muskets and hurried toward him. "The savages have got John!" he cried. "What'll we do?"

Ratcliffe whipped out his sword and waved it about his head. "It's time to rescue our courageous comrade," he yelled. "Gather your weapons. At daybreak we attack!"

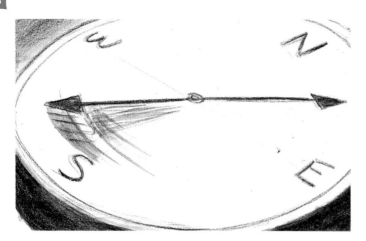

The stars were shining when Pocahontas told the terrible news to Grandmother Willow. "They're going to kill him at sunrise!" she sobbed.

"You've got to stop them," urged Grandmother Willow.

"I can't," said Pocahontas. "I followed the wrong path—I feel so lost."

Meeko tugged her skirt and handed her something shiny.

"It's John's compass!" Pocahontas murmured in surprise. The arrow began to spin. "It's the spinning arrow from my dream!" Suddenly, it stopped and pointed toward the horizon where the sun was beginning to rise.

"You see?" Grandmother Willow said. "Your dream *was* pointing you to John Smith. But, child, you must hurry!"

Pocahontas raced through the brightening woods. In the distance, she could see Ratcliffe's men marching from the fort and her people gathered at the top of the ridge. A sudden wind pushed her faster and faster until she felt she was almost flying.

Powhatan stood over his prisoner and raised his war club.

"No!" screamed Pocahontas, throwing herself over John.

"Stand back, Daughter!" demanded Powhatan.

Defiant, Pocahontas looked up at him. "Father, I love him," she answered. "If you kill him, you'll have to kill me, too. Look around you. This is where the path of hatred has brought us. This is the path I choose, Father. What will yours be?"

A sudden breeze sprang up and leaves swirled around the waiting warriors. Standing silent, Powhatan closed his eyes and listened to the wind. Slowly, he lowered his club and faced his waiting men.

"My daughter speaks with a wisdom beyond her years," he told them. "We all come here with anger in our hearts. But she comes with courage and understanding. From this day, if there's to be killing—it will not start with me."

He stepped back. "Release the prisoner."

The braves, stirred by Powhatan's words, lowered their weapons.

"This is our chance! Fire!" Ratcliffe yelled to his men.

No one moved. Thomas quietly laid his musket on the grass, and the rest of the men followed.

"Fine!" stated Ratcliffe. "I'll settle this myself." He raised his musket and fired at Powhatan. John lunged at the chief, knocking him out of the way. Clutching his side, John fell.

"He's shot John!" cried out Thomas. At once, Ratcliffe was surrounded by his furious men and carried off, shouting and kicking.

Pocahontas cradled John in her arms.

Three days later, the settlers were on the shore, readying the *Susan Constant* to take John home. Pocahontas and Powhatan appeared from the forest, and behind them, their people carried armloads of blankets and corn.

Pocahontas hurried to John, who was lying on a blanket in the shade, and knelt beside him. She tucked a small leather pouch in his shirt. "It's bark from Grandmother Willow," she explained. "It will help with the pain."

"Will you come with me?" asked John.

Pocahontas looked toward her people, standing quietly alongside the settlers. Her eyes brimmed with tears.

"I can't," she answered. "There is peace between our people now. I don't know what might happen if I leave."

John tried to raise himself. "Then . . . I'll stay."

Pocahontas gently settled him back down. "If you stay, you will die. You must go." She pressed his hand to her cheek while he rested.

Later, Pocahontas watched alone from a cliff as the *Susan Constant* sailed from sight.

"Good-bye, John," she said softly. "You will never leave me. No matter what happens, I will always be with you. Forever."

POCAHONTAS
Behind the Scenes

ABOVE: *Glen Keane animates Pocahontas.*

When the animators and artists who worked on *Pocahontas* (1995) talk about their experiences making this film, they use words such as *passion, sensitivity, sincerity*. They talk with hope about the messages of the film: that our existence together is fragile, that we need to see and try to understand one another, that one person *can* make a difference. They express their heartfelt wishes that in some small way the movie might block the road to prejudice. At the same time, they speak artistically of nuance, stillness, and economy of movement. They talk about simplicity of line and subtlety of expression. They speak of growing, through the making of this film, into better artists. "The filmmakers stretched themselves in many ways to make *Pocahontas*—first in its content, second in its design, and third in the level of execution that we were asking of our crew," says Eric Goldberg.

Directed by Goldberg and Mike Gabriel, and produced by James Pentecost, *Pocahontas* is the first Disney animated feature inspired by an actual historic figure. "We felt a lot of responsibility in bringing a story like this to the screen," says director Gabriel, who came up with the idea for the project during a Thanksgiving dinner with his family. The filmmakers drew on some of the finest talent from within the Native American community to voice the native characters, among them Russell Means as Chief Powhatan and Irene Bedard as the speaking voice of Pocahontas. (Judy Kuhn provided Pocahontas's singing voice.) Whenever possible, the filmmakers sought out advice, comments, and participation from prominent Native American educators, leaders, and groups, having several meetings with surviving members of the Algonquin nation in Virginia. They worked to represent the customs, living conditions, dress, relationships, and values of the historical Powhatan nation as accurately as possible.

The filmmakers also consulted historical documents of the period, including John Smith's writings. Ultimately, the moviemakers chose to focus on the love story inspired by the legendary encounter between Pocahontas and John Smith in order to underscore the important themes of tolerance and understanding.

Art director Michael Giaimo, layout supervisor Rasoul Azadani, and backgrounds supervisor Christy Maltese worked as a unified team to create an environment of awe-inspiring beauty. Giaimo wanted the Virginia setting transformed into a mystical paradise. Inspired by the tall pine forests of that state, Giaimo placed an emphasis on strong verticals and simple, clean lines, which extended both to the pristine wilderness and to the design of the characters. Giaimo and his team worked with the natural color palette they encountered on trips to Virginia but heightened and stylized those colors for cinematic and dramatic purposes. Waterfalls and swirling leaves that incorporate native motifs, misty environments, lush pine forests—all contribute an almost spiritual quality to the forest. Says Eric Goldberg, "We wanted to show that this place is so beautiful, wouldn't it be a shame if something happened to it?"

A tonal layout study concept by Rasoul Azadani with cleanup by Daniel Hu.

The principles of simplicity and subtlety that Giaimo and his team were using in the layouts and character designs were matched by the quality of the performances. "One of the things I learned on this picture in terms of design as well as acting is that less is more. Tiny expressions and subtle movements can have great impact," Pocahontas's supervising animator, Glen Keane, observes. *Pocahontas* further opened up the vocabulary of the animated film, requiring achingly fine draftsmanship on the part of all the artists, from supervising animator to cleanup artist. "A pencil-width line could make all the difference in an expression," explains Goldberg. The exquisite work of the artists in refining every detail speaks of their passion and belief in this sweet and winning story of how the love between two people can transcend hatred and intolerance.

Concept art by art director Michael Giaimo.

This Special Edition of
Disney's Treasury of Children's Classics
From Snow White and the Seven Dwarfs to Pocahontas
was exclusively published for initial distribution
by Reading's Fun in 1997.
It contains material previously published
in the following separate volumes:

Walt Disney's Treasury of Children's Classics
Edited by Darlene Geis
First published in 1978

and

Disney's Treasury of Children's Classics
From The Fox and the Hound to The Hunchback of Notre Dame
Adaptations by Gina Ingoglia
First published in 1996